Bear with Me

Novels by Dorris Heffron

Adult Fiction
Bear with Me
City Wolves
A Shark in the House

Young Adult Fiction
Rain and I
Crusty Crossed
A Nice Fire and Some Moonpennies

Bear with Me

A NOVEL

Dorris Heffron

Rock's Mills Press
Rock's Mills, Ontario • Oakville, Ontario
2024

Rock's Mills Press
www.rocksmillspress.com

Copyright © 2024 by Dorris Heffron.

All rights reserved. No part of this publication may be reproduced, distributed, or transmitted in any form or by any means, including photocopying, recording, or other electronic or mechanical methods, without the prior written permission of the publisher, except in the case of brief quotations embodied in critical reviews and certain other noncommercial uses permitted by copyright law. For permission requests, contact the publisher at customer.service@rocksmillspress.com.

Cover photograph copyright © Dorris Heffron.

This is a work of fiction. Names, characters, businesses, places, events, locales, and incidents are either the products of the author's imagination or used in a fictitious manner. Any resemblance to actual persons, whether known to the author, living or dead, or to actual events, is purely coincidental and unintentional, with the exceptions of those individuals who granted permission to the author to identify them by name in this book.

In gratitude to Norman Reed Paterson (1926–2022)

internationally renowned geophysicist,
who in his last years became my tenant and beloved companion,
giving peace and harmony that enabled me to write again.

AUTHOR'S NOTE:

This novel is not about bears. Though because it is set in Canada, they are amongst its inhabitants.

Contents

1. The Dead Ducks of Fort McMurray ... 9
2. The No Name Dog Project ... 14
3. The Hovel in Ottawa ... 29
4. Adventure Canada in the Arctic ... 34
5. The Smiling Wolf ... 42
6. Camping on Ice at the Floe Edge ... 49
7. Back Home Reflecting ... 62
8. Harmony in the Yukon ... 67
9. The First Episode of Violence ... 74
10. Acts of Construction ... 83
11. The Second Episode of Violence ... 97
12. The Consequence in the Year 2000 ... 102
13. Clare's Childhood ... 115
14. Weddings and Grandchildren ... 125
15. The Smiling Wolf Gets Around ... 134
16. Financial Crash ... 142
17. A Good News Story ... 151
18. In Fort McMurray 2014 ... 155
19. Fort Mac People and Pets ... 166
20. Same Old and Worse ... 179
21. The Wake-Up Call ... 188
22. Reflections When Fleeing to Vancouver ... 198
23. Len's Threat ... 206
24. An Unusual Legal Separation ... 215
25. Laying to Rest ... 222
26. Life without Malamutes ... 232
27. The Last Straw ... 241
28. Arbitration Begins ... 246
29. In the Pandemic ... 250
30. The Last Chapter ... 261
Acknowledgements ... 267

CHAPTER ONE

The Dead Ducks of Fort McMurray

In the summer of 2014, Fort McMurray was at a peak of prosperity. It had become a small city of 100,000 industrious workers. It was also at a peak of notoriety, internationally. Global oil prices were high. Fort McMurray, once a small wooden fort dependent on trappers in the ancient fur trade who travelled by canoe or dogsled, was now the oil sands capital of the world. Private and commercial airplanes brought people from across Canada and around the world to work in the oil sands industry. Famous rock stars and film stars flew in on private jets to have photo opps in sight of the oldest refinery, which spouted alarming looking smoke and fumes from its outdated chimneys. The celebrities gave interviews to international media agencies condemning the oil sands as if it were the major villain of the oil industry worldwide.

"It is," said Len to his wife. "Ever since those photos of the ducks drowning in the oil waste pond went viral, Fort McMurray has become the dead duck capital of the world. Sixteen hundred ducks migrating north in a blizzard, desperate for a drink, dive down into what looks like a good watering hole and find themselves in a mass of thick black guck. Not a chance of survival. A slow agonizing death by drowning in oil. Ducks aren't supposed to *drown*, for chrissake! You could see the shock and terror in their eyes as they struggle futilely." Len took a large swallow of scotch. "Too bad you didn't take those photos, Clare. You'd be rich now. And famous."

"I do not photograph pain and suffering," said Clare. "You know that. I focus on character."

"Too bad." Len took another swallow. "Suffering sells."

Clare knew it was stupid to discuss anything with Len when he had begun drinking in early afternoon and was now in his antagonistic stage, but she was intrigued by what went on at Fort McMurray and read any article she could find on it. "What happened to those ducks was a series of natural phenomena, accidents of nature," she said, frying onions for the pasta sauce while Len sat in his favourite chair. "All caused by that freak blizzard in April. It made the warning cannons not work to scare off birds and animals from the tailings pond. When the ducks first began to fly towards the pond the watchmen phoned the environmental supervisor in Fort McMurray. He couldn't get to the oil sands factory for hours because of road blocks in the blinding blizzard. He took photos as was his duty and reported the tragedy to all the relevant authorities and they did what they could. But it was way too late to save the ducks. There was no negligence or willful harm involved. Everyone did their job."

"Repeat!" Len yelled. "Can't hear a word you're saying with your back turned to me."

"It was all an accident," Clare said louder, facing him. "Caused by the freak blizzard. A tragedy, not caused by human neglect or willful harm-doing."

"Tell that to the ducks," said Len. "Tell it to the world. Nobody's listening."

Particularly not you, thought Clare. She turned back to the kitchen counter, sipped some white wine and resumed cooking. Here comes another deadly dinner, she told herself. Zip lip and carry on.

Two creatures that looked like wolves bounded out of the woods onto the path up from the lake and leapt up the steps onto the verandah of Clare and Len's log home on the lake. They stopped at the kitchen door. The thinner one scratched on the screen.

"The wolves are at the door!" Clare smiled as she opened it. "Hello Yukitu. Hello Ikey. Do come in. Smelling supper, are you? Make yourselves right at home."

Yukitu, the smaller one but clearly the lead dog, went to the sofa and put a paw on the end cushion. "Yes, Yuki," said Clare, "Go for it." Yuki jumped up onto the sofa and curled into a circle. Ike, the big long-haired Malamute, did not ask permission. He was big enough to just step up onto the sofa and take his place in the other corner. His paws hung over the edge of the cushions. Len had lowered his newspaper and picked up his scotch to watch the proceedings. The dogs were a form of love still shared by Len and Clare.

Clare had set the table and served dinner on the verandah. "Dinner's ready."

"Is it on the table?" Len said loudly as he put down the newspaper and took a last swallow before getting himself up out of the armchair. Clare refused to answer that as she let the dogs out onto the verandah, Yuki heading for a place on the wicker couch, Ike stretching out on the floor where it was slightly cooler.

They overlooked a small calm lake with several cottages, spaced well apart around its tree-lined shore. Their property, Loghaven, faced the sun setting in streaks of gold and coral across the horizon. The sun was setting on one of the many lakes in the cottage country near Ottawa, the capital of Canada.

"I can't eat all this," Len complained of the bowl of shrimp linguine in front of him.

"Cheers!" Clare raised her glass of red wine. Len accepted her signal of refusing to discuss anything until they had raised their wine glasses in salutation. "Cheers, indeed!" He took a long gulp from his glass.

"You don't have to eat it all," said Clare. "Help is at hand." She nodded to the dogs.

After three mouthfuls Len put down his fork. "Is it any good?" said Clare.

"Of *course*, it's good!" Len yelled. "I just can't eat that much. I'm eighty-two."

It's not because you're too old, Clare said to herself. It's because you're too drunk. "No need to yell," Clare said out loud. "I'm right here. I can hear."

"I yell so I can hear!" Len yelled. Clare laughed. "Don't laugh," said Len. "Your hearing is no better than mine and your memory is worse."

"Get serious!" Clare knew she was rising to his bait. But she couldn't always walk on eggs around him. "I'm only sixty-nine and my faculties are intact."

Yuki got off her comfortable couch and walked away from further discord. Ike smelled the leftovers and stuck around.

"You can't tell your ass from your elbow."

"That's *enough*!" Clare put down her fork. "Just leave. Leave the table if you're going to sit there and insult me."

"I will when you will," Len smirked.

Clare got up from the table, took her food and drink down to the chairs on the dock. Ike and Yuki joined her. They watched the gold and coral colours slowly disappear into darkness.

Len had gone to bed when Clare came in to do the clearing up. Later she phoned her sister, Julie who had a veterinary practice near Calgary in Alberta. It would be early evening there.

"What's up?" said Julie.

"Same old. Drunk and belligerent. Drunk and belligerent. And he won't remember tomorrow a thing that he said tonight. Same old."

"I don't know why you put up with it. It's time you took him to the vet."

Clare laughed. "Others would say, to the courts. But I divorced once. I'm not going through that again."

"I know the feeling," said Julie who had also divorced once but now had a husband she wanted to keep. "I think you need a break. That marriage is bad for your health. Come and visit me."

"Thanks, Julie. I may just do that."

Clare sat on the wicker couch with Yukitu. Ike stretched himself out on the cold flagstones at the bottom of the verandah steps. He was sleeping in the darkness of the late summer night. The mosquito season was over. A half moon reflected a silver path on the tranquil lake.

Clare thought about the last time she had visited Julie, a couple of years ago in early spring. Not a beautiful time of year to visit the foothills of the Rocky Mountains. Snow remained only in ditches and in patches of shady ground. Fields of grass and crops were dead brown, trodden paths were mud. But visiting Julie was almost always like a spring tonic. She had the energy and bounce of a wolf pup at play.

Chapter Two

The No Name Dogs Project

Clare had felt cheered up, just seeing Julie in the Calgary airport, back in 2012. The Calgary airport was Clare's favourite amongst any she had used in the world. It was small. And crowded, not with people but with colourful sculptures. Sculptures of Indigenous artifacts and chieftains, cowboys and horses, buffaloes, wolves, bears and flying eagles. The line-ups were short, the staff likely to smile at you. Julie fits right in here, thought Clare, smiling at the sight of her younger sister. Tall, slim Julie in jeans, running shoes, tee shirt, and an unusually designed necklace of pearls under her fleece-lined denim jacket.

"How's my little sister?" said Clare looking several inches up at Julie.

"Good! Great!" Julie grabbed Clare's suitcase, steering it to the exit. "Let's go, Kiddo. I'm parked using Al's disabled card. Gotta fake a limp or something when we get out the door."

"How did he get a disabled card?"

"When he smashed his shin and had to be chauffeured around."

"But you said he's all better."

"He is. Just hasn't got round to removing the card quite yet." Julie laughed with her peculiar cackle, turning heads towards her. "Here! Take your suitcase. I've got to look disabled."

Julie drove quickly away from the Calgary airport to her home in Scrag Creek. She talked excitedly about her latest project. "So I go onto a couple of nearby reserves twice a year and inject the feral dogs with this contraceptive implant that keeps them from getting pregnant for about eighteen months. And de-worm them, of course.

And leave a bag of dog food with whoever will take ownership of the dogs. If they don't get shot or run over or whatever, they should have a longer life. And the overpopulation problem gets somewhat under control."

"How do you get permission to do that?"

"I knock on doors where the scrawny dogs are hanging around outside."

"Jeez, Julie! Would you keep both hands on the wheel!" Clare hung onto the door handle. "I can get the picture without you drawing it in the air with both hands."

Julie put one hand on the wheel and pointed at Clare. "I want you to take photos. I'm doing a book about this project. I'm calling it No Name Dogs."

Julie turned off the paved road leading up the hill from Scrag Creek and onto the gravel lane winding onto Julie's large country property where she had her veterinary clinic on the west side and her house on the east. Large clusters of evergreen trees obscured the view of the house from the clinic. The lane separated into a wide road clearly marked towards the clinic and a private lane circling in front of the house. As they curved round to the house, a small herd of donkeys ambled onto the road, blocking the car's passage. The donkeys brayed and swished their tails. Julie rolled down her window and started talking loudly to them as Clare laughed and got out of the car. "Hey gang!" Clare called and imitated their braying as they made their way towards her to receive rubs down their snouts and around their ears. It was a cacophony of braying, shouting and laughter as Clare led them into the trees and Julie drove the car to the front steps.

Al, a distinguished-looking, tall, white-haired man, came limping out the front door. "Ladies!" He flourished his cane towards Clare, Julie and the donkeys. "Clare. Welcome to our quiet mountain retreat." A variety of cats and kittens leapt onto the verandah railing. Three or more different-sized and -shaped dogs made their appearance in various places, each barking in different tones.

Clare was lodged in the underground level of the three-storey house, in comfortable quarters with bedroom, bathroom, television room, and a walkout to a view of distant mountains. She lay in bed under the warmth of a duvet, reflecting on her sister's life. Al had made a Hungarian goulash for their dinner. It was his specialty and Clare's favourite of the wide range of cooking Al did. He had had the table set and red wine 'breathing' when Clare and Julie arrived from the airport. Julie and Clare did the clearing up but it would be Al who had things set out for breakfast. When the coffee was made he would take a mug to Julie who would be sitting up in bed checking messages on her iPad. Clare had witnessed that on a previous visit when she had to be up early for a return flight. She had seen Julie smile at Al and he kiss her on the forehead.

It was what Clare missed most in her life since her children had gone off to university and Len retired. Affection. A hug. A kiss on the forehead. Taking her by the arm. Reaching for each other's hand. Oh well, thought Clare. I have the dogs. I'd perish without them to greet me when I come home.

Clare drew up her knees and rubbed her cold feet together. Something jumped onto the bed where her feet had been. Clare sat up. It was one of Julie's cats. "Hello Madam!" Clare stroked her head and back, then lay down under the duvet. "Sleep well. Tomorrow I go to the dogs. The No Name Dogs."

Julie worked in her home office, Al in his, while Clare assembled and ate the healthy breakfast set out on the kitchen counter. Yogurt, fruit, and multigrain toast. After clearing up, Clare took her camera out onto the deck to test the clarity of her lenses. "I want good pictures," Julie had said last night, "but don't be seen taking them."

"Really?!" Clare had laughed. "How do I do that? You providing bushes for me to hide in?"

"Wish I could. But the reservations we go onto aren't known for their fine landscaping." Julie laughed as she wrung out the dish cloth. "What I'm trying to say is, the residents are camera shy. They've had enough of nosey reporters making them and their places look bad. It was hard enough getting permission to touch and treat their dogs.

They trust me now. But not all of them. And not totally." Julie turned to Clare in a rare moment of solemnity. "It will work if you're seen to be focusing on the dogs, how cute and healthy they are. Let the people stay out of the picture. This is a project to help the dogs."

"Julie!" Al had cleared his throat in an exaggerated manner and stomped his cane on the floor. "You are talking to your sister. A highly regarded photographer of…?" Al looked at Julie with his bushy eyebrows raised.

"Oh spit," said Julie, looking chagrined. "Animals. Sorry, Clare. I do get carried away with my own projects, don't I. Sorry. You're a fabulous animal photographer. That's why I need you for this project."

"I'll focus on the dogs." Clare smiled wryly at Julie. She was easy to forgive. Always had been. Her younger sister. So full of ideas, projects, enthusiasms. Some of them turned out to be brilliant. This No Name Dogs project had yet to be proven.

It was a cloudy, damp, and cold day. Clare was waiting with her camera when Julie came downstairs at 7:45 sharp as had been agreed the night before. Julie was super punctual in her business. Running a clinic with staff to lead and client appointments, she had to be. Whereas Clare's work could involve waiting hours, days, sometimes weeks for the perfect focus on an animal in the wilderness.

"Did you have a good breakfast?" Julie reached into the closet for their jackets. "God knows if we'll get any lunch."

"Oh well," Clare put on her jacket. "Maybe there'll be leftover dog food."

The donkeys trotted along with them as they tromped over to the clinic. There were stacks of bagged dog food on the porch of the clinic. "All donated from local businesses," said Julie as the bags were loaded into the back of a black van. She introduced the rest of the No Name Dogs crew. Laura, a vet from the Calgary zoo. Rudi, a volunteer from a local animal shelter called ARF. The ARF man, thought Clare with a smile. And Maud, a retired policewoman.

Retired? Clare wondered. She looks well under sixty. Maud heaved the bags of dog food as though they were small bags of potatoes. When the pile in the van got too high for Clare to lift a bag onto, Maud noticed and said to Clare, "How about a picture of us slaves at work?"

"I'm onto it!" Clare smiled, retrieved her camera and assembled everyone into a working pose. Julie, who had put her pale green coveralls over her clothes, stood tall, with one hand on the van door, the other on her waist, smiling, overseeing the work, wearing dark sunglasses.

Maud got behind the steering wheel of the van, Laura in the front seat. Julie motioned Clare to get into the back seat of the van. "I'm going with the ARF guy." Julie leaned towards Clare's ear before heading to the ARF guy's car. "Gotta check him out. Never know what 'observers' are going to say in the press."

They drove along the highway, past wide flat fields where Clare imagined crops would grow in summer or cattle abound. Today the fields looked barren, cold, dead. The van turned off the highway onto paved secondary roads on the same flat terrain but there were no fenced-in fields. Modest new houses with much open land around each were set back from the road. Vans, or sometimes a pickup truck or car, were parked near the door of the houses. It was very rare to see shrubs, trees, or any kind of garden adorn the houses. Clare had seen Indigenous reserves in most parts of Canada. This one was extensive and apparently prosperous. Though she could not see the inside of any house here, Clare was told the water was good and all utilities, electricity, gas, Wi-Fi, installed. They had not come to examine the lives of the people, only the lives of the dogs.

Scrawny dogs of various mixed breeds, none of them large, skulked around some of the houses. Maud parked the van in a driveway, got out, walked purposefully, as police officers do, to the front door and knocked firmly. Someone pulled aside a sheet acting as a curtain over the large front window. Soon, but not immediately, a young woman opened the door partway, then fully when she recognized Maud. The woman nodded but didn't smile as she exchanged a few words with Maud, then closed the door as soon as Maud turned towards the van. Maud nodded a 'go ahead'.

Laura, who had been making notes in a small book, turned to Clare. "Better just stay here until we locate the dogs and get the inoculations going."

Julie must have said something similar to the ARF guy since he stayed in his car while Julie got out with Maud and Laura. Maud opened a bag of dog food. Laura and Julie filled their pockets and hands with kibble. Soon five dogs appeared from behind the house near a junk pile and from within an old dog house up against the side of the house. Julie assembled her kit in the back corner of the van. "OK, Clare," she said. "Come out and guard the hospital here while we nab the patients."

Three of the five captured dogs were female. Julie injected them proficiently in the back of the lower neck. All five dogs were given worm pills. Maud scattered more food for the dogs, a small pile for each one so there would be no fighting over it, then took the remainder of the bag to the front door. This time, the young woman who had been watching from the window along with an older woman and three children opened the door wide, smiled, and thanked Maud.

They drove on to other houses where permission had been granted to give the dogs contraceptive implants, worm pills and a free bag of food. Medium in size, the dogs were various in colour: black, brown, beige, each with different markings. They reminded Clare of coyotes but their faces were more broad. Some had floppy ears like hounds, others had pointed, erect ears. Clare could see traces of many different breeds in all the dogs she saw roaming the reserve.

"Where do all these dogs come from?" exclaimed Clare. "Or what? They're sure a long way from wolves!" She was most familiar with Arctic dogs in Inuit communities, sled dogs with clear resemblance to wolves.

"These are rez dogs," Laura answered. "Though they aren't all from reserves. Some people from off the rez bring pups and dogs and just abandon them on the reserve, trusting they'll survive or be looked after. So, they're all from abandoned dogs at some point and they breed indiscriminately with each other."

"I wouldn't call it breeding," said Maud. "More like raping. A female comes into heat and is attacked by every male who gets near her."

"She goes into heat twice a year. Could have a litter of six, eight, or more, twice a year. Do the math," said Laura. "A dozen to nearly twenty pups a year from just one dog. Not good!" She was assembling the needle and pills in the back of the van while Maud sat on the fender deftly holding a brown and white dog with large ears pointing wing-like on the sides of her head, her dark eyes apprehensive but her body calmed by Maud's manner of holding her.

"This is Dishwasher Dog," said Maud. "We found her sheltering in a dumped dishwasher last spring. Her pups frozen, dead beneath her."

"Oh my god!" said Clare. "I wish I hadn't heard that."

"That's what usually happens to pups born in winter," said Maud. "Though not always. But Dishwasher here is a good news story. She has survived another year. She's not the scrawny starving dog we found in the dishwasher, traumatized over her dead pups. Her implant has worked. Take a picture. She's fed and secure here on my lap."

Clare positioned her camera. Julie came over to sit beside Maud and inject a new implant. "The guy from ARF likes what we're doing," Julie told them.

"ARF?" Clare sounded the word like a bark.

"Animal Rescue Foundation." said Julie. "In downtown Calgary. If we have their support, we'll have a lot more home prospects for the dogs."

The next reserve they drove onto was also large and prosperous looking with newly built raised bungalows, acres of land separating the houses. There was a community arena, fire and ambulance hall, a sprawling one-storey school, a Peacemaker Centre for the Indigenous police office, and a spectacular Cultural Centre designed in teepee and curve shapes, no rectangles or squares.

"Dare I ask," said Clare, "why the people on the reserve don't take care of these dogs?"

"Some do," said Maud. "And there's this old guy, Jack, we'll get to soon. You'll see what his place looks like and the number of dogs and cats he feeds and shelters. But most people don't want to live like Jack. They have little kids running around and don't want a lot of hungry feral dogs hanging around their house. Packs of wild dogs can be dangerous."

"I don't see any big packs of dogs." Clare was working her camera through the open window of the front seat beside Maud at the steering wheel. "I'm seeing mostly loners, moms with pups, not enough to make a team or a pack."

"You'll see a small pack of five or so in the village where there's more food to scavenge," Maud steered the van onto a gravel road. "Anything larger than that is ... eliminated."

"How?"

Maud turned briefly to Clare and pointed her hand in the shape of a gun.

"Oh." Clare put her camera on her knees as she pictured another scene she didn't want to have in her mind. Dogs being shot because they are too numerous. She had been to the Arctic where that could happen to unwanted sled dogs. Not often, but it did. And then there was that case after the 2010 Olympics in Vancouver, when about fifty sled dogs were shot by their keeper, a non-Indigenous person. The dogs were no longer needed to give sled rides to tourists. The keeper went berserk, took it into his head that they needed to be killed off. One at a time, in front of each other.

Clare couldn't bear thinking of it. But the more you tried to bury a mental picture, the more it would fight for prominence. Best to just let it fade naturally. Vancouver, thought Clare, it's the most beautiful city in the world. Second, in her opinion, was Rio de Janeiro. There were feral dogs there, in Rio. Lots, Clare recalled, big packs of them. Were they culled? Probably. That's what people who justified killing off animals called it, culling.

"This contraceptive implant project is brilliant!" Clare couldn't help exclaiming to her companions, though she knew she was stating the obvious to them. "It deals with the root of the problem. And no execution of living creatures involved."

"Right on!" said Laura reaching forward from the back seat to do a high five with Clare. "Contraceptive implants are used to control the stock in zoos all the time. But they're not yet fully approved for veterinary clinic use across Canada. Trust Julie to get around that."

"How does she do it?" asked Clare.

"She just *does* things," said Maud. "Starts at the top. Went to the federal government. Filled out the appropriate forms, and the implants were made available for use on an emergency drug release permit."

"It's a pioneering project that Julie's conducting," said Laura. "Originating right here in Scrag Creek, Alberta." She smiled then looked serious. "These contraceptive implants only last for about eighteen months. Then we have to do new ones. But I'm sure the implants will soon be improved and approved, across the country. They're a heck of a lot easier and cheaper to do than spay surgery."

Clare thought about that. How far reaching the implications of this pioneering project could be. Feral dogs and cats are a problem the world over. Coyotes and foxes encroaching upon cities or smaller communities. Give them birth control rather than shoot them.

"This is Jack's place." Maud announced as she drove into what looked to Clare like a junk yard.

The driveway was rough, the gravel worn down, pot hole after pot hole splashed up the remains of winter, melted ice and snow. Cats and dogs scattered at the approach of the van and the ARF car. They ran to stand at a safe distance or crouch under various old vehicles and discarded machines placed around the house. There were cats on an old car's roof and hood. Dogs on the seat looking out the windows of the car. Cats on the hood and dogs looking out the window of an abandoned pickup truck. Dogs sitting in old tires, in hockey nets with boards leaning against them as a lean-to shelter. An old tin horse trough provided water for the animals.

"Welcome to our local animal shelter." Julie stood smiling, her arms outstretched. "Take all the photos you want. Jack won't stop you, though he doesn't want any of himself or his house. He's a modest man."

They hauled several bags of dog and cat food up the stairs onto the small porch of his house, then set to work luring the female dogs to have their implants renewed while Clare took photos. Jack came out onto his porch and lifted the bags of food into his house, exchanging some banter with Julie and Maud. He looked carefully at Clare who paused to acknowledge him. A tall man, his face much lined, his long white hair pulled back in a tail. She wanted to photograph him but restrained herself, putting her camera down and her hand up in a wave. He waved back to her then disappeared inside his house.

"That man's face is full of story," Clare said to Julie.

"Sure is. But he's not sharing it with us."

Clare observed the dog being held on Maud's lap after being implanted by Julie. It had brown, tan, and white markings, large round eyes like a beagle, and pointed ears that flopped down. It was surprisingly relaxed, her ears not held back. "She looks like she wants to stay on your lap."

"She does," said Maud. "She's experienced this twice before. Being fed, then gently, firmly held, in a warm place on a cold day. What's not to like!" Maud held her a couple of moments longer, then set her down to do another dog. "You're done, Brandy. Take care. We do want to see you again in October." Brandy licked and slobbered on Maud's gloved hand. "Hey girl! You're *welcome*" Maud turned to Clare. "They don't usually do that. I'm glad my gloves are on. The slobber from these worm ridden, scavenger dogs could do you in. Not to mention fleas!" Maud brushed her pants before taking another dog.

"What are the chances of your seeing Brandy again?" asked Clare.

Maud looked at Laura who was making notes on Brandy. "How many dogs have we found three times running?"

"Brandy's already set the record," Laura flapped the notebook shut. "Finding the same dog twice in a row is a boon. The survival rate for these semi-feral females isn't usually more than two years. Unless they get looked after, as Brandy has been by Jack."

"What do you mean by semi-feral?"

"They tolerate some human touch. They've had some experience of being well treated by humans. Easy to lure or catch, like Brandy. But most are running scared. Won't take food until you're too far away to catch them."

There was no stopping for their own lunch. Laura had brought enough egg salad sandwiches for everyone. They parked in the village in the early afternoon to get out and scatter food to a roaming pack of seven dogs, all of them similar looking, quite big, dark with white markings. "Survival of the fittest and lots of incest," Julie remarked wryly in explanation of the similarity of the dogs. There were only two females but they couldn't be caught.

Julie and her team scattered seven piles of food as simultaneously as they could, to avert fighting for the food. There were warning growls and teeth bared but no major fight broke out. The pack was used to sharing, in its own snarling manner. Worming pills inside a soft pocket of food were thrown into each pile.

Clare noticed that the villagers who passed by or stopped to watch did so only fleetingly. They were used to seeing this or didn't want to give it much regard.

The ARF guy went into a store for coffee, tea and chocolate chip cookies for the No Name Dog team. Then he had to head back to work in Calgary, saying he had a lot of admiration for the project and he would get back to Julie when he had more concrete info on dog adoption prospects.

Julie shrugged when she got into the van, taking over the driving from Maud. "We'll see what he actually comes up with," she said. "Not a lot of city folk want to take on rez dogs. Not if they know they're at all feral."

"Do they have to know?" said Laura. "Everything? Wouldn't the dogs be caged just like all the other dogs for adoption? Why would prospective owners have to know the dog is from a reserve and has never lived in a house? Zoo animals generally come from the wild. They learn to adapt."

Clare wanted to say something about the wrongs of capturing wild animals and putting them into the captivity of a zoo. She couldn't bear to recall the lethargy and boredom, the trapped behaviour of a pack of wolves she had seen in a Washington zoo. But Julie turned and quickly glared at her, making a subtle 'zip lip' signal to Clare that Laura didn't see. Clare backed off. Julie was right in keeping peace in her team. The subject was changed. The afternoon ensued. Light rain drizzled down, on and off.

Clare took pictures of an eccentric property where the yard was full of driftwood sculptures, rough dog houses, new bicycles dropped on the ground after recent use. Over the windows and doorway of the house, antlers were attached. A Canadian flag was draped like a curtain in the front room window. A woman came out of the house wearing a colourful, artistically designed blanket coat. She was carrying a white furry pup. She talked and smiled with Julie and Maud, directing them to a grove of trees where a dog lay with a small litter of pups on some old bedding. The mother was easily lured with handfuls of food and given an implant. She returned to her pups and lay down, licking and feeding them.

"That pup they brought into the house," Julie said, "is, I think, I hope, going to be turned into a household pet."

They drove through two other reserve communities. An older one with well-built, more individually designed houses that looked as though they had been lived in and well taken care of for over a decade. They did not have shrubs planted or gardens for flowers or vegetables. I can relate to that, thought Clare, who did not enjoy gardening but did like flowers and shrubs around her home, so she did the work required. This reserve community had mature trees and no abandoned vehicles or machines in the yards. There were few dogs and they did not appear to be feral. The dogs approached in friendly pet manner.

"No camera work here," Julie instructed Clare. "We're just doing house calls."

A teenager came out of a house wearing sweat pants and a hoodie. He carried a pup that needed de-worming. Julie also gave antivirus injections to it and to other dogs that were brought over to the van by people from the community. Maud and Laura knocked on some doors to let the inhabitants know they were there to administer to any dogs. Some were brought to the van to have implants. Mainly women and older children brought the dogs for treatment. Clare was allowed to take photos of the dogs being treated. A young teenage girl asked to have her photo taken as she smiled and held her pup facing the camera.

They drove on to a very new-looking community of log houses with front verandahs and gabled second stories. The logs were rounded and varnished. There were trampolines in some of the yards. Though it was cold and slightly drizzly, kids came out to show off on the trampolines or wave and watch as the van stopped to turn itself into a mobile vet clinic. It was a Saturday, but no men came out of the houses.

"Where are the men?" asked Clare.

"Let's just assume they're off working, or sleeping after a night shift," said Maud.

"Or just not dog persons?" said Laura, looking skywards.

Clare looked at Julie. "Maud has a dog at home, presented to us by a guy on the rez, right Maud?"

"I do."

"He had run over its hind quarters. An accident. He said he was going to shoot it, put it out of its misery. But his kids said he should give it to us and he did. Drove it to my clinic. He wouldn't hang around. Didn't want to see the dog again. I could save the dog's life. But I couldn't save both legs, just the one. So Maud took on a three-legged dog. Right Maud?"

"Right. We call him Tripod. He gets around like a real trooper."

They drove a distance from the new log houses to the local garbage disposal. "Now for the Dumpster Dogs," announced Julie. There were three large dumpsters. Two with the lids down, One tightly closed. The other was overstuffed with garbage so the lid didn't close. The third one had its lid open. It was about two-thirds full and in it was a medium-sized black dog, scavenging.

Looking carefully in the scrub land and bushes around the garbage site, Clare spotted three other dogs lurking. "What's going on?" she asked. "Why are the other dogs hanging back?"

"One at a time is the law," said Maud. "Otherwise it's a gruesome fight to the death. Sad thing is, scrounging in the dumpster can also be the kiss of death."

"How so?"

"Just think what they're diving into. Shards of glass, of sharp metal. Rotting food, maybe slow poisoning stuff. It's not all steak bones and pizza crusts in there."

"Good thing is," said Julie, "it's not so hard to capture a dumpster dog. Let's see if we have a mom or a dad in here."

Laura brought a cup of dog food. "Hey!" she exclaimed seeing the dog up close. "It's Molly. She's come back for another implant. How many repeats is that for today?"

It turned out to be fifteen. "That's fifteen lives saved," said Julie. "*If* they don't die of lack of water, and food and shelter. Get run over, shot or killed in a fight. And fifteen times litters of eight, twice a year … makes 120 times two … equals 240 pups that wouldn't make it through a winter … to go on and die of the above." Julie put her hands back on the steering wheel. "A good day's work. Let's go home."

They drove over a bridge spanning a creek. Good watering hole, thought Clare. Must be dogs living near here. They saw a fairly big dog, gray-black hair with white markings. It reminded Clare of sled dogs except its ears were floppy and its tail hung down. The dog was walking slowly along the ditch beside the road. It lay down. They stopped the van a good distance in front of the dog. Maud got out and slowly approached with food in her gloved hand. Clare took photos.

When Maud got within two metres of the dog, it got itself up laboriously and moved into the taller grass. Maud halted. Then slowly followed the dog. She halted again. When she came back to the van, she got a pan full of dog food. "He won't let me touch him. I'm just stressing him in trying. I'll leave some food and a worm pill. That's the best we can do for him. He's on his last legs."

They drove off in silence.

Chapter Three

The Hovel in Ottawa

Clare had come home from that visit to Julie's carrying several boxes of pearl earrings and pearl necklaces of unusual design. They were made from different coloured cultured pearls: some with an indigo blue sheen, some silvery black or deep lustrous green, and many ivory or pink pearls. The necklaces were composed of tiny seedling pearls set artistically amidst mature pearls on wire so delicate and indiscernible, the pearls seemed unattached. These were not necklaces for ball gowns or cashmere sweaters. They were to be worn as Julie did, with shirts and tee shirts, jackets and jeans.

"Cowgirl pearls." Julie had laughed when she showed Clare her storeroom of earrings and necklaces. "But you city slickers can sport them too." Julie told Clare how she had found a huge source of inexpensive cultured pearls near Shanghai on a trip to China with Al. Those pearls are perfect for stud earrings, she had thought. And necklaces! Why not string them into casual arty necklaces. Julie purchased as large a supply of pearls as she could afford and brought them home to turn into earrings and necklaces she could sell to make money for her veterinary projects.

"She's made a profitable business of it," Clare told Len, showing him the boxes of earrings and necklaces she had brought home to sell for Julie. "The earrings make cheap but valuable gifts. They'll be easy to sell. The necklaces cost more but they're worth it."

"They don't look worth much to me," said Len after a gulp of scotch. "They look like you couldn't afford to get a full string of real pearls. I thought people were rich now in Alberta. Why, for chrissake, would they buy some cheap cultured pearls strung out along wires? Surely they can afford real pearls from a jewelry store, for chrissake."

"Oh come on!" Clare sank back into the couch. She wanted things to be better with Len when she got home, but he so deflated her and riled her at the same time. "These necklaces are beautiful and original. Julie designs them. She now has someone else do the craft work. Al takes care of the books and business side of things. They sell them at art shows and online. It's a very successful enterprise."

"If you say so." After another large gulp, Len raised his glass. "To Julie, the entrepreneur. Too bad you didn't inherit more of those entrepreneurial genes."

"Just what do you mean by that?!"

"Your sister has a lot of business smarts."

"And I don't?"

"You said it. Not me."

"You know what, Len?"

He shrugged and took another drink in anticipation of 'what'.

"You're right. You're absolutely right. My sister is a fabulous entrepreneur and I admire her for it. Totally."

"Why aren't you jealous? You should be jealous."

"Jealous of someone who does so much good in the world? That makes no sense. No sense at all."

"It sure as hell does. You're just not admitting it."

"And you just want to fight. Well, I don't!" Clare picked up her suitcase and headed for the stairs. "I can tell you there is one thing I do envy about my sister."

"What's that?"

"I envy her having a non-belligerent, sober husband who helps with the bloody housework and the business."

"I pull my weight," Len yelled. "I'm the provider in this household."

Let him have the last word, Clare told herself as she started upstairs. Don't get into it. Don't take the bait. Walk away. She continued upstairs. They were in their house in Ottawa. It was April, not a good time to be at Loghaven on the lake. Too much cold rain and mud to contend with there. The Malamutes had begun to throw their winter fur. When at their city home the dogs lived in the securely fenced back yard. But they had been brought into the house to welcome Clare home. They had jumped up at her in the front entrance, Yukitu first, then Ike was given his turn.

"My dominatrix and my cuddle monster." Clare laughed. "Have you been good dogs?" She gave each of them a crunchy pig's ear, which Ike grabbed and snapped and devoured on the spot. Yukitu took hers off to the kitchen to eat at a more savouring pace. But when Len yelled and Clare started up the stairs, both dogs wanted out. Yukitu pawed the door.

Clare turned at the top of stairs and called down to Len in the living room. "Len, please let the dogs out."

"What? What did you say?" he yelled. "You know I can't hear you when you're round a corner. Come here if you have something to say."

Yukitu scratched louder. Clare breathed out heavily. "Hang on, Yukitu. I'm coming." She put down her suitcase and let the dogs out. Hearing the door close, Len called out from his chair. "I would have let them out, for chrissake. If you had asked."

Clare ran the bath and poured orange blossom oil into the water. A soothing hot bath. So, here I am, Clare told herself, back in Command Central, as her daughters joked about Ottawa, the capital. She was long plane rides away from each of them, her grown-up identical twins, Ali and Megan, both with young families of their own. Ali was a pediatrician at Vancouver General Hospital, Megan a lawyer in St. John's, Newfoundland. They couldn't be further apart in Canada. And she plunk in the middle of the country. Not that they would want me on their doorstep. But it sure would be nice to see more of those bright-spark grandkids. And more of my daughters.

You'd think I'd be used to it by now, Clare reprimanded herself. She felt it as the unforeseen, unending emotional pain of divorce. Her daughters had been born in 1973 in Oxford, where she had gone as a graduate student to marry another Canadian graduate student, Stan, who was doing his D.Phil. at Christchurch College. The plan had been that they would return to Canada after he graduated. But when he finished his D.Phil., Stan obtained a fellowship at Christchurch, an extraordinary achievement at his young age. He thrived in the Oxford life and sinecure. Clare enjoyed it well enough and made lasting friendships, but she did not want to spend the rest of her life there, nor raise her children in the English school system. Nor did she want to, or believe she could, force Stan to go home to Canada. Their relationship suffered and they divorced after thirteen years.

They co-operated with a joint custody arrangement, which gave Clare care of the children throughout the school year in Canada and enabled Stan to have them with him in England during the long Oxford breaks around Christmas, Easter and the summer. Clare thought this would be good for their daughters and it turned out to be so. But she was emotionally knocked over every time by how hard it was to put them on planes and be separated from them. The anxiety about their safety was the worst. Early on she realized and over time genuinely felt it to be true … as long as they're well and thriving, I'm OK with wherever they live.

She put on her bathrobe and went downstairs to watch TV, since she was still on Calgary time, two hours earlier than Ottawa. It was not yet 8 p.m. but Len had fallen asleep in his armchair. Passed out is more like it, thought Clare, as she brought the dogs in to watch TV with her. Len stirred and slowly lifted his head, opening his eyes as the dogs passed in front of him.

"What the hell's going on?" He gripped the arms of his chair.

"Nothing," Clare sat down in the middle of the couch. Yukitu was getting up onto her corner of the couch, Ike heading to the other corner. "Just going to watch TV."

Len considered it all then began to get himself up from the chair. "I'm toast," he said as he gripped the door frame and stumbled upstairs to their bedroom.

Too much of a contrast, thought Clare as she sat between Ike and Yukitu. Too much of a contrast between my life and Julie's. She'll be sitting down to a good dinner Al has prepared, having pleasant conversation, then going to bed with him putting his arms around her. Whereas, when she went to bed, Len would be lying on his back snoring. She would have to nudge him to roll him onto his side and then she would try to get to sleep with his back turned to her.

That was the night she decided to stop sharing a bed with him. She slept on the pull-out bed in the den. Why should I be driven out of our comfortable bedroom? she thought. He's the snoring drunk. But no way would he move from the more comfortable bedroom.

"This is my house," he argued angrily next day. "As is Loghaven. I'm going back there today. This is a goddam hovel. I just bought it to please you."

Clare drew in her breath. His perspective had gone so off base. She would not argue on his terms.

"This is a marriage," said Clare. "This is *our* house. As is Loghaven. We are joint owners."

"Oh yeah? You haven't put a penny into either of them."

"Len, that is so far from the truth."

Len got up, leaving his plate and coffee cup on the table. "And if you don't want to sleep with me, that's your problem. Find another bed."

He gathered up his toiletry kit and briefcase, then drove the Jeep to Loghaven.

Clare followed with the dogs on the weekend. Len came to the door when they arrived. "Welcome home," he said, as though all were well.

"Thank you," said Clare. She believed in civility. She did not move any of her clothes from their bedroom or her things from the en suite bathroom. But she slept in the larger guest bedroom and hung her bathrobe on the hook on the door.

We're not the only old couple who sleep apart, she told herself. But what a lousy way to live the rest of our lives.

Chapter Four

Adventure Canada in the Arctic

The photo that eventually gave Clare some fame and led to her being invited to visit Fort McMurray was taken on a trip, back in 2008, to the high Arctic to camp on ice at the floe edge. Arctic animals, both on land and sea, would gather there in June during the summer solstice. Clare was hoping to see polar bears. Instead she caught an unusual photo of a wolf.

The group of campers was small, ten adults led by two Adventure Canada guides. One of them looked like Prince William, so they called him Prince. Clare paired up with a young photographer who had recently moved to Ottawa. Michelle Valberg. She was strikingly tall with long smooth ginger hair and a radiant inner warmth and strength. Michelle's previous focus had been on African animals, lions, leopards, and the usual safari lot.

The Adventurers gathered for orientation in an Ottawa hotel and would fly next day from there to Iqaluit in Nunavut. The evening before the flight they all had dinner together in the hotel, except for Michelle who excused herself to go home and spend the night with her husband and very young son. Clare observed the other Adventurers at dinner. A professional photographer and his wife from Germany. A couple of travellers who lived in Australia. Some older, apparently fit men and women who seemed to be on their own. Why would they want the discomfort of camping in a tent with a sleeping bag on ice in the Arctic, Clare wondered. Then she realized, my god, they're probably younger than me. It was Clare's first trip to the high Arctic. All her previous work was done in the forests, fields, and mountains of southern Canada where summer involved grass and trees and lakes warm enough for swimming.

Michelle joined them next morning, loaded with lenses and camera equipment that Clare had not seen before and wouldn't know how to operate. This digital stuff is beyond me, thought Clare. And how can young photographers afford such a complexity of equipment?

Michelle was tall and strong. She smiled and laughed as she flung lens straps and heavy lenses over her back and under her arms. Clare offered to help her. She looked Clare in the eye and smiled and thanked her heartily, using a lot of 'wow's and 'hey's and 'amazing'. Clare laughed and decided she really liked this enthusiastic young photographer. They sat together on the plane. By the time they landed in Iqaluit, they knew each other's basic life stories.

After her first marriage did not work out, Michelle married a handsome fireman with warm dark eyes. Clare had noticed how he lifted their little son Ben up into his arms to say good bye to Michelle at the hotel. A modern, work-sharing husband, thought Clare. They were very lucky to have a child since Michelle had been forty when they married.

The sun was shining when they landed in Iqaluit's small airport. Small planes in a small airport within sight of the ocean's edge. There were patches of snow on the ground but mainly the landscape was brown dirt packed down, no trees, no green grass, some rocky terrain and some vegetation along the run-off streams from winter snow, though they were approaching the first day of summer, June 21, the day of most light in the northern hemisphere. The day my twin daughters were born, Clare smiled to herself.

She saw a few sled dogs lying in tethered groups in the brown meadowland along the road into town. These were scruffy, ungroomed sled dogs, clumps of fur protruding from their winter coats ready to fall off or be 'thrown' by the dogs. Her dogs in Ottawa began to throw their coat, much earlier, in March. Clare would groom them regularly for several weeks, pulling the loose clumps out until their coat of smooth hair was established. The dogs along the roadside looked as though they had never felt a comb. They lay listless on the ground in the afternoon sun. But that was typical of sled dogs and wolves. They 'came to' in late afternoon when wolves went hunting and dogs were fed. These dogs looked well enough fed and they had pails of water within reach. Clare concluded they were probably well-trained racing and working sled-dog teams.

It was a short walking distance from the airport to the scattered small houses and pizza/hotdog huts on the outskirts of town. Their group was being led to the home of an Inuit law student near the rocky shore of the ocean. The law student was a sharp-looking woman, Aiya, with short curly black hair, maybe forty-something. Now pushing sixty-five myself, thought Clare, I can't tell anyone's age anymore. They're all just young to me. Aiya's house was crammed with stuff, from furniture to books and knickknacks to Inuit designer fur jackets trimmed with collars, shawls and cuffs of various soft furs. "I'd love to have any one of them," Clare said to Aiya.

"They're all for sale," Aiya looked her in the eye.

"If I could only afford them!" Clare smiled.

Aiya shrugged and turned away. She gave them a talk on Inuit customs and how to make the tea and bannock she served to them. It was like pizza crust with no topping. Clare thanked Aiya, then slipped away from the group to walk around town carrying her simplest camera. She noted kids on bikes or just hanging around the streets. As on the reserves in the south she had seen with Julie, there was almost no sign of pride of place outside the modest houses with large lots of ground between them, though garbage was not strewn and the town looked sanitary. The court house and government offices were new and grand, of Inuit circular architectural design. Nunavut had become an independent Inuit territory of Canada in 1999. Clare felt there was dignity and pride in the atmosphere and in the way the staff of the government offices welcomed her, offering a tour of the building. She apologized for lacking the time to do that.

She re-joined the group boarding the plane north to Pond Inlet.

She sat with Michelle, saying "Could do with a glass of wine about now."

"Not on this plane. Not on this trip," Michelle groaned. "Pond Inlet is a dry zone. But I bet someone in this group has managed to sneak in a bottle of something or other." She looked at the other passengers. "Someone usually passes something around after dinner once we're camped."

Their plane gradually lowered itself below the clouds so they could see out the windows. They looked upon mountains of rock, mostly snow-covered, as was the land of the ocean coast. They circled round and round through fog over the high Arctic community of Pond Inlet until the pilot found his way to land on the small airstrip. Clare stepped down the plane's aluminum stairs, breathing in the air which felt mildly cold, like the end of winter in Ottawa. It was a short walk to the wooden dormitory where they would be accommodated until weather conditions were right for them to begin the six-hour journey by sled across the ice between Pond Inlet on Baffin Island and Bylot Island.

Clare stopped a few steps after putting her feet on the ground. There was a difference in the air. She looked around. They were on the outskirts of a small community of wooden frame houses with much space between them. It was a scattering of houses and community buildings on a hilly landscape sloping down to the ocean edge. A pickup truck or two drove along the roadways. One was being loaded with luggage and cargo from the plane. Some all-terrain vehicles were at hand. To Clare, they looked like children's tractors. This was the smallest airport she had ever seen. This is remote, she said to herself. I'm in a remote part of the country. A remote part of the planet. It's different here. Not just a difference in the air. Colder. And a purity in the air. But there's more than that kind of difference.

Clare was hustled along then by the guides and other campers. Light and bright as it was outside, it was late into the evening. It would never get dark here on this trip into the Arctic. It was a few days until June 21, the longest day. Her companions were eager to settle into their rooms, see if they could make contact on their cell phones with people at home. See what amenities there would be in this wooden dormitory building, the hotel of Pond Inlet.

Clare couldn't make much more than the simplest use of her cell phone in the best of circumstances. She had not advanced much into the digital world. I'm stuck in the darkroom of photography, she reprimanded herself. Still using what is now an old-fashioned camera. I'm going to become extinct if I don't get onto all this new equipment. I'll get onto it after this trip. Best to just stick with what I know for now.

They entered the dark brown building, then assembled in a large room with big windows letting in the light on two sides. It was the conference room and the dining hall and the whatever-other-needs-were-to-be-met space.

"Double up," said Dan, "and choose a room along the hallway over there. Sort your stuff in your backpack tomorrow morning so you're ready to take off in the sleds whenever we say the weather is clear enough. Parkas will be issued after supper here in the grub room tonight. There are showers but not many and they don't work well. They're for special needs really. Remember. You're in the Arctic, the High Arctic, a different part of the planet. Some have called it precious and I would agree with that.

"Your cell phones won't work here. You can leave them in the safe at the front desk. Also your watches. I never need a watch up here. But you can do what you want with yours. See you all back here in about an hour."

Most everyone, except Prince, looked at their watches. He smiled seeing them do so.

Michelle grabbed Clare. "Come on. Let's double up."

They took the room at the far end of the hallway. It had two bunks built into the walls with standing room only in between. A set of shelves built onto the wall at the foot of each bed. This is a hikers' hostel, thought Clare. But luxury compared to the tent we'll have to crawl into for six nights camping on ice.

"Isn't he awesome?" said Michelle.

"Who? Prince William?"

"God no! He's just cute. A lookalike. Sweet guy. But Dan…. He's awesome."

Clare wondered what younger people really meant when they called most everything they liked 'awesome'. "I bet he has stories to tell."

"And knock-out good looking," said Michelle.

"I suppose" said Clare. "I've never been attracted to young men. To me, they all just look like sons I never had. Never had a brother either."

"Dan's gotta be my age," said Michelle. "He doesn't wear a wedding ring. Wonder what his story is."

For supper they had rice and chicken with green peas. "That was good," said Clare to the German couple sitting with her. Michelle was sitting with Dan, asking him questions, smiling and cocking her head this way and that. Busy finding out his story.

"Good?" said Hilda. "You think so?"

"Yes," said Clare. "For dinner at the North Pole. It was hot. Well… warm enough. And don't you think peas taste the best of any frozen vegetables?"

Hilda looked to her husband, who was perhaps not her husband. "I guess we must accustom ourselves to frozen vegetables. Yah?"

Her companion, Ingo, stood up from the table, indicating he had had enough of this conversation. He nodded politely to Clare before turning his back.

When parkas were issued, Clare was given a red one which made her look as though she were wearing a stack of puffy red tires. Michelle was given an orange one which looked similarly puffy on her. "You look like a pumpkin." Clare laughed.

"And you look like a tomato." Michelle put her arm around Clare.

"A tomato and a pumpkin have come to the Arctic," said Prince.

It was strange falling asleep in daylight. Clare thought more about the strangeness. Daylight lingering into the midnight hour. But something else. The quiet! Clare exclaimed to herself. We are in a hotel, in a small town. No sound of traffic or people outside the hotel. Strangely quiet. Like an empty church.

Next day was too foggy to set off in the sleds. Planes were grounded at the airport. Michelle was given access to the phone line to deal with business in her Ottawa photography studio. Clare put on her tomato parka and felt-lined rubber boots to explore the town. With wool socks the boots were warm enough, the temperature being only a little below zero Celsius.

Clare wandered along the slushy roads and over the snow and hard mud pathways. Children played with soccer balls and hockey sticks, whacking pucks into makeshift nets as though the entire terrain were sports fields and arenas. Clare asked them where they got their soccer balls and hockey sticks. "A load of donated stuff from the south last Christmas," was the answer.

She learned later from Prince that Pond Inlet was quite well endowed because it was established as the northernmost tourist destination and a source for Inuit art production. Clare did not see loitering teenagers smoking dope or sniffing gas as was the stereotype of northern Inuit communities. That doesn't mean problems don't exist, Clare told herself, just because I'm not seeing them.

Clare came upon the school which had recently closed for the summer. It was large with several classrooms, modern in design and well maintained. There was a public library attached. Clare went inside and talked with the librarian who was welcoming and took time to show her around. Trained as a teacher-librarian at the University of Prince Edward Island, this young Inuit woman was eager to have Clare see their collection of Inuit-authored books and books about life in the Arctic. The Inuit-authored books were very few, mostly artfully illustrated children's books by Michael Kusugak.

On leaving the library and school grounds, Clare noticed there was no garbage strewn about the school yard, not a scrap of litter. But in other places around town there was a lot of litter. It shocked Clare to see parts of styrofoam containers floating down the rivulets and streams to the ocean shore. On recent television newscasts much attention was paid to how oceans were being polluted with plastic garbage bags and styrofoam containers, which were the toughest and took longest to disintegrate wherever they were dumped. Our group should organize a couple of hours to go around picking up this litter, Clare thought. And immediately thought better of it. It would be an insult to the people of the community. The litter free school yard indicated the young were taught not to litter.

Instead she focused on the shoreline which met with the ocean, its surface deeply frozen over with ice. A few dog teams were tethered out on the ice, pails for food and water nearby. There were fishing holes and ice huts with people fishing or just sitting on folding chairs around them. Children playing. They looked like people on holiday, everyone wearing waterproof boots. Fishing camp, Clare smiled to herself. Arctic style.

She walked along the shore then up the hill where a scruffy looking sled-dog team was tethered, the dogs lying listlessly on the ground as dogs do in the afternoon. A few boys were making their way up the hill on the far side of the dogs. One boy, carrying a broken hockey stick, went over and poked a dog, making it get up. Then it lay down again listlessly. Clare stopped in her tracks and stared at them harshly. The boy looked at her, shrugged his shoulders, and moved on up the hill with the others.

Chapter Five

The Smiling Wolf

Next morning Dan assembled the group to instruct them on their departure for the floe edge. It would take six hours being pulled in large wooden sleds across the ice by Inuit drivers on snowmobiles. Each person could bring a knapsack of personal belongings. Photographers could bring only enough equipment to carry on their own. Easy for me, thought Clare. All I have is my old digital camera and a couple of zoom lenses. Change of underwear, socks, journal, face cloth, face cream, toothbrush and paste, deodorant and comb in my knapsack. It would be five nights of camping on ice. Then the return trip.

More sleds would be loaded with camping equipment: tents, portable toilet, cooking equipment and food. It would take about an hour to get everything loaded before they could set off across the ice towards a place they could not see. Clare contemplated the endless ice with shallow pools and cracks of ice water extending as far as could be seen from the rocky hillsides of Pond Inlet.

"It's these 'cracks' that bother me." Clare said to Michelle when they stood on the shore watching the lineup of sleds perched over a shoreline crevice full of icey water. "Are these 'cracks' actual cracks in the ice? How deep do they go? Right down to the ocean water? Can they move? Or increase? Making this icefield one great flat, floating iceberg? That takes us into the Atlantic or Pacific? I'm not ready to go out in that manner. Not yet! I plan to have a big party first. *Then* catch the ice floe."

"My God, Clare!" said Michelle. "You have an amazing imagination. Too much for a photographer. These are just cracks in the ice, Arctic style."

"Full of menace," said Clare. "Full of menace."

Clare climbed back up the hillside to get a picture of the shoreline of ice with the sleds perched over the long shoreline crack, their runners pointing out over the endless ice, as they were loaded up by the Adventure guides and Inuit drivers of the powerful Ski-doos that would pull them to the camp and floe edge. She imagined six hours driving through fog and whatever else lurked out there. Dan carried a rifle. The Inuit guides and drivers had rifles stashed in the sleds.

I don't mind being scared, thought Clare. It's the thrill part of any adventure. Seeing a polar bear, getting a good picture of it is what she hoped for most. "That's what everyone wants," Dan had remarked during the discussion period. "But not up close. You all hear that? You don't want to be up close with a polar bear."

Michelle laughed. "We need up close, Dan. You can protect us."

Smart guide, thought Clare. He's planted the expectation. We'll see polar bears, but at a safe distance.

Before boarding the sled, Clare went to check on the sled dogs. She thought of how sled dogs were replaced by roaring Ski-doos. She missed Yukitu and Ike and the Malamutes she had before them, Yukon Sally and Jake. They had been named after her grandmother's Malamutes. Yukon Sally was her first Malamute. She was the most regal and most wolflike. She was large, with long skinny legs, too wolflike to qualify as a Malamute show dog. Clare had been intrigued by her from the first moment she saw her as a pup. The rest of the litter had already been selected. Yukon Sally was left over, her siblings taken to new homes weeks previously. Yukon Sally sat in the corner of the kennel, observing Clare observing her. She didn't crouch, cower or make a move, just stood her ground. Clare judged her to be intelligent and sensitive, as smart dogs are, yet stand-off-ish and empathetic as Clare understood wolves to be.

Yukon Sally was still small enough for Clare to lift up and carry her in her arms to the car. The breeder, Alison, had handled her well. Yukon was calmed by Alison. She did not struggle but kept silent in Clare's arms as Len drove them home. Clare noticed the sleeve of her jacket was soaked in Yukon's saliva where Yukon had rested her chin. She must have been terrified, thought Clare, but hadn't let out a whimper. She wouldn't eat for the first couple of days but she drank water and soon, gradually, ate the kibble Alison had recommended for her.

Clare took Yukon to their cabin on the lake for the first week and paid her constant attention while respecting that Yukon didn't like to be petted. She responded to praise and enthusiasm and some playfulness. She needs a companion, thought Clare. She is a pack animal. By the end of a couple of weeks, when Yukon Sally indicated that she accepted Clare and showed her affection by pawing Clare and nodding her head, Clare felt honoured in a unique way. The honour was something to be treasured and respect for Yukon's independence of thinking was to be given in return.

Clare did not use food treats to train Yukon to 'sit down' or 'come'. She praised Yukon and showed how pleased she was with her when Yukon did as asked. But it wasn't really obedience. Clare could see that each request was something Yukon first thought over and then decided, OK, I don't mind doing that. But decision making was involved. Sometimes Yukon just didn't want to do it. For instance: fetching. Clare tried throwing a stick for Yukon to fetch. Yukon understood what Clare expected of her. And she did it. Twice. On the third throw, Yukon sat down, indicating, I've had enough of that. It's boring and stupid.

"You're right." Clare laughed. "You're absolutely right. How about learning 'stay'. That's a useful one."

It took two tries. Yukon understood what was requested. She 'stayed', for a short time. Good enough, thought Clare. She knows what is requested. But Clare had the feeling Yukon would only do it if it seemed reasonable to her. That proved to be true. Clare had no desire to try to teach Yukon humiliating tricks, like 'roll over' or 'beg'. Yukon had her own way of making requests to Clare. Yukon would come to the table when Clare and Len were eating meat. She would sit down politely at the edge of the table and put her paw on the table.

"Yukon Sally!" Clare exclaimed. "How dare you!" She laughed and began cutting a piece of chicken.

"Here, Yukon." Len put a piece of chicken on the floor near him. Yukon went over and ate it. "Don't make us regret feeding you at the table," he said.

"She's beyond dog," said Clare. "She really is."

Yukon Sally would not take a bribe. If Clare gave Yukon a rawhide bone when Clare had to leave the property for a few hours, Yukon would chew the bone only after Clare returned.

It was the darkest day, December 21, the winter solstice, when Yukon Sally, aged ten, suffering from a cancer, had to be laid to rest. Five years prior to that, Clare had bought a male Malamute pup, Yukon Jake, to be Yukon Sally's pup and companion. Jake would do most anything for food. When the vet came that winter day to lay Yukon Sally to rest in Clare's arms, outside in the snow that Yukon Sally loved, Jake was diverted from the scene by being given a large rawhide bone. He snatched the bone and ran around the corner of the house to chew it. After he discovered Yukon Sally had gone and did not return, never again would he accept a rawhide bone.

Clare was remembering those scenes when she looked at the scruffy sled dogs lying on the rocky hillside. In the distance, on a patch of snow and ice, Clare saw a dog emerge. Or was it a wolf? It looked like Yukon Sally. Clare slowly turned her back to attach a better zoom lens to her camera then turned slowly to find the wolf or dog still standing there. It's a wolf, thought Clare. It's so unlike any of the dogs I've seen in Pond Inlet. Or am I having a vision? No. I don't have *visions*. Clare scoffed at the idea. She looked more intently through the lens. The wolf was smiling like a Malamute. Entirely like Yukon Sally, Clare thought as she saw the expression on her face through the lens. Entirely! She clicked the shutter again. And again. She was mesmerized. The animal stood still a moment longer, then turned and disappeared behind the hillside. That's no dog, Clare concluded. Though perhaps it was.

She began to walk towards where it had been but there was a gulley in between. It was too far and difficult to get to where the dog had been. It would take too long to pursue whatever she had seen. Clare could hear Michelle calling for her.

"What were you doing?" Michelle said as they clambered over the wooden sides of the sled and sat down on the wooden seat at the back. At the front end was a covered hood over the supplies giving the sled the shape of an old baby buggy with long wooden runners instead of wheels.

"Taking a photo," said Clare. "Maybe the best I've ever taken."

"Of what? You didn't spot a polar bear, did you?"

"It was a wolf. Smiling, like a Malamute. It had to be a wolf. We'll look at it later. Once we get this sleigh ride going."

The snowmobile drivers took off like the start of a race, each pulling a sled on a long yellow rope cord. The Inuit drivers were agile and expert. Most of the route was through ankle-deep water on the surface of the ice. It sprayed up behind the snowmobiles like the wake behind a motor boat. The drivers veered to spray some wake in one another's path. When they came to a crack, the drivers sped up to leap over it, yanking the long sled quickly across it. When Clare and Michelle became more at ease in the sled, they stood up, leaning on the hood of the sled, their binoculars in hand.

"These guys are having fun." Michelle laughed. "Competing and showing off."

They were driving over a vast frozen channel with rocky cliffs and mountainous terrain rising up on either side.

"Oh my god!" Clare put down her binoculars. "There's a crack wider than the sleds. We can't get across *that*."

The snowmobiles slowed down. Dan, on a snowmobile of his own, drove up to what must be the lead drivers. They conferred. Then they set off to the right, pulling the sleds alongside the crack, looking for where it might be narrow enough to get across. A couple of snowmobiles took off in the opposite direction. Dan drove over to Clare and Michelle's sled. "I'm trying to herd a lot of *cats*," he said.

But he smiled. "Patience is required. Don't worry. These guys always come through."

Far to the right, the crack narrowed enough to get the sleds across. But it wasn't easy. They had to stop with the Ski-doo close to the crack. Then the Ski-doo, in a spurt of power, flew over the crack and stopped when the sled was spanning the crack. It was expert positioning. The passengers got out and used the front runners to get onto the ice with the help of the driver. Then the sled was more easily pulled over the width of the crack. It took a while to do this with all the sleds, especially the sleds carrying heavy supplies.

They carried on until early afternoon when they stopped for lunch on the rocky shore. People went discreetly behind rocks to relieve themselves.

There were ham and cheese sandwiches, tea, coffee and water in thermoses. Raw carrots and celery. Cookies. Everything served in containers that would be re-used.

"So show me that image again," said Michelle.

Clare lifted her camera from the strap around her neck.

"Incredible," said Michelle. "Totally awesome. You've got a genius eye. I've never seen a photo of a wolf smiling."

"You know how it feels … that you've been let into another world, when you get a picture of the character of a wild animal." Clare looked again at the photo she had taken. "In this case it was different. I don't believe in literal visions. Ghosts visiting and all that. But in this case, the photo came to me. It was so like an actual visit from my Malamute Yukon Sally. It chokes me up. Completely chokes me up," said Clare, her voice breaking up. She pressed her fingers hard on her forehead to regain control.

Michelle put her arm on Clare's shoulder. "Weird things happen," she said. "No doubt about that."

Later she advised, "You're the old pro, Clare. Well … not *that* old, But you've been at this game much longer than I have. I just want to say … that doesn't look like a dog. It may remind you of your dog. But to everyone else it looks like a wolf. And there's a lot of wolf huggers out there. They want photos of wolves. There are also some wolf killers. They need to see this photo of a benign, smiling, innocent wolf. A photo like this can do a lot of good. A lot. You've got to market it as a wolf."

"Hey!" said Clare. "Will you be my agent? No pay of course. I'm just a poor old photographer." They were laughing as they headed back to the sleds, sloshing through the ice water.

CHAPTER SIX

Camping on Ice at the Floe Edge

It took more than six hours to get from the town of Pond Inlet across the inlet itself to the campsite. Bright yellow two-person tents were set up in a row on the north side of the inlet with mountainous Bylot Island in the background. The ice on the campsite had no layer of water on it. Tent ropes were attached to pegs which were hammered into the ice. Clare and Michelle finished hammering their tent pegs then laid out their sleeping bags inside and sorted out their knapsacks and camera equipment. Michelle's advanced digital equipment was surprisingly lightweight and compact except for one long lens.

"I have a lot to learn from you," said Clare.

"You mean from my equipment." Michelle smiled. "So do I. Some of it's new to me too. I have a very supportive father. He loaned me the money for this new camera. It'll come off my inheritance. He assured my sister of that. But I have the camera now when I need it. Lucky, eh."

Michelle's father was a prominent surgeon who appreciated the need for advanced equipment. Clare thought of her own father who had died of acute leukemia at age fifty. Certainly not a prominent man. But a kind, good person, with a weakness for alcohol. Otherwise entirely unlike my current husband. My weakness, thought Clare wryly, is for alcoholics.

A large dark green tent was set up in the middle of the row of campers' tents. This was the kitchen and dining tent. There was enough space for all the campers to stand up and sit down on canvas folding chairs where they could eat meals from bowls or plates held in their hands. A supper of beef stew was being cooked in the kitchen. The chef was a thin, lively guy experienced in Arctic expeditions, which he referred to often. Further back from all the tents was another green one, designed to accommodate two separate toilets with canvas privacy walls surrounding them. They had environmentally friendly waste-disposal units. If I have to get up in the night as usual thought Clare, with no night darkness here in the Arctic, at least I'll be able to see my way to the toilet.

This is not a rowdy bunch, Clare observed as they all sat around the dining circle at supper. The few couples stuck to each other, the singles were reticent, quiet explorers. Probably full of their own interesting tales. Except for that tedious retired teacher who thinks everyone wants to listen to her. She could drive me crazy. Clare turned from her to enjoy Michelle who sent kibitzing remarks into the circle, making Prince blush a bit and break into his wide smile. Dan seemed well practiced at deflecting any baiting, teasing, flirting, or probing remarks. An experienced, good-looking, intriguing guide like him has to be, thought Clare, but he likes Michelle. Who doesn't! She knows how to bring out the life in people. She's a natural-born good photographer.

"Tomorrow," Dan stood up ready to retire for the night, "we'll put our feet on dry land. We'll hike up the shore here of Bylot Island. Look as far as we can. Next day, the Ski-doos will take us to the floe edge. We had a good safe journey today."

"That was ominous," said Clare after they had crawled into their tent and shoved themselves into their sleeping bags, using their down jackets for pillows. "That remark about having a good safe journey today. Did he realize how close we came to sinking into those perilous cracks? Or was he expecting an attack from a herd of walrus or what!"

"A herd of walrus," Michelle laughed. "I'd like a picture of that."

It's strange, Clare thought, all this light through the night, the cold air of a mild winter day though we're at the peak of summer. And the silence of this world … no sounds in the campsite, no animal or bird sounds in the vastness all around. Clare and Michelle fell into the silence of their own sleep.

When they woke in the morning and dressed to crawl out of their tent, they noticed the tent pegs had shifted and needed to be re-staked. The ice was melting imperceptibly underneath them.

A mug of hot coffee and oatmeal porridge was all Clare chose for breakfast. Coffee and porridge never tasted so good when she made them at home, standing in slippers and housecoat in a warm, machine-equipped kitchen. Standing on ice in felt-lined rubber boots, long underwear, pants, and parka, with her cold hands warming around the hot coffee mug, awaiting porridge steaming in the pot, Clare looked across the ice to the distant dark rock cliffs and the distinct blue of the Arctic sky, thinking breakfast had never felt so good. Even the milk made from powder tasted alright.

Dan led the expedition. Wearing no hat, his hair shaved close to his scalp, he carried his parka bunched up in his hand. He wore sunglasses and a fleece pullover, an impressive rifle slung over his shoulder. No gloves or mitts. "It's a warm summer day, to him," said Michelle.

"The white explorers thought the Inuit had some peculiar body temperature because they were, like Dan," said Clare, "used to the cold temperatures,"

They sloshed through surface ice water towards the high rocky shore of Bylot Island. Clare carried Michelle's long zoom lens, trying not to stumble and fall into the ice water with it. Dan led them to the narrowest part of a long crack winding along the edge of the shoreline. The crack of endlessly deep ocean water was only inches wide at that point but Clare felt her heart leap as she stepped across it carrying Michelle's precious lens. They climbed to a plateau of rocks with large patches of moss that was soft to sit on. Michelle assembled her equipment, setting up lens and camera on a tripod. Clare stepped away from the group to explore the panorama before them. She sat down on the soft moss, seeing in front of her a vast expanse of ice with majestic black rock mountains rising up in the distance on either side. It was a passage towards the central horizon where light emanated in sunrise hues.

Clare thought of the grand and graceful sea creatures swimming beneath the ice. Powerful whales and fish. Seals and walruses emerging onto the ice. Flocks of birds inhabited nests in the cliffs and rocks of the mountains. Clare used her binoculars to scan the scene. A creature was moving over the ice on the shoreline of the passage. She adjusted her binoculars to maximum. Yes! It surely was a polar bear. A lone polar bear.

Clare lay down, feeling her back supported by the soft moss and ancient rock. She closed her eyes to feel it more intensely. She opened her eyes and sat up, observing and memorizing the scene. The polar bear was still there, lumbrously crossing the passage that led to the light emanating in pale yellow and coral colours on the central horizon. The black mountains now had a purplish hue.

"This is it," Clare said out loud. "This is where God lives."

She smiled at herself. She knew that if she said this to others they would laugh. But she felt it as true and unforgettable.

Rejoining the group, Clare found everyone peering through cameras or binoculars to follow the polar bear. They were excited. "Too far away," Michelle said to Clare. "Even with my longest lens, it's blurred and I can't get the expression on his face. Damn! But hey! I've got his image. A real, live polar bear. And we see him on our first day! Talk about good omens,"

Clare was frustrated because the bear was too far away to be more than a spot on her camera. But she had spotted her first live polar bear. And she did get a clear landscape shot that was meaningful to her. She showed it to Michelle. "I know it's a cliché landscape," she admitted to Michelle. "Sun rising between two mountains, ocean in foreground, but it has a strange power to it. I'm calling it 'Where God Lives.'"

Michelle looked closely at it. "Definitely a cliché scene," said Michelle. "but if you don't use that title, it could sell."

Before supper, Michelle and Clare wandered onto the stony terrain behind the campsite. They saw the remains of recent and ancient stone campsites. Two young Inuit guides and snowmobile drivers were standing there, with their guns. Must be hunting geese and whatever else comes their way, Clare surmised. The men lowered their guns and looked 'caught' when the women approached.

"Don't worry about us," said Michelle with a smile. "Do whatever you want to do. We're not reporting." She moved on with Clare. "Dan told them not to be seen hunting in front of us, because of all the issues around hunting seals and Arctic species," said Michelle.

"But they hunt for food, not trophies," Clare said.

"I know," Michelle agreed. "They have families to feed. They're just food shopping really." She smiled then stopped. "Hey! I want to talk to those guys. I'd like to interview them for a TV station back in Ottawa. I know some people there. This could be good. I have a recorder and camera. Let's do it." They went back to the guides and arranged to interview them after supper.

Michelle brought a recorder, handheld microphone, and video camera. Clare had her own camera. They found the guides coming back from hunting seals near ice holes where they might appear. The guides were reserved and unforthcoming until Michelle got them laughing and unconscious of their accents and speech. Clare held the mic and asked some questions while Michelle used the video camera and furthered the interview.

The guides had been riding snowmobiles from a very young age, competing with others and winning challenges of manoeuvring and speed. They were taught hunting skills by family members for as long as they could remember. They would not talk about hunting seals except to say yes, they killed adult seals for food.

"Thanks guys," said Michelle. "You are amazing. Just amazing."

"Awesome," said the one wearing blue sunglasses. "Aren't we awesome?"

Interviewers and interviewed laughed with each other.

The tent pegs had to be adjusted before they settled in for the night. Then again in the morning. Should we be alarmed? Clare wondered. It's melting a lot. Could this campsite break off into an ice floe and take us out into the ocean? It seemed too preposterous to voice aloud. But she saw that Dan and Prince checked every day how much the tents had to be adjusted.

The next day was June 21, the summer solstice of 2008. This day they would spend at the floe edge. Enough snowmobiles and sleds were assembled to transport them over the ice to where the free-flowing water of the Arctic Ocean met the frozen edge of ice near land. It was where sea and amphibious animals gathered at this time of year. Clare didn't fully understand why. It had something to do with mating and birth and likelihood of food. Clare knew she was not a proper tourist. She liked to experience things afresh, find and observe what interested her, then read up on it afterwards. She let others carry and consult their guidebooks.

This experience of the floe edge suited her perfectly. There were no guidebooks for this. There were no other tourists apart from their small group from Adventure Canada. Not another person in sight on the mountainous land, the icefields, and the indigo-blue ocean. Then Prince introduced an Inuit elder to the group. Clare hadn't seen him at the campsite. But somehow he had got there and came to the floe edge in Prince's sled. He was a friendly, short man with wrinkled face, wearing sunglasses and a leather and fur hat with ear flaps, quite like the leather and fur aviator hat Clare was wearing. It was her favourite winter hat. The elder was introduced as Ike.

He did not speak English but he made himself well enough understood with nods and frequent smiles. He carried a long metal pole with a sharp tip. It had various uses, one of which was to point at and test the thickness of the ice at the floe edge and along a large wide crack that met with the floe edge. Ike looked at Clare, tapped the pole to his own hat and then to Clare's and smiled and laughed with much delight. It was contagious. He had most everyone smiling or laughing. He led them to the floe edge, carefully. Everyone was cautious, if not outright scared. What if the edge were too thin or broke off?

Clare trusted Ike. Wisdom of the elders, she told herself. He stopped five feet from the edge indicating they should do the same. Then he walked them along to a place where he had hooked up a wire, microphone, and battery device, allowing the wire to drop down under the floe edge. One at a time they were invited to use the hearing end of the device to listen to the sounds in the ocean depth.

Michelle gasped as she listened to the device. "It's fan-friggin'-tastic!" she said, passing the device to Clare. "You won't believe it!"

Clare also gasped, her eyes widened. It was sonorous and haunting, echoing and deeply mellow. The sound of whales and whatever other ocean animals, near and far, high and low. "*That* is awesome," she said as she passed the device to the next person. "Truly awesome." Throughout their time at the floe edge she returned to the device several times to hear again the sounds from the ocean depths. Ike was delighted at her appreciation and led her to spots where she might get a better glimpse of sea creatures.

Narwhals were the first big sea creatures they saw at the floe edge. Clare was fascinated by the odd-shaped protrusion sticking out of their foreheads like a spear. A unicorn has something similar. But the unicorn is a mythical fantasy, pink and white, prancing about in dreams. The narwhals were very real, like small whales, charcoal black with yellowish mottling on their sides, their tails large, powerful and graceful when they rose out of the ocean and flapped on its surface as they dove to swim beneath. "They're playful!" Clare moved fast along the large channel the narwhals were swimming up at the floe edge. She tried to get camera shots of their tails and silhouettes in the water. "They're having fun. Putting on a show." But with her old camera she couldn't get more than the flap of their tail above water.

Someone spotted a bowhead whale out in the flowing water. Michelle had her equipment set up near the mouth of the channel and the floe edge. She could pivot and catch the snout of the bowhead whale. Her camera was powerful enough to catch it distinctly in the distance.

Clare's was not. I don't have the equipment to capture the sea animals, she realized. I have to hope for polar bears or walrus on the ice or seals out of water, though seals have had so much international attention with the focus on the hunting of baby seals, I don't want to get into that. It shows a lack of respect and understanding of Indigenous culture. Better I should just take a break and enjoy the wonder of this place and its life. She observed Ingo and his mate vying with Michelle for best position with their cameras. Clare went over and offered to help Michelle with anything.

"Thanks," said Michelle, "But I just need to keep sharp and work fast. Oh my God! There's a whale about to flap its tail. Right in front of me. Oh … my … God!"

Clare watched Michelle position and focus her camera. She caught the nose of the whale and then its tail coming up and flapping the water with strength and a graceful whack that sent the surface water in a unique fountain spray of water droplets.

Michelle worked with agility and joy. And diligence, Clare noted. She has what it takes to be great. It's a joy to watch her. Like watching my daughters, Clare reflected, remembering them graduating from university and each getting into professions they were good at, then become good mothers, though stressed with the problems at work and at home. They have helpful husbands, Clare concluded. I tripped up in that area. But I'm not going to moan about it. I'm here. And this is marvellous.

The chef called the group to lunch on sandwiches and soup in a mug. They sat on the folding canvas chairs brought from the camp, watching various shaped icebergs float by at varying distances. Over the five days they camped on ice at the floe edge they saw icebergs up close and far away. White ice structures, some curved with hilly chunks, some more block shaped, or a curious mixture of both. One was built up in blocks but had a large space like a square tunnel in the middle of it. "Now what we want," said Clare, "is a large flat iceberg carrying a polar bear and cubs, have it parade by us en route to catching seals."

No such luck, Clare reflected wryly to herself getting into her sleeping bag that night.

Clare awoke feeling mildly anxious. They would have this last day at the floe edge and then they would pack up in early morning for the long sled ride back to Pond Inlet. It was a bright sunlit day. She had taken enough photos of the magnificent landscape. They had seen numerous narwhals, some whales, seals in the distance, icebergs and flocks of birds that lived in rock cliff nests. And the one, faraway polar bear.

The previous morning, shortly after they arrived at the floe edge, near the ice-crack channel, two things had appeared coming out of the water onto the edge of the ice. Then a head emerged, and the shoulders of a man who hoisted himself up onto the ice. He was in full Arctic diving gear. A mask, helmet, and body suit that left no skin exposed. Air tanks on his back, flippers on his feet. He stood up and waved at the group. Then another slightly smaller man appeared, in similar attire. Both waved, enjoying startling the group. Everyone gathered round them. Dan and Prince tried several languages to converse with them. The divers were enjoying keeping their identities uncertain. Then they put their masks back on, waved goodbye and slid back down into the water. Much further along the floe edge could be seen a Zodiac boat with a few passengers.

"Russian spies?" Michelle said to Dan.

"They didn't want to say," Dan answered to the group. "More likely, wealthy European tourists, come by private plane, helicopter, and all."

On this, the last day at the floe edge, Clare was hoping for something more dramatic than an apparition that turned out to be wealthy tourists with a sense of humour. And yet this trip to the High Arctic she knew would affect her for the rest of her life. The scenes would come back to her. That sense of 'this is where God lives,' silly as it might be to other people, would remain a truth for her. Of all the countries and famous places she had seen, this would remain the point of the origin of species for her. It was her sense of where life began, not in the

Garden of Eden, somewhere in the Middle East or in Africa. It would emanate from here in the magnificence of the Arctic horizon, the indigo ocean, the strength of the rock mountains, the beauty of their darkness, the sparkling light of snow and ice. This is not the last frontier, Clare concluded, it's the first. My children and grandchildren cannot have the opportunity of such a pristine experience here as I have had.

"Lucky us," she said to Michelle.

Sitting up in her sleeping bag, Michelle looked perceptively at Clare. She cocked her head like a Malamute sled dog figuring out what has been said to her by a human being.

"Yes!" she said, "I know what you're saying. I'll never do lions and tigers on safari again. I'm doing our Arctic."

There was a trough of melted ice water around their tent. Michelle and Clare were already shifting their tent to a not yet melted spot when Dan and Prince came round with the order. "Move your tents before breakfast, Adventurers."

They were taken to the floe edge for the last time. It was sunny. Everything was intensified. The indigo colour of the water. The snow on the ice where they stood and on the snow-capped mountains, snow sparkling with ice diamonds. There was no night sky at this time of year, no darkness sparkling with stars. She imagined other times of year when there would be so much darkness, the winter solstice with twenty-four hours of darkness. Then the sky could have that grand display of a colourful explosion of green-hued waves called the Northern Lights.

"There's a walrus, a rogue walrus!" the word spread amongst the Adventurers. It was more like a rumour being passed around as they took up different positions along the floe edge. But it wasn't long before everyone had spotted the rumpled water movements of the rogue walrus, within sight of the floe edge but not very close to it. Then interest in it died down. The rumpled water movements disappeared into the distance.

After lunch, Dan appeared outfitted in an orange Arctic water survival suit, paddling a kayak.

"Where'd he get that!?" "How'd he get it here?" "He's snuck out of nowhere!"

"It's his final-day party trick!" Michelle exclaimed and laughed.

Dan was indeed grinning as he paddled along the floe edge in front of them. As was Prince when he emerged from the direction where Dan had been.

"Anyone want to join me?" asked Dan as he drew the kayak up to the edge. "It's a two-person kayak."

Not one Adventurer volunteered.

"Michelle?" Dan paddled near to Michelle and Clare.

"No. Not me," Michelle said with a laugh. "Can't take my camera in a kayak. I kayak enough at home, on warm lakes. I'm here to take pictures."

"What about you, Clare?" asked Dan. "You been in a kayak before?"

"Sure she has," said Prince.

"She's finished taking pictures," said the school teacher. "I've been watching her."

"She's Canadian," said Ingo. "She can kayak."

"I canoe!" Clare protested. "I've only been in a kayak a few times." And I don't canoe with a rogue walrus in ice water! she wanted to yell. But they all looked at her expectantly.

"You don't have to do it," Michelle spoke quietly to Clare.

"It's not something anyone should be forced to do," said Dan, sizing up the situation.

"The hard part is getting into a canoe," said Clare. "Or a kayak. I'm used to wading in. Can't do that here." There was mumbling and muffled laughter around her as they stood on the floe edge of the Arctic Ocean.

"You have to wear a survival suit, " said Dan.

"We'll help you," said Prince.

"I'm thinking about that rogue walrus," said Clare loudly.

"Long gone," said Dan.

"How can you be sure?" Clare surveyed the calm dark blue water.

"Can't be sure about much," said Dan. "But if you don't trust me, stay where you are."

This guy is trustworthy, thought Clare. Total expert in a kayak. He just doesn't want anyone freaking out with fear in the front.

"OK," said Clare. "Let's do it." Have I ever been more scared? she asked herself.

Prince helped her into the survival suit. Dan and others held the kayak against the ice of the floe edge. As she sat on the ice and aimed at getting her legs into position under the bow and her arms ready to hold both sides of the kayak, she saw the gap of ice water between the floe edge and the kayak. Never forget this one, she thought as the Prince and Adventurers helped get her awkwardly and gracelessly into the front compartment of the kayak. She gripped the paddle in the middle but was too fear-frozen to operate it until Dan had paddled and steered them out from the edge and they were gliding smoothly along. Fear subsided. Confidence grew. She paddled in poor synchronization with Dan. But the thrill, fun, and magnificence of this adventure lodged in her mind and would be recalled for as long as she lived.

"Champagne!" she exclaimed as she stood up after crawling out of the kayak and was lifted up by Prince and Ingo. "Champagne all around."

They had to wait for the fog that settled in next day to lift before they set off for the return journey to Pond Inlet. It didn't matter that they had to wait until mid-afternoon since there would be no darkness of night to fall upon them. The level of water on top of the ice seemed deeper but Clare and Michelle did not feel the apprehension and fear that beset them on the outward journey. They relaxed on the back seat of the sled or stood up leaning on the hood, taking in the scenery that lay ahead.

"Once I've gone over all the photos and made selections of anything good," said Michelle, "I'm going to have an exhibition at my office in Ottawa, turn it into a gallery. I'd like to exhibit your photo of the smiling wolf for you. You cool with that?"

"That's very generous of you, Michelle. Very! Not many artists offer to share in their limelight. I'll help with the work and costs. I'm near hopeless at flogging my own work. Just ask my husband about that. He reminds me of it constantly."

"Really?!" said Michelle. "My guy thinks I'm hot. He's with me all the way."

A larger airplane flew the Adventure Canada group plus others directly from Pond Inlet back to Ottawa. Wine was served and a small hot dinner. This was a plane to Ottawa, which was no 'no alcohol zone'.

"I'm not against luxury," said Clare, clinking her plastic glass of wine with Michelle. "But primitive camping on ice in our High Arctic was … the best." They clinked glasses again in agreement.

"Awesome place," said Michelle.

"Interesting, dignified people we don't know enough about," Clare waxed on. "The wildlife and magnificent landscape. You're right. It's awesome. Much better than luxury. It was our privilege. Our privileged experience. More wine please…."

Chapter Seven

Back Home Reflecting

The mountains and snow were left behind as they flew through clouds over terrain of sparse trees, then forests and lakes. Then villages and towns amid farmland and resorts. They could see the green trees of summer and the many lakes with cottages on the north side of Ottawa where Clare and Len's Loghaven was. The plane descended over Rideau Hall and the Prime Minister's residence, then over government buildings, museums, the high peak of the National Gallery and the Parliament buildings. They flew over the river and the canal where Len and Clare's townhouse was, then landed at Ottawa's airport.

Although Ottawa's airport is not large, it felt very large, grand, and modern compared to the landing strip and wooden building at Pond Inlet.

Michelle's husband and son were smiling and waving to her at the bottom of the airport escalator. Nice, thought Clare as she made her way to the taxis. That's how it should be. And that's how it was in my marriage to Len … until he retired.

Len had begun working with an investment company after graduating from university with a degree in Commerce. The investment company was later bought by the Bank of Confederation and Len continued working there until he reached the retirement age of 65. That was in 1997, when retirement at the Bank was compulsory and abrupt. Len told everyone he was looking forward to retirement when he would be a "free man with a good pension in his pocket."

Seeing how immersed in his work Len had always been, Clare worried that he would be lost and bored in retirement if he didn't get involved in some charitable work or worthy causes which could benefit from his expertise in investments. When he turned sixty, she urged him to choose something he liked. "You could get on the board of the National Gallery," she suggested, "or the Museum of Nature."

"Those are your interests," he replied. "I'm no culture vulture. I'll just enjoy investing on my own. No pressure from anyone." But when asked by the Cancer Society, he did say he would serve on their board.

As he neared sixty-five, Len's successor was chosen and would take over his position the day Len retired. The Bank gave Len a retirement lunch with appreciative speeches. His secretary helped clear out his office.

Clare redecorated his home office and added a larger filing cabinet and bookcases. She organized a dinner and dance party for him at the country club. The twins were nearing exam time at their medical and law schools, so they could not come home for the event. Len smiled and laughed at the amusing speeches. He looked pleased with the leather swivel desk chair Clare presented to him. He was not given to making eloquent or heartfelt thank you speeches himself but he obviously enjoyed the large elegantly dressed gathering in honour of him. He loved to waltz and polka with Clare who moved in perfect synchronization with him. They danced until they were breathless and collapsed on chairs smiling and holding hands.

For the past several years, Clare had been working part time at a camera and photography shop. But she took the first Monday of Len's retirement off to be at home with him. Len slept in until past 9 a.m. While Clare was out with Yukon Sally, Len made himself his usual breakfast of cereal, toast, and coffee, then settled into his new home office. When Clare offered him lunch, he was sitting at his desk with a glass of scotch. "No," he said, lifting his scotch. "This is all the lunch I need."

"Not very nutritious," Clare remarked from the doorway.

"Who the christ cares!" Len leaned back in his swivel chair. "From now on I can do what I want."

Clare recalled some of his remarks at his retirement parties. He said he was never going to have to get up in the dark again. She could understand and sympathize with that. He had been disciplined about getting up at 6:40 a.m. every working day, making his own breakfast, and leaving the house before the twins got up for school. He walked along the canal to catch public transport to his office, winter, spring, summer, and fall. But it was as though he threw the rules of civilized behaviour out the window with the alarm clock. He began swearing, drinking, and sleeping in like a teenager.

He had always worn a suit and tie to the office. He had ten tailor-made suits and silk ties with elegant shirts that Clare had selected. He had good black shoes and brown shoes. Clare was used to seeing him well dressed, dignified, and distinguished looking. But he was not good at putting casual clothes together. Clare helped by buying him well-coordinated slacks, shirts, and sweaters. Suddenly in retirement he didn't want to be told what to wear. He bought himself some sweatshirts and jeans. He took to wearing jogging shoes and moccasins.

At his office retirement party, he had made a speech to colleagues and invited wives, saying now that he was retired, he was going to take over household chores so Clare could spend her time in her darkroom doing photography. There was some quipping by colleagues about locking his wife in the darkroom but Clare was more than surprised that he would even consider taking over any chores. At home from that party, Clare had joked to him that Wednesday was laundry day if he wished her to give him a lesson or two. "No," he replied. "I'm not going to do that shit work. But I will do the shopping sometime."

"The food shopping?"

"Sure. Why not!"

He went one week to No Frills on the far side of town and came back with a load of No Frills yellow boxes and packages of 'family size' staple goods, from laundry detergent to cereal and toilet paper.

"For god sake, Len! There's only the two of us living here. I can't even fit those monster boxes into the cupboards."

"If you don't like the way I do it, do it yourself. At least I know how to be frugal."

"Frugal?! Why do we have to suddenly be *frugal*?"

"Because I'm on a pension now."

"But it's a very good pension. We're not poor!"

"You can go on being extravagant. But I'm the one who has to cover the bills." He walked out of the room.

Clare looked at the large can of the cheapest kind of cooking oil from the shelves of No Frills. She went into the hallway and shouted at Len on his way upstairs. "I cook with olive oil. First cold pressed. I'm taking this stuff to the food bank."

She did so. Right away. Clare loaded the oil and the monster boxes into the car and drove it to the food bank. Back home she made a dinner of beef stroganoff which Len ate in silence until he said, "You make a damn good beef stroganoff."

"Well, thank you," Clare raised her glass of red wine to Len.

"No Frills is not a pretty place to shop." Len raised his glass of wine to Clare. "I'm not going there again."

"Good!"

"But I am going to start making our own red wine."

"I won't drink it," said Clare. "Stan and I tried making our own wine when we were students in Oxford. It was awful. Especially the red. Couldn't make it without too much tannin which gives awful headaches. I'm not prone to headaches but that wine always gave me a headache. We stopped making it. Of course, when Stan got the job at Christchurch, we had access to really good wines from their cellar."

"Nice life you left behind," said Len. It was not the kind of remark he had made before.

Len went to a winemaking shop to make and bottle his red wine. Clare refused to drink it. She bought moderately priced wine from the wine and liquor store. Sometimes Len tried to slip some of his homemade red into her wine glass but she could always taste it and gave it back to him. After a few months, Len got tired of the work of making and bottling his own dinner wine. Instead, he went to the wine and liquor store and bought the cheapest red wine on the shelves. "As long as I have my scotch first," he said good humouredly to Clare, "I don't really care what the dinner wine tastes like."

If only our differences had remained at that trivial level, Clare lamented to herself.

Chapter Eight

Harmony in the Yukon

The first summer of Len's retirement, when they took a long trip to the Yukon, was Clare's last memory of their marriage as harmonious. They had been married nearly twenty years by then. It was Clare's idea to take Yukon Sally to the land of her ancestors, in the western Arctic. The Yukon was where the Klondike Gold Rush had taken place in the 1890s. It was also where Clare's grandmother, Meg Wilkinson, went as the first woman veterinarian. Clare was eager to follow on her grandmother's trail. She wished she could be the trail blazer her grandmother had been but it was Julie who was most like her. And Megan and Ali, thought Clare. I haven't even made a living off my profession. As Len so often reminds me.

Clare and Len flew to Vancouver with Yukon Sally and then up to Whitehorse in the Yukon where they rented a van and equipment to camp when necessary and stay in accommodations along the Klondike Gold Rush route. Len had always liked to travel and they had vacationed in famous places in Europe but always stayed in comfortable hotels. Len was no camper and never stinted on vacations.

But when he retired, he liked the idea of a cheaper vacation and he shared Clare's interest in seeing Yukon Sally in the land of her ancestors. So, in the summer of 1997 they flew to the Yukon. They stayed longest in Dawson City, the well-preserved and restored historic town of the Klondike Gold Rush. Len enjoyed the saloons and dancehall shows, spending nights in simple cabin accommodations, walking around the unpaved streets and boardwalks with the colourful nineteenth-century wooden buildings, and hiking along the narrow trail of Moosehide Gulch overlooking Dawson City at the convergence of the Klondike and Yukon Rivers.

Len didn't mind a few uncomfortable nights tenting in campgrounds when it was a small part of the larger interesting adventure. He enjoyed driving the big rental van along the unusual wilderness highway with Yukon Sally sitting like royalty in the back seat. He didn't appear to mind that he couldn't have his scotch until the end of the day. Clare was having her favourite kind of holiday, exploring unfamiliar territory of her homeland and taking expert photos.

When in Ottawa, Yukon Sally was always wanting to escape, hunt down small animals or find suitable dogs to play with. In the Yukon, where teams of sled dogs abound and dogs are welcome in hotels, Yukon Sally strutted around like a show dog and stuck close to Clare, like a well-trained dog in the ring. And she was much admired by people who saw her because purebred Malamutes had become a rarity in the Yukon. Their glory days were in the 1890s, at the height of the Klondike Gold Rush, when teams of Malamutes were as expensive and prized as the most luxurious vehicles of today. When the Iditarod and Yukon Quest sled dog races were established they were always won by teams of Malamutes … until the early twentieth century when the smaller and slightly faster teams of Siberian Huskies were brought to the races and began to win more often than the Malamutes. Since then, the racing sled dog teams were nearly all smaller, mixed-breed dogs.

Clare took a photo of Yukon Sally sitting with two Indigenous men and Len on the steps of the Malamute Saloon in Dawson City. On the outskirts of Dawson, the log cabin of the poet Robert Service was preserved. His long narrative poems about people and stories of the Klondike Gold Rush became internationally famous, most of all his poem "The Shooting of Dan McGrew" which begins: "A bunch of the boys were whooping it up in the Malamute Saloon." Clare had Len take a photo of her standing on the porch of Robert Service's cabin with Yukon Sally.

They drove the Dempster Highway north, over the Arctic Circle to Inuvik. It was a long magnificent route through landscapes of purplish, rounded mountains, verdant tundra valleys, and pale gray, jagged rock mountains gleaming in the long days of sunlight. Then came the flatlands of the Mackenzie River delta where they took a ferry across the wide river. Human life and visible animal life were so scarce, Clare put her camera down in surrender. Then she saw in the distance an eagle swoop over a swampy area. As she lifted her camera, it disappeared from her sights. Clare groaned. Though wondrous in its scenic landscape, the Dempster Highway trip turned out to be a dud in terms of wildlife photography.

Inuvik was a prosperous-looking town of new, colourfully painted homes and buildings. Indigenous children rode new bicycles in the streets, adults drove pickup trucks. There was a small-plane airport. Central to the town was a large white igloo-shaped church, artistically designed and furnished with traditional polished wooden pews. It was a Catholic church.

"Must have cost a lot to build that sucker!" said Len.

They had good fish dinners in the restaurant which featured in its lobby an enormous taxidermied polar bear standing on its hind legs. Clare handed Len her small camera. "Take a shot," she said as she reached out to hug the bear. The bear was too big to get her arms around so Clare turned, pressing her back and head into him as she clung to his outstretched front legs. For some reason, his paws were covered in cloth. Perhaps his claws had been removed. The look on Clare's face and the look on the bear's had a comical similarity.

Clare captioned this photo: *Me and the Arctic Wildlife*.

On the outskirts of Inuvik, Len and Clare stayed in a bed and breakfast chalet. It was of polished logs, run by a young German woman who was trying to establish a breed of white-furred Arctic dogs she planned to sell in Europe. Her chalet was immaculate, with a huge 'environmental toilet', high off the floor, requiring a step up to it and flush instructions so complicated, Clare had to ask the woman to do the flushing for her.

They drove back to Dawson City and up the Alaska Highway,

through a place called Chicken Alaska, down to the infamous Gold Rush town of Skagway and then north back into Canada to hike in the mountains of Kluane Park. At the entrance to this grand national park was a sign saying, "No tenting. Bear warren."

They were able to get a new, simply but nicely furnished log cabin, with a porch facing the King's Throne Mountain. The wooden bed had a patchwork quilt. "Isn't this perfect!" said Clare, setting her glass of wine on the bedside table then stretching out on the bed. "This cabin, the view, the mountain air."

Len put down his emptied glass and went to the bedside. He took off his shoes. "Let's try out this bed."

"Before supper?"

"Why not! I'm retired."

"As Vonnegurt said," Clare got up to pull down the covers, "Make love whenever you can. It's good for you."

"*While* you still can," said Len.

The long sunny days of the Yukon summer continued into mid-August. Each day they hiked the narrow mountain paths from morning until late afternoon. Yukon Sally carried their lunches in her saddle sack. Len had no fear of heights but Clare did. Mount Kathleen became so steep, Clare told Len she would wait for him while he went on to the summit. But Yukon Sally would have none of that. She waited just ahead of Clare, howling at her to continue on with them, until Clare said, "Alright. Alright, Yukon, but you have to catch me if I slide off the trail."

Clare made it to the summit and thanked Yukon Sally for leading her to do it.

They returned safely to their cabin and had a celebratory supper of canned baked beans with weiners and wine. Len had his scotch.

On their last day, a sign on the notice board at the beginning of the trail said "Grizzly Bear warning."

"What the hell is that supposed to mean?" said Len.

A young couple of hikers standing nearby said, "It means a Grizzly has been sighted on this trail recently. You can hike. But keep a watch out."

Len looked at Clare. Yukon Sally sensed the fear in the air and howled sharply.

"Yukon wants us to go," Clare said. "And I want a photo of a Grizzly. At a distance!"

"OK." Len started on the trail.

"Our Malamute will be our bear watch," Clare said to the young couple.

They all set off together. Yukon Sally took the lead.

They hiked until noon, then sat on the trail eating their sandwiches together. The two cans of beer Len had put in Yukon's sack were shared amongst the four of them. They sat enjoying the vast view of mountains and valley where a river ran through.

"Doesn't get any better than this," said Len. Clare put her hand on his shoulder. The young couple nodded in agreement. Then the girl, Tina, said, "Might be better without the bear scare."

"Are you very scared?" asked Clare.

"Aren't you?"

"Not very," Clare said. "Animals aren't normally predators upon human beings. They usually react in some kind of defence or protection of their young. I'd love to get a photo of a Grizzly. From a safe distance."

"I get what you're saying," said Tina. "Haven't thought about it like that. Animals not being predators on human beings."

"People do get mauled and killed by bears," said Dacks, her companion. "You never know what sets off a wild animal. We'll keep carrying bear spray."

Two guys came along the trail.

"We saw a Grizzly about an hour ago," they reported. "But it was way off the trail." Then one of them looked at Yukon Sally and said.

"That dog looks too much like a wolf. A Grizzly won't want to tangle with it."

Clare and Len conferred. "I'm good for another hour uphill," said Len. "Then let's head back for Happy Hour."

The young couple accompanied them for another hour and then continued on further up the mountain.

Back in their cabin, having drinks, Clare scratched Yukon Sally behind the ears. "I forgive you," she said, "for keeping us safe." She took another sip of wine. "But for making this trip a complete washout in terms of wildlife photography…" She shook her head in mock reprimand.

Home in Ottawa, Clare looked over all her photos of landscape and Yukon Sally in the Yukon. The photo she laughed over and kept going back to was the one of herself with the big stuffed, laughing, white polar bear. She enlarged and block mounted it on her office wall. There's so much story in this photo, she told herself.

That's what I want to do. Photography that tells stories. Stories of the rapport, the connection, the similarity, yet difference, the whatever, between animals and people.

She kept mulling that over and as she woke one morning thinking about it, the expression "A picture is worth a thousand words" kept running through her thoughts. What a good title that would be, she concluded, for a collection of photos, a book, a coffee table book, of photos I take. Or have taken.

With that in mind she worked hard over the months and year that followed to produce a book that would be ready for the next Christmas, the Christmas that heralded the turn of the century.

After they returned from the trip to the Yukon, Len took up his old habits, became his own boss. He spent most of every day in his office going over his accounts and investments. In the years and events that followed, Clare came to see their trip to the Yukon as the last happy and harmonious time they had.

Chapter Nine

The First Episode of Violence

The first episode of violence occurred in Len's second year of retirement. That summer the twins were doing graduate work and had come to the cabin on the lake for the weekend with their boyfriends. When Clare came back from food shopping in town, Ali came up from the dock where they were sunbathing and swimming. She came into the kitchen wearing her bikini cover-up, asking Clare if she needed help bringing stuff in. "Sure," said Clare.

As they carried more groceries in, Ali asked if they could have some friends come to dinner and stay over on Sunday. "Why not," Clare said, smiling at her pretty daughter. "No reason Len and I can't go back to Ottawa in the afternoon and keep out of your way. You're all good cooks, even the guys."

"Of course the guys are, Mom. This isn't the nineteenth century. And we'll leave no clean-up."

Clare found Len upstairs, standing with scotch in hand, looking out the bedroom window at the girls and guys in swim suits on the dock. "Len," she said, "OK if we go back to Ottawa a bit earlier tomorrow? The kids want to have friends over."

Len turned to her, swallowing the rest of his scotch. It was three in the afternoon. "Why?" asked Len. "So they can have another of their orgies?"

Clare reacted by doing something she had never done before, though she had seen it done without repercussion in old movies. She slapped his cheek. Len put his glass down and beat her over the head and shoulders as she crouched in self-protection. He flailed with both fists, hitting hard as he could. Then he walked fast from the room, downstairs, out the back door and drove off in the Jeep.

Stunned, with her head hurting, Clare stood up. She made her way to the bed and sat there in shock, trying to figure out what to do. She closed the bedroom door. She looked out the window at her daughters on the dock, their beautiful young figures. Leading healthy lives, with beautiful minds. Why would he say such a thing, she thought. Her daughters having orgies. Because he was standing there picturing it!

Twisted, she concluded. He's twisted. He's been a father to them for twenty years and he comes out with that. And the violence within him! Beating me about the head and shoulders. He's been drunk before. Every day for the past two years. But he's never come out with something like that. Still … it had to be within him. She thought of what her friend Liz said about drunken words and behaviour. "What they say and do when drunk is what's within them."

I need advice, Clare thought. I need some help with this. I'm a liberated woman. I don't let a husband say such a twisted thing about my daughters then beat me about the head and shoulders, without doing something about it. She looked up the number of the Women's Help Line. She went downstairs as Megan came up from the dock.

"Just getting some beer and chips for down on the dock," she said to Clare. "Want to join us?"

"Not just now. I'm going to take Yukon for a hike."

"That spoiled dog," Megan said ruefully but smiled at her. "Hey, where's Dad? The Jeep's gone."

"He's gone home. Decided to do some work on his computer."

Megan looked at Clare, scrutinizing her. "That's pretty sudden. And rude. Doesn't even say goodbye to us. Mom, are you OK? Did you have a row or something? Did you tell him off for drinking so early in the day?"

"No. It would do no good. And I'm fine."

"Well, he isn't fine. He shouldn't be drinking and driving."

"I know. I'll be back soon." Clare turned and went out the back door with Yukon Sally. She was afraid of breaking down in tears.

Clare did choke up at the kindness in the woman's voice on the Help Line. "Sorry," she said to the woman. "I'm just upset. Bear with me. A bit choked up. Just catching my breath." Clare breathed out. "Yes, to answer your question … yes. It's a first offence. And maybe I provoked it, because I slapped his cheek, after he said something offensive and very untrue about my daughters. I've never done that before and he … I guess reacted … as he never has before."

"A counsellor will phone you in about fifteen minutes to talk this over and tell you your options. Is that alright with you?"

"Yes. Thank you. Thank you very much." Clare sat on the trail bench waiting for the next call; Yukon went sniffing in the woods.

The counsellor who phoned was also kind, and calm and gently informative. Clare listened and memorized the options. "Inform the police, so it is on record and you can lay a charge. Inform your doctor. Be aware that intimate partner violence occurs in all income classes. Your husband needs counselling. You would benefit from attending some sessions with him."

When Clare got back to the cabin, she wrote the options down. The counsellor said she would do a follow-up call in two days but she gave Clare a number to call if she had need before that. The options and advice so dominated Clare's thoughts, she excused herself after dinner saying she needed an early night. Her daughters and their boyfriends exchanged quick glances. They had no doubt discussed Len's sudden departure and scotch drinking but they didn't question Clare further.

I don't want them involved in my marital problems, Clare resolved. I'll work this out and fix it up. They weathered my divorce of twenty years ago exceptionally well and maintained a strong relationship with their father in England. Now they need to live their own lives and make good marriages for themselves.

Something the counsellor said that disturbed and surprised Clare was that violent intimate partners often come from a family in which they witnessed the father abusing the mother. They hated him for that but then in growing up found themselves doing the same thing.

That's twisted, thought Clare. And recalled with a smile her own mother's wise response when other parents asked her how she raised two such well adjusted teenagers. "By the supreme example of what *not* to be," her mother had responded.

In thinking about her own father and the drinking problem he developed after his store went broke, Clare realized two things. Her father was a benign alcoholic. It made him sad and quiet, never abusive or belligerent like Len. Her father drank in secret, always tried to hide his bottles. Clare hated it when her mother made Julie and her go on bottle hunts to expose and shame him for drinking. That was partly why Clare couldn't bring herself to confront Len about his drinking. Also, Len had so much defiance and retaliation in his nature, she was sure that telling him not to drink would make him drink all the more.

Clare drove back to Ottawa after breakfast next morning. Her daughters were still in their pyjamas. Ali gave her an extra affectionate hug. "The guys will drive us back tomorrow afternoon," she said. "We could take you out to a movie in the evening."

"Don't take guff from Dad," Megan said quietly, hugging her. "There's something wrong with him."

When Clare returned to their house in Ottawa, Len was sitting at his desk. He remained there until Clare came into his office and sat in the armchair on the other side of his desk. He clicked his ballpoint pen closed and set it down on his desk, resting his arms on his leather swivel chair. He made her say the first words.

"We need to talk," she said.

"Go ahead."

"I've spoken with the Women's Help Line."

"What did they have to say?"

"I should report what you did to the police."

"The police!" Len scoffed, leaned back and folded his arms across his chest. "Go ahead. You hit me first."

"A slap on the cheek doesn't warrant what you did to me."

"All I did was push you out of the way so I could get away from you."

"Really! So, you're willing to lie?"

He shrugged his shoulders.

Clare breathed out hard and shook her head. "Len, I already decided not to go that route. I'm not going to the police but I will report this to our doctor."

Len shrugged as though that wouldn't bother him.

"Also, I want you to go for counselling and I'll go with you."

He thought about that. "I could go along with that. Might learn something interesting." He picked up his pen. "The Bank actually offers six sessions free to retirees."

"Good God, Len! Why didn't you tell me? Why didn't you take them?"

"You need them more than me."

They both attended all the sessions. Clare found the counsellor distant to the point of being disinterested. Len was forthcoming with the woman, telling her things about his upbringing that he hadn't told Clare. He had told Clare his mother thought he could do no wrong and was immensely proud of him, whereas his father, though proud of him, never gave a word of praise, never talked personally with his children. Family meals were for eating, not conversing.

Len told the counsellor there were no displays of affection in his home. His father was harsh with him and his brothers, as well as with his wife who had a lot of fun-loving Irish in her. Though Len thought his father loved his mother and provided well for his family. His parents never quarrelled in front of the kids. His father didn't drink much. His mother smoked and enjoyed scotch at parties. There were a lot of Rekai family parties in Winnipeg. The Rekais were a well-known family in the business and cultural life of Winnipeg. Len's uncle had become outstandingly wealthy and influential in the city. Len thought his father was envious of that brother, Stefan, to the point of being bitter about Stefan's success. Not that he would ever voice his jealousy in an overt way.

Clare had never met Len's father. He had died in his early seventies. But she met Len's mother and his brothers at a Rekai family reunion just after she and Len had married. She found Len's mother delightful. But she was alarmed at his brother Pete's treatment of his wife, a kind, submissive woman. She made a remark to which Pete replied "Oh, you stupid cow."

No one but Clare seemed surprised at this. Later, Len said, "That's just Pete. He's actually very good to his wife. Though she's not the sharpest knife in the drawer. My dad had no tolerance for stupid remarks either. None of us do in our family."

"Don't ever call me a stupid cow."

"Why would I. You're not a cow. And you're not stupid."

Clare was surprised at Len saying after a session, "So I am my father's son after all."

"What do you mean by that?"

"I'm a good provider but an uptight, lousy father. Just like my own. Got to wonder if I'd be any different if I'd actually fathered a child."

"Len, what is all this coming from? You've never talked like this before."

"You never wanted to hear it. That counsellor knows how to get things out. You see it but you just don't want to say it."

"What? What are you talking about?"

"Megan and Ali. We go to their graduation. Their father lives way the hell over in England. They have a great relationship with him. But it's me at their graduation, And I don't even know what to say to them."

"You leaned over to each of them when they sat down with their degrees and said 'Proud of you.' I heard you."

"OK. I guess I managed to do one better than my dad on one occasion."

"Len, I think we should have had some counselling years ago. You seem to get a lot out of it. You talk more easily to her than to me. I actually hate the process. Sitting there every week, dragging up a list of grievances. I don't have that many. I just want you to stop drinking so much and never ever beat me like that again."

"Don't hit me and I won't hit you."

Clare seethed in silence. Let him have the last word, she told herself. There was no good end to this discussion.

"You've got the problem," Len carried on. "You can't cope with me drinking and doing what I want in retirement. As the counsellor said, you're the daughter of an alcoholic and that creates problems for you."

"My father managed to control his drinking after a time. He got a good job and was then promoted. My mom was a terrific school teacher. By the time I went to university we were a prospering, happy family."

"Then stay off my back and we'll both be fine."

After the fourth session, the counsellor informed them she was taking leave from her job. She had lost a young patient to suicide and she needed time away. Clare and Len could have had two more sessions with a new counsellor but they agreed they didn't want to do that.

"Thanks," said Len, "But we've got things figured out well enough."

Clare didn't think so. Nor did she think another counsellor in a couple of sessions would be much better at figuring out the causes of such sudden violence in Len. Clare suspected it had to do with more anger and frustration within him than she could fathom. She thought if he could find more purpose, some kind of healthy project, he would be busier, happier, drink less, and be nicer to her. She recalled the counsellor saying Len seemed to have anger within him and that his sarcasm was a form of anger.

Len needs a project, Clare decided, something to work on that will make our lives better.

"Let's build onto the log cabin," she proposed one evening at dinner. "Let's turn it into a really convenient and comfortable country home, without destroying its genuine antique character. We could buy that big empty lot behind it, give us more scope. We could even put in a tennis court. We both love tennis."

"Better than golf," said Len.

Well, that's not a no, thought Clare. She took it further. She had put thought and some investigating into this plan. "You know the condo you bought for me to fix up and rent out…"

"I bought it for investment and extra income."

"But it's in my name and I do all the work on it. Are you trying to say, it's not mine?"

"I paid for it with my inheritance. It just makes more tax sense to have it in your name."

Clare was quiet as she thought over the implications of what he was saying. She had renovated the condo, increased its value, and rented it out at good profit.

Len interrupted her thoughts. "I've got an even better idea. Sell this bloody big house that's forever needing repairs and yard work. Then we could do a big, bang-up job on the country home. Sell that dingy little condo and buy one of the new luxury condos along this street."

Now you're talking, thought Clare. This is better than divorce. "Downsizing in town is a good idea with the twins away in grad school. But a condo won't work with Yukon Sally. We need something like a small townhouse with a bit of back yard to let her outside. And some kind of extra bedroom for visiting kids. And grandkids, if we ever get some."

"Kids would want to be at the lake," said Len. "But an extra bedroom wouldn't hurt if it could also be my office."

"With a pull-out bed." Clare began to picture it. "I'll start looking for something like that. Maybe in the old part of town, one of those little carpenter cottages."

"It has to have two bathrooms," said Len. "Two pots to pee in. And two parking spots."

"That's getting expensive."

"Two hundred thousand has got to be the limit if we're going to do all that we want to with the cabin property."

That's not realistic, thought Clare, but she didn't want to discourage Len's new enthusiasm. She had a real estate agent friend, Christine, who was very good at her work and liked a challenging search. Christine put their house on The Driveway up for sale and began negotiations for purchasing the lot behind their cabin on the lake so the renovations could begin.

It involved complicated financing with a bridge loan but Len was excited by the venture and puffed up by the evaluations of their properties and seeing his net worth added up in front of others.

"Can't say I'm rich as Uncle Stefan in Winnipeg" he told Clare. "But I've outstripped my father, that's for sure."

They secured the adjacent property behind their lakefront lot. It had been on and off the market for several years. That gave them four more acres to expand upon. "This is one hell of a good investment!" Len looked at their new lot from the cabin bedroom window. "The real estate around here can't go anything but up and up." He got into bed with Clare and made vigorous love.

CHAPTER TEN

Acts of Construction

Within a year they had sold their four-bedroom house overlooking the canal in Ottawa and purchased what Christine called a 'hidden treasure' in the old part of Ottawa. It had been renovated in the 1970s in an exposed brick wall fashion that was no longer popular. Christine negotiated a buying price of $185,000. It had a fenced-in, very small, brick patio backyard, with a patch of soil for dogs to 'leave their mark' when necessary. Behind that was just enough room to park the Jeep and car, if you had some practice at it. It was an old attached row house near a small park.

"It's a perfect *pied à terre*," said Clare. "I love it!" It had two rooms and a bathroom upstairs. On the main floor was a living room with a floor-to-ceiling brick fireplace, a window looking onto the front porch and street, and a kitchen with attached solarium dining area. The basement had a sitting room with fireplace and built-in bookshelves around it, a toilet and sink room near the furnace room, and a small laundry room. It was otherwise a stinky mess from a recent basement flooding. The upper floors had dirty carpets, poor lighting, malfunctioning old appliances. Clare thought the kitchen cupboards and the bathroom were ugly. But she saw what potential the little house had.

"Perfect!" Clare laughed at it with Christine. "More renovating." In her mind, she was already replacing carpets with hardwood floors, repainting the rooms in her own colours, putting in a pedestal tub, new fixtures and cupboards, lighting and appliances. She told her friends it was not to be called their *'pied à terre'*, but Paws à Terre. They planned to get a pup companion for Yukon Sally.

Len showed little interest in the townhouse project. He was focused on their lakefront property with the tennis court and walking paths through the woods. He bought a chainsaw and an all-terrain vehicle to create and maintain the paths.

Their house on The Driveway sold quickly, for five times what Len had paid for it twenty-two years previously. Over the twenty years Clare had lived in it, she had renovated, restored, and decorated it so attractively the buyers remarked they liked it 'as is'. Everything had been kept in good working order. In consultation with Christine, Clare had done some repainting and bought new towels, some lamps, and an entrance rug so the home 'showed' at its best. Len never found fault with Clare's taste and décor. He left the design of the addition to the log cabin almost completely up to her and the log home builder. Len stipulated he wanted his office to overlook the lake. The old log cabin became their large living room looking onto the lake with an open concept kitchen. Working from the kitchen counter, Clare could see the old stone fireplace, the sitting area, and the lake. Four bedrooms, three bathrooms, two offices, and a recreation room with fireplace were built onto the old structure.

"We can't call this place 'the cabin' anymore," said Clare. "It's a handsome log house. Let's call it Loghaven."

"That's a good one," said Len. He built a wooden sign saying Loghaven on the fence by the road along their property.

Before the building on the house began, Clare had started the work on the tennis court. "It doesn't work the other way round," she explained. "If you do the house first, you might not end up with enough money to do the court."

"We have enough," said Len. "But I want more for investing. You'll have to sell the rental condo."

Clare was leery of that. It was the one area of finances that was in her control. The money they had received from the sale of their house on The Driveway went straight into Len's bank account for him to look after and pay for the townhouse and for Loghaven. Clare knew it was more than enough to pay for both. But she trusted Len in controlling the money. He had always taken care of the bills and invested safely. He was the opposite of extravagant. The President of Confederation Bank enjoyed calling Len his careful 'church mouse' whereas the head of marketing was known as the flamboyant 'town mouse'. Also, the house on The Driveway was in Len's name only. Len had bought it with his first wife, Karen, just before she was diagnosed with ovarian cancer. Treatment failed and she died less than a year later.

Len had been living alone in that house for over a year when Clare met him on a trip home to help her mother move to a seniors' retirement building in Ottawa. Her mother had been living in a small house behind Len and Karen's house on The Driveway. Their back yards shared one fence. Clare's mother, Vi, had written to Clare about her new neighbour who had become ill with cancer. Karen had befriended Clare's mother as though clinging to her own mother when she knew she had to let go of life itself. It surprised Clare that her mother had been so attentive to a young woman neighbour who was so needy.

"Oh for God's sake, Clare," said her mother when Clare came to Ottawa to help her with the move into the retirement residence. "The poor thing was dying and lonely. She was just ten years older than you. It could have been you at my door. Just how hardhearted do you think I am!"

Clare smiled and gave her mother a hug. "Hey Mom, did you just tell me you miss me and sometimes even worry about me?"

"Just stop giving me so much to worry about. You've been in Oxford too long. It's time you and Stan came home and brought those bright little twins for a good Canadian education. They're beginning to sound like British fishmongers."

"Stan will never come home," Clare had responded solemnly. "He's got his dream job in Oxford. He's come to think Oxford is the centre of the universe. And we can't afford to send our kids to private school. They go to the local state school full of working class kids, which is OK in itself. I don't like the accents either but I'm not going to complain about that. I did complain to the teachers that my kids are coming home with incorrect grammar. The teacher responded quietly but firmly. 'That's the way these children speak and we're not to make them feel badly about the way they speak.'"

"Are you serious!" Vi reached for her cigarettes. "If I hadn't corrected bad grammar in my classes, I would have been fired."

The day Clare helped her Mom move into her new residence, Len invited Vi and Clare to come to dinner. "It will be spaghetti," he warned them. "That's my one specialty."

Since they hadn't as yet unpacked the kitchen boxes, Vi accepted the invitation. Len welcomed them into his house. It struck Clare as ill-arranged, gloomy, in need of new paint and updating. Len was struck by his first sight of Clare. "Vi," he said, well within Clare's hearing, "You never told me your daughter was so good looking."

"She didn't get her good looks from me," Vi retorted, "I still have mine."

Len and Clare laughed. "That's my Mom," said Clare. "As she's no doubt already told you … call her Vi, for she's 'no shrinking Violet.'"

Vi was tired from the day of moving and wanted to go home early before it got dark at nine o'clock. It was obvious Len and Clare weren't ready to end the evening. Len said he could bring Clare home later, so Vi drove herself home. Len offered Clare some cognac but she stuck with wine. Len helped himself to cognac and spoke freely of his marriage and his life as a widower. He was a dozen years older than Clare.

"We married in the fifties," he told Clare. "No sex before marriage. Not like today! Discovered on our honeymoon that sex was painful for Karen. There's some medical term for it that I forget. Then she didn't want children. Maybe couldn't have them. I'd always wanted three or four kids. It was not a happy marriage. But in those days you stuck it out. Karen was a lonely person. Her parents died in their early sixties in a car accident on holiday in Europe. Her sister lives way the hell off in California. Then she got so sick with cancer and didn't have the strength to even begin to do all she wanted to renovate this house."

"I'm sorry you didn't have children," said Clare. There seemed to be years of pain in Len's voice when he spoke of that.

"Yeah. I'm forty-eight now. I suppose I could marry someone younger and have a child or two. I've actually joined a dating service, an expensive one. They keep me busy with dates. All nice women. But no real spark yet. And no one I can share good memories with." He looked away pensively and then back at Clare. "I guess you have a pretty good life over there in Oxford."

"It is a good life," said Clare. "It's the perfect life for my husband. A real sinecure. I enjoy a lot of it. I have good friends there. But I'm Canadian. I miss my homeland. It's the real inspiration for my work. I'm a wildlife photographer. But there's not much more than foxes and hounds to focus on in England. And I'm worried about bringing up my daughters in the English school and class system."

"You should come home," said Len.

"Maybe I should." Clare took a long sip of wine. "My marriage has become a seventies mess. We've tried everything. Counselling. Brief separation. Getting together again. Something happened just before I left to come help Mom move, that was a last straw for me." Clare looked down at her knees then up, trying to smile at Len. "But how can one ever be sure it is the last straw?"

"I had a lot of last straws," said Len.

They smiled at each other. "I guess I better get you home," he said.

They arranged to see each other the next day, and again the next evening, and again and again. Just before Clare was to fly back to Oxford, Len asked if she would consider marrying him. She answered yes, she would.

Clare and Stan lived in north Oxford in a house owned by his college, Christchurch. The evening Clare returned to Oxford, after putting the seven-year-old twins to sleep, Clare sat down in the living room to talk with Stan.

"What's going on?" said Stan. He was tense and wouldn't sit down. "Something has happened to you in Canada."

"Yes," said Clare. "I've come to a decision. I think you feel it too. We need to divorce. I want to go home, back to Canada."

"You're always like this after a visit to Canada," said Stan impatiently. "You always want to go home, 'back to Canada,'" he mimicked her.

"Stan, I'm serious. I'm filing for divorce."

"Then *go*!" his face was flushed with anger. "Just go! But you can't take the kids. They stay with me."

The next day, when Megan and Ali were in school, Clare met with her lawyer. She had been to her almost a year previously for a temporary separation agreement. Divorce papers were drawn up. The divorce was uncontested but a battle for custody ensued. Six months later, joint custody was granted, with care and control of the children given to Clare. Then Clare flew home to Ottawa with Megan and Ali, each with a suitcase of clothes and small possessions. The girls would fly back to be with their father at Christmas, March Break, and six weeks in the summer. The financial settlement was a token $100 to Clare.

From then on, Clare understood why war veterans wouldn't talk about their time on the battlefield. The custody battle was nothing compared to the battle fields of the two World Wars but it was to her an emotionally terrible time that she wanted to forget, but never could.

While waiting for Clare's return to Canada, Len had behaved with unwavering support, good humour, patience, and love. He wrote gently amusing letters to Clare while she was going through legal procedures in Oxford. Phone calls were not practical because those were the days of dial phones and there was only one in the front hall of the college house which Stan and Clare continued to share until the custody was settled. Len flew to Oxford for two weeks so he could meet the girls and also the social worker who was doing a report for the custody decision. Clare noted that Len let the girls observe and approach him rather than foisting himself upon them.

Ali and Megan liked him well enough. They liked the idea of going to Canada where their grandparents lived, both Stan's parents and Clare's mother. Also aunts and uncles and cousins. They had no relatives in England. Their new school was said to be very good. They could keep their home and friends in Oxford with their dad and have a new home in Ottawa which sounded interesting, overlooking a canal and all, near the Parliament buildings. There was also a little old log cabin on a lake which sounded like something out of story books about settlers in Canada. They hoped to see 'Indians' wearing feather headdresses. Their mother and Len would have a wedding very soon after their arrival in Canada. And their mother promised them a puppy.

Those things came to pass. Clare looked back on the first years of life back in Canada with her daughters and Len as very good. Though not without times of poignant pain. That first Christmas putting her little daughters on a plane back to Oxford. And then doing it three times a year until they were at university. She never got over the gut-wrenching pain of doing that. Though it was ameliorated by knowing their father looked after them well and encouraged their education and ambitions. But Clare never forgot overhearing Ali saying to a playmate one day after coming back from Oxford in that first year, "I miss my dad in England, very much."

The twins were outgoing and made friends easily. They excelled at school and enjoyed various sports. They both loved skiing in the Laurentians and swimming and canoeing at the cabin when they didn't have to be in England. They got to know and enjoy time with their cousins and grandparents on visits to and from Kingston. They found their Gramma Vi the most fun.

After some years of impermanent relationships, Stan married a younger Canadian woman, Marta Brooks, who worked as a journalist in London. They had no children, other than Ali and Megan. Clare learned that Marta was a good stepmother to the twins and over time she and Clare came to like each other.

A serious disappointment for Len and Clare was not being able to conceive a child. Clare was only thirty-six when they married. Not conceiving was surprising since Clare had confided in Len that 'the last straw' for her with Stan had been what happened just before her trip to Ottawa to help her mother move. She had been on a different form of birth control, the coil. She found herself pregnant in spite of it. Stan went to the doctor with Clare to hear the results of her pregnancy test. The doctor said yes, Clare was pregnant but it sometimes happened that in a very early stage, the coil would expel the fertilized egg.

"That would be good," Stan had replied.

"Why?" the doctor and Clare said simultaneously, in surprise.

"The marriage is on the rocks," Stan said without looking at Clare.

"I see," said the doctor.

Clare stood up, thanked the doctor and left the office. Stan followed her out. He caught up to her on the sidewalk. She turned and said in a low voice. "I hate you for that. Absolutely hate you."

Two days later, Clare stared down in the toilet at a clot of blood expelled from her womb. The following day Stan drove her to the airport to visit her mother in Ottawa and help her with the move into a retirement condo. En route to the airport, Clare sat with the twins in the back seat, trying to talk naturally with them, not speaking to Stan except to say good bye at the departure gate.

"You're trying not to cry, aren't you Mummy?" said Ali. "It's OK. We'll see you in three weeks. Daddy will look after us."

Megan hugged her mother and burst into tears.

Clare saw there was no hiding the tension between her and Stan from the children. She pulled both girls into her arms to reassure them. "Don't cry Meggy. Ali's right. I'll see you in three weeks." She kissed each of them on the forehead. Then stepped into departures turning to wave once more with a smile meant to hide her anxieties.

After the divorce proceedings and custody settlement, when Clare returned to Canada with her daughters and married Len, she expected to conceive very soon. But a year passed without conception. Clare and Len then took tests that revealed Len had a very low sperm count.

"Maybe it was me all along, not Karen, who couldn't have children," said Len. "Oh well. No use talking about it. Does no good."

"It's healthy to talk things over," said Clare.

"Not for me," said Len. "Doesn't help. Let's move on."

"It's Friday," said Clare, thinking diversion might help. "We could go out to a movie, if my mom is willing to babysit." But Vi was having dinner with other people in her building. "I'll make a pizza and we can watch *The Cosby Show* with the twins."

The twins cheered at the prospect. But Len didn't enjoy *The Cosby Show*. It was all happy family stuff with a comedian father. Len left halfway through it. Said he needed to get something done at his desk. He took his scotch with him. Clare enjoyed just being with her daughters, no matter what they were doing. They were enough for her. It became an unspoken sadness in their marriage that they were not enough for Len. Though he was unstinting in providing for them and sharing with Stan in their university costs. Clare had worried that Len might lose sexual interest or confidence after the results of the sperm test. But not so.

"I was deprived," he said to Clare on a Saturday morning when they could linger in bed while the twins watched kids' TV. "Deprived for too many years. I'm enjoying making up for lost time. And turning fifty, I've no time to lose. It's good to sleep with someone who doesn't like pyjamas."

Good years followed. Len became a top executive at Confederation Bank, with appropriate salary increases. Clare began to have more time for photography as renovations were being completed and the girls graduated from elementary school and could get to high school by public transport. Len took no share at all in helping with the twins, or housework, meals, gardening, or arrangements for their social life. That was the norm for men of his vintage and for his colleagues at the Bank. Clare accepted this division of labour and lifestyle because Len was so well paid and she earned so little from her photography.

Ali and Megan graduated from elementary school with top marks, then from high school with prizes. Megan's prize was in the arts, Ali's in science. After high school, Ali chose to go to the University of British Columbia in Vancouver, Megan went to McGill in Montreal. Len paid for the girls to come back home to attend their high school graduation and the party afterwards in their house on The Driveway. It had become the teenagers' popular party house. Clare got on well with her daughters' friends, and parents could trust that parties there would be sufficiently supervised.

By then the puppy they had grown up with in Ottawa had become old. Frowsie was a cross between a Newfoundlander and a Labrador, a big dog who could swim across the lake at their cabin. Everyone loved the big, friendly, lumbering dog with the brown and black coat forever in need of more grooming. Frowsie lumbered around at the graduation party enjoying the attention of old friends. But she could no longer climb stairs and she needed to lie down often. Megan and Ali cried when they hugged her goodbye. They feared what Clare couldn't bear to face, that they would never see Frowsie again.

Clare drove Megan to the train for Montreal and Ali to airport for Vancouver. Back home, Clare sat with a drink and her arm around Frowsie. She reflected on how well things had gone. The girls off to the universities of their choice. Len had risen to the top of his field at Confederation Bank and would retire in the new year with a good pension. She had an exhibition of her photos of wolves and bears of Algonquin Park opening at the Museum of Nature. A calendar of the photos would be on sale in the gift shop. She got another glass of wine and sat closer to Frowsie, the one who had always comforted her when she had to part from her daughters. Frowsie stirred. "Do you need out, Frowsie Dog?" Clare helped her off the couch and took her to the back door. Frowsie got down the one step and onto the grass. She lay down and couldn't get up. Clare went back into the house calling for Len to come and help. He came out of his office and went to look at Frowsie. "We have to get her to the vet," he said, looking at her collapsed on the grass.

It was a Sunday afternoon. They phoned the veterinarian. The vet on duty said they could meet her at the clinic. Len and Clare lifted Frowsie into the car on a blanket and drove her to the clinic. The vet came out to the car with her stethoscope and travel case. She examined Frowsie as best she could. She looked solemnly at Clare and Len. They instinctively drew together, shoulder to shoulder.

"We could give her oxygen to give her more time," offered the vet. "But her lungs are full of fluid. She hasn't much longer. She's lived a long life for such a big dog."

"Can we take her to our cabin?" Weeping, Clare stroked Frowsie's head. "Let her … die there? Peacefully. Naturally? Or will that make her suffer more?"

"I'll give her a strong sedative." The vet reached into her case.

Clare sat in the back seat with Frowsie as Len drove them to the cabin. They made it there after the sun had set. It was mid-November. Darkness took over early. As they lifted Frowsie out of the car and lay her on the grass, her four big legs stretched out and stiffened, as did her big soft body. Clare lay down beside her and put her arms around Frowsie, burroughing her face into Frowsie's warm but lifeless body. Len patted Frowsie's head.

They pulled and lifted her into the cabin, laying her near the fireplace. Len made a fire. They had wine, some bread and cheese. Raised their glasses to Frowsie's great character traits. Clare phoned her best friend, Lizzie. They prepared the pullout bed and slept by Frowsie and the fire. In the morning they prepared to bury her near a cedar tree. Clare stood beside Frowsie's body wrapped in the blanket. Len began digging. A new neighbour they didn't as yet know well came over with a shovel.

"That's a hard thing to do," he said. "Let me help." When they finished digging, the neighbour whose name was Tory, Tory Sanderson, went back to his cottage and lowered the flag which he had raised on a proper flag pole near his dock. Clare noted that Tory was tall and carried himself well, like a man who had been in the military.

Back in Ottawa, Clare phoned Megan and Ali at the end of the day so they would have the evening to absorb the news. With Len back at work, Clare was alone in the house. No big lumbering, empathetic, companion to talk to. Clare knew she had to do something about the grief and loneliness overcoming her. She phoned Len at his office.

"I'm a basket case," she said to him. "I don't want to get up in the morning because Frowsie isn't here to share my toast, or walk along the canal with me, or greet me when I come into the house. It's all so empty and silent. Tomblike."

"What are you going to do about it?"

"Get another dog."

"OK."

"I can't go to the dog shelter. In my state I'd come home with every one of them. Can we spring for a purebred?"

"What kind?"

"I want an indigenous Canadian dog. A Newfoundlander needs too much grooming. And it would remind me too much of Frowsie, make me weep. I'd like to have a Malamute sled dog, like the ones my grandmother Meg kept."

"We can't have a team of sled dogs! We live in a city, for chrissake."

"We could start with one. Get a companion dog, if necessary, down the road."

"Twin dogs, eh?" Len said in good humour. "One for Ali. One for Meg."

Such a long time ago that was, when they got their first Malamute. Clare named her Yukon Sally, after her grandmother Meg's first Malamute. Clare was intrigued by how wolflike Yukon was compared to all the dogs she had known and grown up with. Yukon was cautious and strategizing, working her way around the outskirts of their enclosed back yard in Ottawa, figuring out where was best to cross into its centre when she wanted to. She listened to a command to 'come here', clearly understanding what was being asked of her, but taking her own time to consider whether or not she should do it. It was as though she were saying, "I'll get back to you on that."

Clare read up on the breed, its history and traits. Alaskan Malamutes as they were officially registered in the Kennel Club. Yukon Sally was indeed a lot like the Arctic wolves the Malamutes were descended from. Malamute sled dogs were bred originally from wolves across the Arctic, not just in Alaska. But the Malamute-speaking Inuit in the western Arctic got most of the publicity or credit for it. Yukon Sally had the fur, colouring, and stature of Malamute dogs, but her legs were long and thinner, like wolves'. Her breeder explained that Yukon wouldn't succeed as a show dog because of that. But Yukon was regal and had the intelligence of a lead dog. Or lead wolf, thought Clare. She's a bit of a 'throwback' but good breeders don't delve into that. They know that people fantasize about wolves. And not all good comes from it. Breeding wolves with dogs produces an unpredictable pet and a captive wild animal.

Once Clare understood that a Malamute's intelligence should be respected and encouraged since it is they who know sooner than the musher when thin ice is being approached, she saw that Yukon acted well on co-operation rather than obedience. Then she found Yukon Sally easier to understand and work with. "She's like a teenager," Clare explained to Len. "Respect her intelligence and independence, then you'll find she understands and wants to co-operate, rather than please you by obeying, as a Lab does."

Len never fully understood that. He had been raised to simply obey his parents. He didn't much like modern teenagers with all their independence in attitude and ideas. But he tried to keep quiet about that.

Yukon Sally was six years old when they sold their house on The Driveway and built the addition onto their old cabin. Part of the plan was to get a Malamute puppy, a companion for Yukon Sally. They got a male puppy, Yukon Jake, from Yukon Sally's breeder.

Len had been pleased by the renovations Clare did on the house on The Driveway and how much it had sold for. He saw the benefits of her renovations on the small rental condo and was satisfied with her putting the rent money into the joint account where he kept close track of it and did not mind her using it for small improvements on the house or cabin and then for a second car, a Jeep which she and the twins used most. He was proud of the tennis court and grand addition to create Loghaven.

But he was irate when Clare had the real estate agent deposit the money for the sale of the rental condo into her bank account. Extremely irate.

"This is grounds for divorce!" Len raged at Clare. "Give it back to me. That money is mine."

"I'll give you $50,000 to invest," Clare answered calmly. "The rest I'm keeping to use on furnishings and landscaping and any leftover could be for a bit of investing on my own." She had thought it over carefully and at length. After twenty years of marriage, she decided she had the right to control the money from a small property given to her in her name.

CHAPTER ELEVEN

The Second Episode of Violence

All the work on Loghaven was completed, apart from landscaping, by Christmas of 1999. They moved the furnishings in and brought Yukon Jake home from the breeder's kennels. Len couldn't help but like the puppy and was willing to share in having to get up in the night to let Jake out of his crate and take him outside to urinate, then put him back in his crate until morning. Jake always howled in complaint when put back in his crate but soon settled down. They kept the crate in the recreation room.

Although Len had become more civil to Clare over the holidays with Megan and Ali home with their boyfriends, Clare knew he still harboured intense anger at her for taking control of the money from the sale of the rental condo. He was drinking more than ever. Vi came for New Year's, the celebration of 2000, the beginning of the twenty-first century. Vi got along well with Len, had always admired his strength of mind and success in business. "He had to put up with a lot during Karen's illness," Vi had told Clare, "also her weakness of character."

"What do you mean?"

"She clung to him like a vine. She could have pulled him down. But he remained strong and good at his job." Unlike your husband, my dad, Clare knew her mother was saying to herself. But that New Year's, when Len staggered up to bed, Vi remarked to Clare, "Len never drank like that when he was working."

Clare didn't feel she could tell her mother how bad it had become. Clare couldn't bear to tell her mother that Len had beaten her about the head and shoulders a year and a half earlier. She couldn't bear to tell anyone about that except the Help Line counsellors and her sister Julie. "Divorce him," Julie had said firmly, "before he does it again." But Julie was then in the midst of divorcing her first husband. Clare thought her advice was too influenced by that. And Clare didn't want to divorce again, ever.

Clare did inform her doctor about the pummeling. He put it in her medical records and said sympathetically, "Let's hope it was a one-off. Be careful not to rile him when he's had too much to drink."

Clare thought the counselling sessions and then their constructive building of Loghaven and moving into Paws à Terre had done the job of giving Len a better focus and more purpose in retirement. It had, but his rage over her taking control of the condo sale money was still seething within him. She was being very careful to avoid the subject and avoid any contention with him. It had been nearly a year and a half since he had beaten her about the head and shoulders. She would never raise a finger to him again, lest he retaliate like that. And she had become good at not rising to his antagonizing comments, which usually moved on to belligerence when he got drunk.

They stayed on at Loghaven after the celebration of the new century. It was beautiful there by the lake in the fresh snow of early winter and an easier place to toilet train Jakey. Len wasn't keen to go to the small townhouse. He liked the spacious comfort, the views and quiet of Loghaven. He did not miss the cultural and social life of the city. He did not phone colleagues or friends. He spent his days in his office avoiding interaction with the young people and his evenings by the fire, drinking and reading *The Economist* while Clare joined her daughters and their boyfriends watching movies in the rec room. Len waved them off when Clare drove them to the airport after New Year's.

It was January 5, 2000, about three in the morning when Clare heard Jakey howling in his crate. She tapped Len's shoulder to see if he would wake from his deep sleep. He had had a lot of scotch that night. "Can you let Jake out?" she said when Len stirred. "It's your turn. But I'll do it if…"

Len threw off the covers. "Jesus Christ!" He got up and put on his bath robe. Slammed the door as he left the room. Clare heard Jakey stop howling when Len approached. Good dog, thought Clare, he's learned to call us when he needs out.

It seemed a longer time than usual before Len returned and went into their ensuite bathroom. And why almost no protest when Jakey was put back in his crate? Clare got up and went into the ensuite to ask what had gone on.

"Why is Jakey so quiet? What did you do?"

"I fed him." Len yelled at her

She was standing in front of him. "You fed him at three in the morning?" she said incredulously, genuinely astounded.

Len lifted his right arm, holding it out stiff with his fist closed and slugged her hard in the left temple. She put her hand to her temple and reached to the door to hold onto for support as Len stepped around her and walked quickly through the bedroom to the hall and into a guest room, slamming the door. Clare lay down on the bed, reeling, trying to think what to do. The side of her head hurt.

She phoned no one. He could have killed me, she thought, knocked me onto the tile floor, or onto the hard edge of the toilet. She lay there thinking until morning light when Jakey needed to be let out with Yukon Sally.

As she sat at the kitchen counter drinking coffee, Clare came to some conclusions. I didn't touch him. Just asked him a question in genuine astonishment. What he did was so out of the blue. Unprovoked. Unreasonable. Of course at the heart of it is his anger at me for keeping control of the condo sale money. I'm not giving in to that. I can't live with him controlling everything and slugging me if I don't obey him. When he comes down this morning, if he doesn't give a full apology, and show some remorse, some real resolve never, ever to hit me again … I'm going straight to the police. I can't let this happen again.

Len came down to the kitchen. He had showered, shaved, and dressed for the day. He didn't say a word or look straight at her. He put on the kettle for his instant coffee and put a mug with powdered coffee and sugar into it on the counter, then prepared his bowl of cereal.

"Do you have anything to say to me?" asked Clare.

"What do you want me to say?" He carried on with his breakfast, not looking at her.

"About last night."

"What about last night?"

Clare stood up, went for her coat and purse, put on her boots and talked to the dogs before she got into the Jeep to go to the police station in Ottawa.

It was now fourteen years since Clare went to the police station but Clare could remember the scenes as clearly as snapshots in front of her. She had breathed deeply to calm herself before going into the police station. "I have to report some violence" she said to the receptionist. "to me. I mean violence done to me."

"By...?" The receptionist looked at her expectantly.

"Sorry. By my husband. Last night."

Clare was interviewed by an officer in a room, then taken to another room where two women officers interviewed her. They listened to her account of what happened, then gently but firmly cross questioned her. When they learned this was a second offence and with a closed fist to the temple, the officers looked at each other. Then they spoke with more concern and kindness, making Clare's eyes well up with tears, and she couldn't speak for some moments. One officer sat with her while the other went out of the room for what seemed a long time.

Two male officers came into the room saying they wanted to bring her husband in for questioning. They followed her back to Loghaven in their cruiser and accompanied her to the door. Len came from his office to the door where the police stood.

"What the hell...?"

"Is this your husband?" The officer addressed Clare.

"Yes," Clare answered, but her voice wasn't working well, so she nodded.

"Sir," the officer spoke to Len firmly but politely. "Will you come to the station for some questioning?"

"Yes." Len's voice was suddenly submissive. Clare couldn't bear the look on his face. Such a mixture of dignified and docile.

"Officer Pitt will accompany you to gather your things in case you should be required to stay away from your wife for a time. "

"Have charges been laid?" Len did not look at Clare who shook her head in a no.

"It's possible they may be," answered the officer.

Clare sat down on the front hall bench feeling weak in the knees and signalled the officer to also sit down. "No. Thank you, ma'am."

The dogs had remained silent outside at the approach of strangers, as Malamutes do. Now Yukon Sally and Jake were scratching at the door. Clare let them in. They vied for pats from her then turned their attention to the officer. "Down boys," the officer said with authority.

"Sit down. Yukon Sally. Jake," said Clare firmly. "Sit down."

They were sitting by Clare when the officer came downstairs with Len, who got his coat and hat. He would not look at Clare as he was escorted outside. He handed his car keys to one officer and got into the back of the cruiser with the other. Clare watched the cruiser and Len's car drive down the lane. Clare sat down on the couch. Sally and Jake got up on either side of her. She put her hand on each of them. It took effort to hold her own head up. It felt like all the air had been taken out of her. The cottages on either side were empty. She was alone with her Malamutes overlooking the snow-covered lake.

Chapter Twelve

The Consequence in the Year 2000

Len was charged with assault, required to stay away from Clare for six weeks, take some psychological tests, and stop drinking alcohol. He stayed at their townhouse, Paws à Terre, in Ottawa. He would be required to stand before a judge.

The day after he was arrested and released to go to their Paws à Terre, Clare drove into Ottawa for some cash and supplies. She had only one credit card which was authorized by Len and paid in full by him each month. She found the card no longer worked for her. Len had changed the pin number. He had also emptied the joint account.

Jazuz! That was quick action, Clare said to herself. How bloody stupid of me not to have obtained my own credit card. I'll do so, asap. How right I was to put the money from the sale of the rental condo into my own bank account. It's a wonder he didn't cut off the credit card when I did that. I guess giving him $50,000 and paying for all the Loghaven finishing things staved him off.

She made an appointment to obtain her own credit card and an appointment with a recommended lawyer, Mr. Cane. When she explained her situation to him, he told her her few options. Separation, or divorce, or attempt reconciliation after Len was brought to trial. "Being married for twenty years," he said, "your settlement should be good." He gave her separation papers to fill out if she took that route.

Clare laid the papers on the desk beside her laptop computer. She read through the forms to be filled out ... her monthly income, her monthly expenses, her dependents... Clare stopped there. She couldn't go through this again. Wouldn't do this to her daughters again. After years of graduate work, Ali in paediatrics, Megan in law, they were just beginning their careers. Ali in the paediatric wing of the Vancouver General Hospital. Megan on the other side of the country had just begun practising law in St. John's, Newfoundland. Ali would be getting married soon. This was no time for Clare to be even mentioning divorce.

She put the forms into a file folder to be taken back to her lawyer.

Len phoned her at the end of the week. Clare was amazed at his being in good humour and talkative.

"I'm following orders," he said. "Got a lawyer. Can't think of his name right now. Seems to know his business alright. Told me to restore the credit card pin for you. Doesn't look good on me, cutting that off. So I did that right away. I was going to do it soon anyway."

"Thank you."

"You're welcome. Also answered a lot of questions on some psychological test they gave me."

"What was that about?"

"Oh, some funny questions about what I'd do if I encountered some guy begging on the street. Stuff like that."

"And…?"

"What did I say? Said I'd pass him by, of course. I give lots to the United Way, don't I?"

"Yes you do. How did it all turn out? The test."

Len laughed. "Seems I'm an arrogant, unsympathetic son of a bitch."

Clare laughed. And laughed. "Oh Len…"

"I know," he said. "Seems I'm not a perfect guy. Do some things I shouldn't. Shouldn't be phoning you. They told me no contact for six weeks. Or until I've appeared before the Judge, or whatever."

Clare felt a heavy dread.

"You OK with me talking to you? No one else I want to talk to."

"Yes. You can talk to me. But you'd better follow the rules."

"You're not going to report this, are you? For chrissake."

"No, I won't report this." Though I wouldn't lie if questioned about it, she thought.

* * * * *

The neighbours came up to their cottage on the weekend. Tory and his wife Hetti were a sociable couple often bringing family or friends to their cottage. They had grown-up kids and young teenage grandkids from afar. Clare envied the apparent happy marriage and social life going on in their place as she sat with her dogs wondering what her future was going to be.

Ali phoned her on Sunday as she often did, if not having to be on duty at the hospital. Ali was planning to marry another paediatrician, Morton Thordarson, who had grown up in the Icelandic community of Gimli, Manitoba. They were the same age and had a love of sports as well as careers in common. It looked like a very compatible marriage but Ali was anxious about where and when they would marry. Her wanting to talk about that was a relief to Clare because it allowed her to not tell Ali what was going on in her own life.

She talked with Megan less often but Megan had an almost uncanny sense when something was being covered up. "Mom, what's wrong?" Megan said when they talked on a Sunday. "You sound funny."

"Nothing. I was just clearing my throat."

"No. you sound nervous. On edge. Why are you spending so much time at the cottage?"

"Because I love it here. So do the dogs."

"Where's Dad? Len."

"Why do you call him Len now?"

"That's not answering my question. Where is he?"

"At the townhouse. He has things to do in Ottawa."

"Mom, you're fudging something. Is he drinking more than ever? Have you separated?"

"Am I being cross questioned?"

"I just want to know what's going on. The truth."

Clare considered the situation. Soon Len would be brought before the judge. Clare's lawyer told Clare that the police would likely have the charge dropped if she wanted them to. It would mean that Len would then have no criminal record. Clare certainly wanted that.

She did not want Len to have a criminal record and be written up in the papers as such. It would prevent him from doing various volunteer work and volunteer work was good for him. A criminal record would shame him and their family. It would ruin him. Definitely she wanted the charges dropped.

The judge would demand conditions, Clare's lawyer explained. Likely Len would have to have a year's counselling and show desire to reform himself. That's exactly what Clare wanted. She fully consented to the charges being dropped. She knew she would have to tell her daughters basically what happened before and unless it became a public event, a newspaper story. 'Retired Confederation Bank executive convicted of wife assault'.

"OK, Meg, I'll tell you the truth. I was going to soon in any case. It's just hard to do." Clare choked.

"Mom, I'm your daughter. I can help you."

"You can help me by breaking it to Ali. I couldn't bear to tell her. She's so happy now with wedding plans."

"Of course. What's the truth?"

"Len hit me. Hard. On the side of my head. My left temple. I didn't see it coming. He just got mad because I questioned his judgement about feeding Jake in the middle of the night. He made no apology. So I reported it to the police. They charged him with assault. He has to appear before the judge in three weeks. I'm asking for the charges to be dropped. He'll likely have to have counselling for a year."

Megan passed the phone to someone at hand. "Mrs. Rekai, this is Nate, Nate Logan. I'm a … a friend of your daughter's. She just wants a moment to absorb what you said."

"Mom," Megan took the phone back. "You have to make very serious decisions now. Dropping the charge for something that actually happened. What will be the consequence of that? Continuing to live with an alcoholic who slugged you? What if it happens again? It's likely to."

"Then he'd go to jail. He's not going to let that happen. People should be given a second chance." Clare stopped there, realizing she had already given him a second chance.

"OK, Mom. It's your decision. Do you want me to come home before or for the court appearance?"

"No. Thanks Meggy. I'll do this on my own. Inform Ali for me, please. Don't let it spoil her happiness. I'll talk to her right after you do. Nothing important is going to change. Len won't strike me again. Things are going to be better. We've both learned from this. It's late where you are. Get a good night's sleep."

"You too, Mom." Megan choked and hung up.

Three weeks later, Clare sat in the benches of the courtroom. Accompanied by his lawyer, Len sat in the front row. He was called to stand before the judge. Len wore his gray business suit and tie. His head was slightly bowed as he stood before the Judge then he faced the judge respectfully. Clare felt such a rush of emotion and sympathy for him, she clasped her hands tightly together on her lap to stop herself from moving.

"How do you plead?" said the Judge, himself a gray haired man.

"Guilty, your Honour." Len said quietly but clearly, bowed his head then looked up again at the judge.

After further statements from the prosecution on behalf of the police about the charge being stayed and Len agreeing to a year of counselling sessions, the Judge accepted dropping the charges and court was adjourned. Clare stood up as Len approached her. She took his arm as they walked out of the courtroom.

"Glad to get that over with," said Len when they arrived back at their townhouse in separate cars and walked into the house together.

"Yes," said Clare. "Me too." Yukon Sally was pawing and Jake jumping up at the solarium door. Len opened the solarium door for them. Yukon Sally jumped up and put both paws on Len's shoulders. Jake barged in to do the same but his paws as yet reached only to Len's waist.

"Down boys," said Len, but he was smiling and flushed at the welcoming. "We'll take you back to Loghaven tomorrow."

He waited until 4 p.m. to pour himself a scotch and had only two before dinner. Clare had prepared Len's favourite meal, schnitzel and brussel sprouts with mashed potatoes. She had also prepared a toast. She raised her glass of wine. "Here's to us. Let's put this behind us and, as they say, move on."

"Suits me," said Len and took a large gulp of wine.

There were some tense times in that first year, usually during the dinner hours. During the day they had separate activities, Clare with photography, Len at his desk becoming more and more focused on his investments. He volunteered with his financial expertise on cancer fundraising campaigns. They skied together two or three afternoons a week. When summer approached, they played doubles with friends. Those were good times. Their neighbours, Tory and Hetti, were excellent tennis players but Tory was away for long periods working on projects in developing countries for international organizations like the United Nations and CIDA. He seemed to have had an impressive career as a geophysicist who worked long after retirement age, picking and choosing his projects. But he was not one to talk about his achievements.

Len always poured himself a scotch at 4 p.m. and would take it to his desk unless people were coming to play tennis at four. Then he would put his drink in a 'traveller' and take it to the court along with the large thermos of water brought for everyone. When there was no tennis and Clare came into the kitchen to prepare dinner between 5 and 6 p.m., Len would sit in his armchair with his scotch and want to have a conversation, an argument actually. He would ask Clare her opinion on something he had read in the day's newspaper. Busy preparing dinner, she would remind him she hadn't time to read the paper until after dinner.

"Sure you do," he'd say. "You just choose hiking with the dogs, swimming, playing with your camera…"

"I don't 'play' with my camera, you know it's my … work."

"OK. I won't say that again." He got up for another scotch.

Back in his chair, he tried another angle. "So who do you think's going to win at Wimbledon?"

Clare didn't watch television tennis, unless it were a final dramatic game or involved an up and coming Canadian. "Len, I'm making a cheese sauce here. Can we talk about this at dinner?"

"Can't talk and cook at the same time?"

Here we go, Clare seethed. Antagonism time. Her fantasy of pouring a bucket of cold water over him came to mind. It released some of her tension and reminded her … don't engage. She exhaled and said "I'd just rather have something to talk about at dinner."

"Why can't dinner be for eating?"

This is too stupid, thought Clare, too stupid to respond to. She kept silent.

"Can't you just answer the question?"

Clare put the wooden stirring spoon down hard on the counter. "Yes," she said. "We can eat at dinner. *And* talk."

"Right then. I'll just say nothing," Len yelled at her.

"Len," Clare turned to him. "If this is a serious issue, take it up with Dr. Bodker."

"I will. He wants you to come to some sessions."

"I will. I'd like to."

They sat down to dinner with nothing further to talk about.

Len never spoke about what was said at his sessions with Dr. Bodker, other than "He's a good guy. Asks a lot of questions. Doesn't tell me much. But when he does comment, it's not too far off."

Clare found Dr. Bodker much more engaged than their previous counsellor. Clare guessed he was near Len's age. He said he had obtained his doctorate in psychology after an earlier career in engineering. Dr. Bodker invited Clare to attend three sessions with Len. When Len's year of sessions was finished, Clare paid privately for two more sessions alone with Dr. Bodker. It did not surprise Clare to learn from Dr. Bodker that Len had unresolved issues from his first marriage and had not adjusted well to retirement. Also, Len did not think he had a drinking problem.

Dr. Bodker did take her by surprise when he said, "Len believes your problems stem from you having had an affair some time ago."

"What!" Clare exclaimed then fell silent. She knew she was sounding stunned and stupid. She was stunned. Memories long laid away, carefully, painfully, sadly, lovingly, rose into her mind. Dr. Bodker waited for Clare to gather her thoughts and respond in her own way.

"Sorry," She looked at him sitting patiently in his leather arm chair. "It was so long ago. Eleven years. Len hasn't mentioned it since. It happened when he was still working." As Dr. Bodker made a note, scenes from eleven years ago came to Clare's mind. The International Association of Wildlife Photographers conference in Puerto Rico. The elegant and eloquent French chairman. Constantine. He was of Russian ancestry. He lived in Paris. "It was so short-lived," said Clare. "So impossible." And yet so intense, thought Clare, I'll never forget. And never want to. "He was twenty-one years older than me." Oh God! Shut up Clare, she told herself. She recalled a saying of her mother's, using the image of a cowplop, 'The more you step on it, the wider it spreads.'

"A father figure?" Dr. Bodker smiled. His demeanour was benign, a measure of sympathy but very controlled. He looked at the clock. The session was nearing its end. "A past affair, particularly a brief one, is generally regarded as a consequence of a weakened relationship, rather than a cause of it."

"Has Len really harboured this … this grievance all these years, and never brought it up to me?"

"Apparently."

Len had some affairs before his wife died, Clare wanted to say, but held herself back. She didn't want to do that kind of 'ratting' on him. It had happened back in the seventies when the birth control pill was brought into popular use and many marriages were affected by the new attitudes to love and fidelity that it brought. 'Make love whenever you can, it's good for you,' became a slogan, for some.

"In our next session," said Dr. Bodker, "would you like to talk about your relationship with your father, in regard to his drinking?"

"OK," said Clare. "Yes." But her mind was full of the memory of Constantine.

She couldn't bring herself to raise the subject with Len at dinner that evening. Or ever. She had kept Constantine's letters and the long poem he wrote for her after their first meaningful encounter at a previous conference. She kept them in a box under the chaise in her office for six years.

Then, after their house on The Driveway was sold, Clare saw a film about a woman who had had an affair. She later died suddenly in an accident and her grown-up children found the journal she had kept recording the mutually fulfilling affair. That made Clare think deeply and realistically about her hidden box of correspondence with Constantine. Did she want her children, Len, or anyone, to find and read the letters meant only for her? No!

When she was alone in the house, she burned them in the fireplace. As she watched the small flames and sacrificed more letters to them, the feeling that she was committing an act of violation and cowardice began to grow within her. When she had put the last letter into the fire, the feeling of violation and cowardice was overriding her sense of 'I'm protecting my husband and children from' … what? Shame? No that's too strong. I don't feel shame about what happened between Constantine and me. I just don't want it to affect others, especially my family. I don't want it known publicly. It would be an embarrassment to my children and husband.

The evening after Clare came home from the session with Dr. Bodker telling her Len had brought up the subject of her long past affair, Clare took some wine after clearing up from dinner and went to her new office in Loghaven. She looked through the album she had of that conference in Puerto Rico. There was a photo, taken by the press at the opening reception, of her in a long black gown with Constantine beside her in a white jacket. He was tanned, tall, striking blue eyes, thick dark hair graying at the fore edges, brushed back in European style. A stereotype of a handsome man, but with an unusual broad smile. Clare was then forty-five, also tanned, with shining auburn hair, smiling in conversation with two men looking with pleasure at her.

Jazuz! thought Clare, what a flattering photo! I look in my absolute prime. And Constantine a perfect peacock. No wonder they gave me a copy of this photo. Constantine had made a beeline for her at the beginning of the reception and escorted her around, introducing her to various people from different countries. He was gallant and humorous, making people smile, even laugh. He was very good at making brief, relevant conversation and moving on. He allowed himself to be drawn away from Clare but later returned to her. She was clearly the chosen that night.

And then again next day at the general assembly. During the first coffee break, Constantine came down from presiding at head table, shoulders back and striding like a general. He went straight to the row of chairs where Clare was sitting on the aisle. He stopped, clicked his heels, bent over, took her hand and raised it to kiss. Clare was surprised and embarrassed. It was a gesture from another century. She felt people seeing it might burst into laughter. She quickly rose to her feet so that she was standing up as Constantine kissed her hand. Hers was a gesture of equality, friend to friend. They both started talking then Clare let him have the lead.

It was a scene she carried with her through the years. Constantine, eager and excited as a school boy. Unabashedly so. He was a playful man. Amusing and self-mocking, yet deeply serious in his dedication to his work and pursuits. At that conference, he dined and conversed with her whenever his schedule allowed. He invited her to his suite and ordered room service dinner so they could have an evening of privacy. It became a night.

He explained he had observed her at two conferences in the past two years. He had chatted and danced a waltz with her but he had been accompanied by his wife and was attentive to her. His wife was pleasant, well groomed and expensively dressed. Not outgoing or showing much interest in where she was. She was introduced to Clare as Natalia. Clare learned Natalia was close to Constantine's age; they had been married nearly thirty years and had no children.

After that night together in Puerto Rico, Constantine said to Clare, "I'm sorry, I was not at my best. Will you give me more time?"

"But…" Clare didn't know what to say. She had enjoyed talking and being with him more than she could say.

He put his finger towards her lips, saying, "Hush. Please. I'm thinking of a plan. The conference is to end tomorrow. I'm thinking of a possible photo-taking excursion. Have you been to Cuba? Could we arrange a week, or at least five days? I know a small hotel in Cuba. It makes sense to attach a professional trip to see what wildlife we can find in Cuba. He smiled with a mischievous look in his eyes and embraced her. "Oh my love. My Rosalinda."

"Rosalinda?!" Clare laughed gently. "I'm no Rosalinda."

"You are to me."

They had five days and nights together in a small hotel, as luxurious as hotels get in Havana, Cuba. It was not a torrid affair, Clare smiled as she reminisced. Everything they did was infused with conversation, amusing or thoughtful comments, quiet enjoyment of each other's presence, knowing it was so time limited. Walking arm in arm along old streets, intimate dinners in the hotel dining room, drinks in Hemingway's favourite bar, trips to the beach, watching the sunset, taking photos of crocodiles confined to putrid pools, snorkeling in clear ocean water. His playfulness, intensity, and tenderness in the bedroom and everywhere.

In the departure lounge at the airport she was afraid she would cry. But he held her shoulders and whispered in her ear, "No tears, my Rosalinda. Where ever you are, we are … forever and a day." He smiled and brought her hand to his lips, looking intently at her. She had to smile. "You're not real," she said.

"Mais oui," he said. "Je suis … forever and a day."

When she returned home, little interest was shown in her added on photography excursion to Cuba. Len was not inquisitive at dinner and the twins were wrapped up in high school concerns. When Clare showed them the photos she had developed of the snorkeling bay and the crocodiles, the twins remarked it would be cool to visit Cuba sometime.

"Too socialist for me," said Len. "But it would be a cheap holiday. Maybe we could all go on a March Break."

"But we go to Oxford on March Break," said Ali. The conversation stopped.

Before the end of a week, Clare received a letter from Constantine, then every week, sometimes two came through the front door mail slot while Len was at the office, the twins at school. She sent letters to Constantine at a general delivery address in Paris he had given her. He occasionally phoned her as her new friend and colleague from Paris. When he phoned to wish her a Happy New Year, Len picked up the phone then handed it to Clare. "It's that friend of yours in Paris. Why does he have an English accent?"

After talking to Constantine and returning his good wishes, Clare explained to Len. "He's actually Russian-born and Jewish. His family immigrated to Paris when he was a child. He was sent to boarding school in England for safety sake before the war."

"Before the Second World War? How old is this guy?"

"Sixty-seven," said Clare.

"Jesus!" said Len. "He could be your grandfather." Len dismissed him as any competition.

Months of correspondence passed. Constantine wrote of plans for a photography trip to Canada. Then the inevitable happened and yet it came as such a sudden shock to Clare, she felt she couldn't breathe.

Constantine phoned on a Saturday morning when Len was still in bed and Clare had just come out of the shower. Clare picked up the phone.

"Clare…" Constantine's voice cracked and he hesitated, then said, full of strain. "Natalia is standing here beside me. She found a letter from you in my suit pocket and took it to a lawyer. She will divorce me if I do not cease all correspondence with you." He took a breath. "Immediately." He took another breath. "You have my full apologies. Forever … and…" The phone was taken from him.

"I could hear most of that," said Len. "What the hell is going on?"

Clare slumped in the chair.

"Just tell me the *truth*," Len yelled.

Clare put her face in her hands. Drew in her breath. Then looked at Len. "I spent time with Constantine in Cuba. We corresponded. I can't believe he would consent to do this. In this manner. His wife standing over him. But he has. I'm sorry."

"You're sorry for him." Len got out of bed and put on his robe. "I guess you should be. What an old fool to think he could have you."

Len had a shower and dressed. Clare was still in the chair, absorbing the blow, wiping her eyes.

"It's over," Len said to her. "Just make sure of that. I don't want to talk about it again." He turned his back on her and got dressed.

Clare wrote a letter to Constantine at the general delivery address in Paris, asking him if he was alright and saying she understood if he wanted no further correspondence. Her letter was 'returned to sender', the delivery address no longer functioning.

Near Christmas, Clare received a card from Constantine saying, "Live long and well, my Rosalinda. Forgive but don't forget. Forever … and a day."

Clare did not burn that card.

After a very long time, Clare was able to tell herself, we should be grateful to Natalia. She prevented us from causing anxiety, anger, and grief for the families we love. Constantine sometimes remarked about people 'playing the fool'. That was us.

CHAPTER THIRTEEN

Clare's Childhood

In her third session with Dr. Bodker, Clare talked about her father.

"I was eight years old, my sister Julie five, when my parents bought a clothing store in my mom's home village of Blyth, Ontario. Dad was a lovely man. Gentle, smart, a peacemaker, a do-gooder, kind and handsome with Irish good looks. Tall, black hair, warm brown eyes. Of course he dressed well. I don't think I ever heard him yell. People liked him. And he liked them.

"He had different occupations. Was a lumberjack, became a teacher in a business college. That's where he met my mom, who took a course from him when she was an out-of-work teacher. Those were the 1930s, the Great Depression years. After they married, Dad became a travelling salesman for Canada Packers in northern Ontario and Quebec. It must have been a lousy time for each of them. Dad on the road all the time and Mom stuck in a small apartment way up in Kapuskasing, looking after me and Julie as babies and little kids. Washing our clothes in an old wringer washing machine, hanging them on the line outside in winter at twelve below zero. You should hear her descriptions of it! She does know how to tell a good story.

"But Dad made enough money as a travelling salesman to buy that store in my mom's home village. Trouble is he was too kind to make relatives and friends pay their bills. The store went broke within a year. Dad thought it would be dishonourable to declare bankruptcy. He felt himself a failure, became depressed and started drinking too much. We left Blyth with a huge debt. Had to move from place to place over the next ten years because Dad kept losing jobs on account of his drinking problem.

"It was actually a very rich upbringing for Julie and me because we learned to make our way into every kind of community, always being the new kids at school. We moved from the village of Blyth to renting a house in the big city of Toronto, then when Dad lost another job, we moved to a rural community north of Toronto and lived in two rooms in the top of a friend's house. Julie and I attended a school called Vellore with eight grades in one room. We rode bikes along gravel roads to get to it. Dad worked in a gas station and a butcher shop. Then we moved to rent the back half of a grand old red brick farmhouse on a big farm in the same community. Did Julie and I ever create adventures there. We put on a circus in the hay loft of the barn. We rode on the back of a couple of retired work horses we were paid to look after. Meaning, shoveling manure out of their stables before breakfast. We burned down the old icehouse because of leaving a candle burning on a shelf above the floor thick with sawdust. We had captured a wounded blackbird and were secretly keeping it in the icehouse. The fire could have spread to the farmhouse but firemen came and doused it out before the flames hit the house.

"Julie and I kept quiet about how the fire had started. But I bet our parents just didn't want to know and the firemen didn't investigate too far, out of kindness. Everyone knew we didn't have the money to pay any damages."

Dr. Bodker smiled. "Continue about your father."

"Things improved after that because our mom got back into teaching and got a permanent job in the neighbouring town of Woodbridge. Dad got a better job. The debt was finally paid off and we were able to buy a modest house in Woodbridge. My dad finally got hold of his drinking problem. He became president of the Lion's Club and found a job he really liked in food sales. He was promoted to supervisor of sales at headquarters in Ottawa so we moved there and Mom got another teaching job.

"I went off to Queen's University in Kingston. When I was in second year, Dad turned fifty. Everything was going well for him and Mom. At last! They were happy. But when I went home for

Christmas, Dad was feeling unwell. He told me his bones felt sore. Back at Queen's, in January, Julie phoned me. She broke down as she told me, 'Dad has acute leukemia. He has to go to hospital for blood transfusions.' I took the train home on weekends to visit him. Then I was called home the week before exams in April to attend my dad as he died in hospital."

"That must have been very hard for you." Dr. Bodker looked carefully at Clare.

"Yes. But I learned something important from it." Clare held her shoulders back and lifted her chin from the slight slump she had sunk into. "You see, Dr. Bodker, people were kind. The dean, the padre, my teachers at Queen's were sympathetic and helpful to me. I was on student loans and they got a bursary for me. They set private exams for me and I did quite well on them. That taught me: no excuses. No matter how badly you're feeling inside, you can still function, do what you have to do. Maybe not so well as normal, but you can still do them." Clare sat back with a small smile.

Dr. Bodker made a note. "You said your parents were happy 'at last'. How unhappy were they? How did your mother deal with your father's alcoholism?"

"We never called him an alcoholic," said Clare. "It wasn't a term we would use. We evaded talking about it. He just had a drinking problem. He was a secret drinker. And we kept it secret. He never drank in front of us. But we always knew when he had been drinking. We would freeze when he came in with a flushed face and tried too obviously to be normal. He had gestures. Shuffled his feet. Didn't join well in the dinner conversation. All of us were stiff, ill at ease. I felt sorry for him but wasn't much good at getting us all to ease up."

"And your mother? How did she deal with it?"

"My mother is strong. She can be tough. Though she was also given to what we called 'fits'. She would get suddenly mad and stomp upstairs to their bedroom, crying. Childish tantrums really. Or middle-age stress. She developed eczema in her ears, had to go to the doctor because of it. Definitely stress-related illness, we would say now.

"Sorry, I'm not answering your question well. Mom wouldn't talk about his drinking. But every so often, she'd get mad and make us go on a bottle hunt. We hated that. Julie and I. We'd have to go down to the basement with her and we'd find empty liquor bottles hidden here and there. In rubber boots, stuck behind stuff on the shelves, hidden under the stairs. We'd have to take them upstairs and when Dad came home, Mom would confront him with them. Julie and I would clear the scene.

"Then, when we were in high school, I walked in on a scene that keeps coming back to me. I think it was the time when we started doing something really effective about his drinking."

The scene played out in Clare's mind before she related it to Dr. Bodker. It took place in the kitchen. Clare's mother, Vi, had been confronting her father, Gene, with three empty vodka bottles she had found. Vi was angrily berating him. Clare saw her father lie down on his back on the kitchen floor. "I give up," he said. "You might as well just stomp on me."

"Dad!" Clare rushed in and grabbed at his hand. "Get up! Just *get up*!" She pulled as he got himself up.

"Dad, you have to go to AA." Clare grabbed the phone book from the hallway phone shelf. "I'm calling AA." She fumbled with the phone book.

"He won't," said Vi, dramatically putting her hands on her ears. "It takes guts to go to AA."

"Mom! Stop it. Give him a break. Just *stop it*!"

"Don't you *dare* talk to me like that!" Vi stomped her foot. "I've tried everything I know, for *years*, to help him. Everything! You always sympathize with him." Vi was both screaming and crying as she ran upstairs to their bedroom.

Gene sat down at the table, looking helplessly at Clare. Clare sat down opening the phone book. She wrote down the number then phoned AA.

"There's a meeting a week, Wednesday at 7 p.m. In the Presbyterian Church hall. I'll go with you."

"It's OK, Clarey. I'll go on my own."

Gene came home from the AA meeting looking discouraged. "It's not for me," he said. "I don't like public confessions."

"What eventually worked for my father," Clare told Dr. Bodker, "was reconnecting with his long-time friend who had become a Catholic missionary priest." Gene's father was a Catholic. His mother was Anglican and remained so after marrying. Gene chose to go to the Catholic Church with his father as a young boy. He grew up Catholic but Gene had a falling out with the local priest when their clothing store went broke in Blyth. He stopped attending church.

When his friend, Father Jack, came back to Toronto from a mission in Brazil, he looked up Gene and visited him in Woodbridge. They had more visits and phone calls. Before Father Jack returned to Brazil, Gene decided to start going to mass again. Vi would not. She had married in the Catholic Church for Gene's sake, but never took to Catholicism. "Celibacy is unhealthy," she said, even to Father Jack whom she liked and got along well with. "And how ridiculous to call the Pope 'Holy Father'. He's celibate, isn't he? And probably corrupt like the lot of them in that Vatican."

Father Jack just laughed and said, "Glad to see you're humorous as ever, Vi."

Gene went on a few retreats sponsored by the Church. Clare could see that the Catholic retreats made her dad feel better about himself. She attended mass with him when he wished to go. But it was Gene pulling up his own bootstraps, summoning up his own inner strengths and discipline, that got him away from his drinking problem and led to him to getting a job he liked and was good at.

"Your mother was a strong force in your life," Dr. Bodker remarked. "Is she alive?"

"Oh yes. She lives in a retirement community here in Ottawa. She's the entertainment centre."

"The entertainment centre?" Dr. Bodker smiled as he queried.

"She should have been an actress. It's part of what made her such a good teacher. She likes to keep people entertained. One of my favourite memories of her goes back to when we lived in Blyth. My Mom put on a play in the town hall theatre across from our store. Julie and I had front row seats. She hadn't told us what part she was doing in the play. So we were sitting there when Mom came on stage.

"She was wearing rubber boots, overalls, a plaid shirt, her hair piled up under a battered fedora. She was chewing on a straw, revealing two of her teeth blackened out. I shrieked and laughed. Julie and I both clapped and laughed, cheering her on. So did most of the audience. But not all. Next day at school, a girl I didn't much like approached me and said, 'Your mother was trying to make a fool of farmers but really she just made a fool of herself. My mother said so.'"

Dr. Bodker raised his eyebrows in restrained amusement. "You do a good imitation of others yourself."

"Yes. I'm afraid I have some of my mother's genes."

"Do you recall how you reacted to that girl?"

"I chased her down the hall telling her she's all wrong and to *get lost*."

Dr. Bodker raised his eyebrows in restrained amusement again, then asked, "Do you think your mother became any kind of role model to you?"

Clare couldn't help smiling at that and saying, "I'll tell you what my mother had to say about that. Julie and I both did well in high school. At graduation, when I had an Ontario Scholarship for university and was given an award for all-round contribution to school life, some parents asked our mom how she had managed to raise such good teenagers. Mom replied, 'By the supreme example of what *not* to be.'"

"That's a good one." Dr. Bodker nodded. "A lot of psychology involved in that."

"Of course it wasn't easy after Dad died." Clare had one more scene she wanted to tell Dr. Bodker about. It involved an aspect of her mother that Clare found so foreign to her own nature, she was sure she could never do it. She didn't want to be the sort of person who would.

It occurred that summer, after her father's death, when her mom said things that disturbed Clare and wouldn't leave her memory.

"You wish it was me who died, not your father."

"Oh for godsake, Mom. Don't say such a stupid thing."

"It's true. You always favoured him."

"He's the one who needed help. I just tried to help him. And now he's dead. Just let it be, Mom, please!"

Vi began to cry, then went upstairs to the bedroom. Clare was sitting in the chair her dad had always sat in. She thought of going up to comfort her mom. But tears came to her eyes and she laid her head back on the chair.

Another evening that summer, Vi said to Clare, "I helped your dad. Far more than you'll ever know. You think me harsh. But sometimes being harsh is what works. You remember when the store went broke? You know your dad just lay in bed for days."

Clare remembered it too well. She was then nine years old.

"He told me he felt so badly he didn't want to live. 'Really?!' I said to him. It made me so mad, I went down the hall and got his hunting gun out of the closet. And I handed it to him."

"Oh Mom. You didn't."

"Yes I did. But he wouldn't take it. He just rolled over with his back to it."

Clare pictured him with his face in the pillow.

"But that was the day he got himself out of bed," Vi said pointedly. "And I helped him begin to deal with the bills. And I got myself that damn job waitressing in Frank Gong's, to get food on our own table. And you got a job picking up pins in the bowling alley. Remember that?"

"Of course," said Clare. "It wasn't a bad job and I liked earning money."

"I damn well *had* to," said Vi.

"You have a good job now," said Clare. "You're a terrific teacher."

"You bet I am," said Vi. "And I'm going to be even better."

"What do you mean?"

"I'm thinking of going to Paris, get a diploma for teaching in French. I could get a grant to do that. And a hike in my salary when I get back."

"Fantastic!" said Clare. "Go for it!"

Vi amazed everyone who knew her, by actually doing just that. She had never travelled anywhere outside her province, but suddenly at age fifty, Vi got the grant. Flew to Paris, lodged in a student hotel, made friends with other students, especially a young gay man, Jean Paul, and travelled with him and his partner to Austria at Christmas. She missed Clare's graduation from Queen's, but Julie was home from her university for it. Both Clare and Julie were deeply impressed by their mother's venture and praised her for it.

Dr. Bodker listened to Clare's recollection of the scenes without interruption. Time, in this final session, was running out.

"My mother never married again," Clare concluded. "Didn't even have an affair, so far as I know. I'm not much like her." Clare smiled wryly. "And my husbands are not like my father. Except that Len has a drinking problem."

"There's enough to keep reassessing your parents and their relationship all your life. But I want to say this before we end. Your mother took a great risk in handing the gun to your father. He could have used it on himself. Other personalities might have used it on her and then on himself. If you children were in the house…"

"We were at school."

"You are living with an alcoholic of a complicated nature. He has now a history of violence. You should consider leaving."

"I did. But I just cannot go through divorce again. I won't do that to my children again."

"Are they not adults now?"

"Yes but…"

Dr. Bodker looked at his watch. "We must conclude. Others are waiting. Remember, you have the right to happiness." He stood up.

Clare stood up. "Thank you, Dr. Bodker." She shook his hand.

* * * * *

In the years that followed, Dr Bodker's words replayed in Clare's mind. The right to happiness was not very meaningful to her. Clare had never sought happiness as a goal in itself. To her it was a byproduct of doing other things. Doing well in life made her happy. Doing some good. Loving and being loved. Friendships. Having children, healthy children who did well. Doing well at her work, facilitating her husband to do well at his. Interesting adventure. The whole gamut of things produced happiness for her as it did for other people.

Her relationship with Len after retirement did not improve. It was definitely not happiness producing. She believed he would not strike her again because he knew he would go to jail if he did. Also the year of counselling had surely done him some good. His drinking was more controlled during that year. But less and less so as time went on.

Clare remained wary. She became good at not responding to his increasing verbal antagonism, belligerence, and disparaging remarks. She learned to avoid him and walk away. I'm not the cause of his frustration and anger, she concluded, but I'm the one at hand and so I'm the target of it. I need to keep out of his range as much as I can.

After a dinner with former colleagues and spouses at which Len came out with unusual vulgar remarks about a woman's breasts and what he would do with them, a colleague phoned him next day and told him to "Get back in control. And *stop drinking!*"

"Will you?" asked Clare.

"Get serious," said Len. "Scotch is my preservative."

After tennis doubles at Loghaven when they came in for drinks before dinner, Len served wine and beer to the others as they requested, then brought out his large jug shaped bottle of scotch, lifting it by its handle. "My doctor told me I need to get a handle on my drinking." Len poured himself a big one. "And so I did." They all laughed but not heartily.

Clare turned to the other aspects of her life which were very good. Friendships, especially Lizzie in whom she could confide. They had been roommates at Queen's. Lizzie also had spent her first married years abroad, in Africa, but now lived in Ottawa. Clare's work as a photographer became more productive. She was becoming known for her wildlife photography and her photos of people with their pets. Family photos with pets was easier and brought in the most remuneration for her. Wildlife photography was expensive in terms of time and travel investment but it was her natural love. That and her children.

Chapter Fourteen

Weddings and Grandchildren

Shortly after that year of counselling, Ali phoned to say her wedding plans had to be put on hold because her fiancé, Morton, did not get the internship he expected at Vancouver General Hospital. Ali did get hers. The best internship Morton could get was on the other side of the country at a children's hospital in Halifax. They would be parted for two years.

Clare flew to Vancouver after Morton left for Halifax. Ali seemed in good spirits. "Two years isn't so long at this stage of life," Clare told her. "You're just twenty-eight."

"I know, Mom. It's just hard to be so far apart. But we'll marry when I'm thirty, not too old to have children."

Cell phones were coming into common usage. Ali and Morton talked on their phones every day. It seemed weird to Clare that she would be walking down the street with Ali in Vancouver and suddenly Ali would receive a phone call and continue walking down the street talking to Morton as though he were there with them.

During the second year, the phone calls became less frequent. Then Ali phoned Clare to tell her, "Mort has fallen for a nurse. A nurse! Can you think of anything more cliché!" Then she broke down crying. So did Clare, briefly.

"The jerk!" said Clare. "I thought one of the things that was so good about you two was that you're such equals. Not that nurses are inferior to doctors. But they do work on different levels."

"He was very apologetic, Mom. But let's face it. He's just another guy who likes to be looked up to. Some nurses do that with doctors. They really do. I can just picture it."

Ali went through stages of anger, sadness, loneliness but she kept busy, as she had to. And she had good friends she did triathalons with in summer and skiing in winter. One was a pharmacist, divorced, no children, nine years older than Ali. Aristotle Kapelos, Ari, everyone called him. He owned two pharmacies. Ari flew with Ali to Ottawa at Christmas to meet her parents. He was tall, with black curly hair and a ready sense of humour. "I've had my eye on Ali for two years," he told Clare and Len. "Me and every other guy. Why wouldn't we! She's the best at everything she does. Never expected she'd pay attention to a lowly pharmacist, so I had to push myself harder than I ever had. I came out ahead of her in the triathalon." He smiled widely.

"Not by much!" said Ali.

They walked about arm in arm. He often stroked her thick sable hair. They laughed and played with the Malamutes. "Most beautiful dogs I've ever seen," said Ari.

They were both marathon swimmers.

"Makes me happy just watching them," said Clare.

"He sure looks like a stud," said Len.

On New Year's Eve, Ali and Ari returned from a dinner and dance downtown. Ali was wearing a remarkably designed gold diamond ring. Ari smiled proudly at her as she held up her finger to show Clare and Len. Clare couldn't speak, she felt so happy for Ali. Nor could Ali speak as she looked at her mom. They hugged.

"This calls for champagne," said Len. "But we don't have any. Scotch anyone?" He held up his glass. They all laughed. Clare got white wine from the fridge.

"We want to marry very soon," said Ari. "I'm eager to start a family. We can afford household help so Ali can keep on with her work. And I with mine."

"What do you think?" Clare asked Len after Ali and Ari had departed for the airport.

"About Ari?" Len considered. "Could be too good to be true."

* * * * *

They married in May when Ali had finished her internship. She would continue working at Vancouver General Hospital in the paediatric ward. It was a large church wedding with Ali's father Stan and Marta flying in from Oxford, Ari's parents and siblings from Vancouver, plus other relatives and many friends. Costs were shared by the bride's parents, Stan and Clare.

"What a contrast," said Clare to Len as the plans were worked out. "What a contrast to Stan and I getting married as graduate students in Oxford. I doing my thesis for Queen's, Stan doing his D. Phil. at Christchurch, living on student loans and scholarships, our parents with no money to spare. We married quietly at the Registrar's office in Oxford, then threw a party on our little houseboat with home made beer and wine. It was 1968. We thought we were liberated in not making a fuss over getting married. We didn't even tell the guests it was a wedding party. Though our two witnesses at the Registrar's let the secret out. It was a fabulous party. People jumping into the river, some swinging by the rope we had tied to a tree over the river.... Until toilet paper began to flow by! Someone had dumped our chemical toilet when it got full, straight out the bathroom window and into the river."

"And what about us?" said Len. "We got married at City Hall, kids around us. Then we had the luncheon on Captain John's boat on the river. The following week, Captain John's *sank*!"

"But they pulled it back up and it's still afloat," said Clare. "And this is twenty-three years later."

"Makes you wonder," said Len, "how long it's good for."

Megan attended Ali's wedding with her friend Nate Logan. In telephone calls prior to the wedding, Megan gradually told Clare about Nate. They had met at Dalhousie where Megan studied law. Nate was in architecture. He had grown up in Black Pickle, Labrador.

"Black Pickle!" Clare laughed. "You're making that up."

"No I'm not," said Megan. "It's a small community on the coast. Sometimes polar bears wander into the village in spring. Nate's father has a team of sled dogs. Every winter he used to do a run with them down to Happy Valley–Goose Bay."

"I've heard of Happy Valley–Goose Bay," said Clare, "on TV weather forecasts about Labrador. Sounds like a place I'd like to see."

"It's not what you'd imagine. Nate has shown me pictures. Quite flat, not a valley. I don't know if it's the geese or the people who find it happy. Hopefully both. Nate says it could do with more imaginative architecture."

"Sounds like he cares about where he comes from."

"Absolutely. He's very involved in the culture and heritage. He's Métis."

"No kidding! Is he talented, as an architect?"

"Sure is. He's on a big scholarship at Dal."

"Love to meet him," said Clare. I wonder what he looks like, she thought. My daughters live in more interesting circles than I did. Though she recalled when she was at Queen's University, she had befriended a black student from Nigeria in her literature class. Out of interest, Clare had joined International Club where foreign students could gather socially. She was elected secretary of the club.

Clare was phoned one weekend by a member of the club who was an older African student with the too likely name of Rufus. He told her he was in bed with the flu or something. Any chance she could bring him some soup?

"Don't!" said her roommate Liz. "It sounds like too much of a set-up, a seduction. Or let me go with you." Liz thought, then said, "No. Sorry, I can't. I have basketball practice this afternoon."

Clare mulled it over in her mind. She had met Rufus just a few times, had hardly any conversation with him. He seemed a shy, well-mannered, reserved guy with wrinkles in his face. A 'mature student'. He smiled and said hello whenever he encountered Clare. I have to do it, Clare decided. I'm being put to some test here. He's ill and lonely. He's not going to rape me. If he tries to seduce me, I'll talk myself out of there fast.

He did not try to seduce her. When Clare opened the door of his room, Rufus smiled as he sat up in his pyjamas in bed. He did seem weak and ill. She handed him the soup in a plastic container she had carried in a towel to keep it warm. He had a spoon on his bedside table.

"You're a kind, nice girl," Rufus said.

He lived in a dingy rooming house. Clare had left the door of his room a little open, just in case… "I'm just doing what anyone should do, Rufus. You must really miss your home. Everything feels worse when you have a lousy cold or whatever. I'll just sit on this chair while you finish the soup." The chair was by the open door. Clare kept her coat on, buttoned up. Rufus smiled at her again and ate his soup then handed her the container. "I'll be alright now," he said.

"Are you sure?"

"Yes. A friend is coming over after five."

Before she closed the door, Rufus said. "Thank you, Clare. I won't forget this."

"It's nothing, Rufus. Just normal. Call the Student Health Clinic on Monday if you're not better."

Clare had no call from Rufus again until the end of the year. They had waved and nodded to each other a few times in passing on campus. At the end of the year, Rufus came to her apartment to leave her a small gift, wrapped. He didn't want her to open the gift until he had left. He was graduating that year. In the box Clare found a dainty, exquisite necklace. It was an extremely fine gold chain with a small charcoal black stone, set in gold with three tiny diamonds. She was flabbergasted.

Clare still had that necklace. She sometimes thought of getting it evaluated. But then decided that would be crass. Let it remain the valued gift, she decided, from a lovely guy who may or may not have been testing me out, back in 1964 when Black students were a rarity on Canadian campuses.

"Are you and Nate serious about each other?" Clare asked Megan over the phone.

"We'll let you know," said Megan.

"You're thirty, Megan. You don't want to be wasting time with guys you're not serious about, or vice versa."

"I know how old I am, Mom. You should be worrying about yourself in old age."

"I'm not quite sixty, which is not really old these days. But I'm not afraid of getting old. It's lucky to get old. My dad died of cancer at fifty, so I thought I would. I've been grateful for every day since."

"Yes, Mom," Megan laughed. "You've told us that many times. Repeating yourself is a sign of you know what."

"OK, Meg. Answer me this. Where does Nate want to practice architecture?"

"In Labrador, but there's not enough work there so he'll have to be based in Newfoundland, here in St. John's."

"Ahah! So that's why you chose to work with a firm in St John's. You two sound very serious about each other."

"Mom, I'm not *that* dependent on a guy. I like living in Newfoundland. It's refreshingly different here. And my firm is highly respected. A lot of work is brought to us. Most of mine is Legal Aid but that's to be expected in my areas of law. I'm not a corporate lawyer."

Clare was surprised and somewhat disappointed at Nate Logan's appearance when he came with Megan to attend Ali's wedding. He was good-looking, medium height, dark eyes, dark hair in a conventional short cut. Conventionally dressed in dark suit and tie for the occasion. His tie was unusual, with beadwork on it. Megan was always classy and dignified with an air of glamour. Ali looked stunning in a long deep red, sleek satin gown with a copper sheen to it. Ari the Greek couldn't help being a knock-out.

After the ceremony when drinking, dining, and dancing got underway, Nate and Megan came over to Clare and Len. Clare and Len were good dancers but Len needed to sit one out. Nate sat on one side of Clare, Megan beside him. Clare talked with Nate about his architectural ambitions and expressed admiration for his desire to work on buildings that would incorporate Inuit heritage. He took interest in her photography of wild animals.

"You should come to Labrador and the Arctic to see interesting wildlife," said Nate.

"I'd love to," said Clare. "Can you swing me an invite?"

"Mom!" Megan interjected.

Nate laughed. "I don't have a lot of pull. I'm still a student. But Adventure Canada is a good safe way to start."

They all got up on the floor, dancing in a group. "So what do you think of Nate?" Megan said as she brushed up against her mother.

"Good looking," said Clare as Nate passed near them. "But I don't see much Inuit in him."

"Mom!" Megan's brow wrinkled. "Just don't say that!"

"Why not? We could do with some more interesting eyes in the family."

"Mom!" Megan spoke with pent-up exasperation. "Could you please not be embarrassing! This is Ali's wedding."

"What's so embarrassing about that?"

Megan moved away from her mother. Not much later, Nate made his way to Clare and asked for a dance.

He was smiling when he said "Megan said you're sort of disappointed in my appearance."

Clare wanted to say, Damn, my daughter lets me get away with nothing, but Nate intercepted her thoughts. "Not to worry," Nate was almost laughing. "I try to make up for my looks in my actions. I'll do my best to get you to the Arctic."

It was Nate who told Clare about the Adventure Canada trip to the Artic in 2008. By then Nate and Megan were married and had two children, a girl and then a boy. Ali had had two boys. They hoped for a girl on the third try but the third was also a boy. "I give up," Ali told Clare. "I'm done. Ari thinks we should try once more."

"Don't!" said Clare in alarm. "Twins run in your family. Remember, men do only the fun part."

Ali laughed. "Good point, Mom. But I have no complaints. I have lots of little girls to tend at work. A full-time nanny at home. And Ari enjoys cooking."

My daughters have got it right, thought Clare. I had no home help with the twins when they were babies. Stan and I planned it out. I didn't get pregnant until after Stan had been given the job at Christchurch. The salary was low because he was so young. But the perks were great, for him. He was given a very nice College house and all meals and an office in the College. The plan was to stay there for seven years then return to a good job at a Canadian university and Clare would develop her work as a wildlife photographer.

It was a shock to find she was pregnant with twins. She did have a fabulous midwife who visited regularly to make sure she was getting the breastfeeding right and an expert doctor who did regular checkups. Stan came home early from Christchurch for the first six months, helping with supper and the twins and pitching in on the weekends. Getting out to go food shopping was Clare's big treat.

Clare's mom, Vi, had come over for two weeks in the summer when school was out. Vi played with the babies on a blanket and in their bouncy chairs. But she found the double baby carriage too unwieldy on the street sidewalk. And it was clear she had had enough of looking after babies in the days of cloth diapers and hanging them out on a clothes line, winter and summer. Clare remembered her mom describing that. She told Stan about it. That's why the first major thing Stan and she bought when they moved into the Christchurch house was an automatic washer and dryer.

I got through those first two years with twins, thought Clare. No nannies and housekeeping help like my daughters, but then I had no other job. I just wished I did.

Visiting her children and grandchildren regularly and having them visit occasionally was Clare's deepest joy. But she couldn't share that with Len. From the first announcement from Ali that they were having a baby, Clare saw the sad reaction in Len.

Clare had got off the phone with Ali. She went excitedly to tell Len in his office.

"Ali and Ari are expecting a baby in April!"

"That's great," said Len. "You'll have grandchildren." A deeply pensive and pained look came gradually over Len.

"So will you," said Clare. "It's your step-grandchild. Your first."

Len didn't answer that. He remained pensive. Then he got up from his desk.

"This calls for a drink," he said, heading for the bar in the kitchen.

Clare thought and realized, it's probably hardest of all at the grandchildren stage, when you have to fully face that your 'line', your lineage has stopped with you. She felt very sorry for Len.

But as more grandchildren came along, she thought, come on! Kids are kids. And these aren't ill behaved or stupid or ugly kids. You should take some joy and pride in them. At least *interest*. But Len did not. He wouldn't join Clare in visiting them. When Ali or Megan came to Loghaven with their kids, Len didn't interact with them. He kept mainly to his office. He found young kids a noisy nuisance.

It was early evening when Clare arrived home from her trip to the Arctic in June 2008. The dogs were in their kennel, leaping at the thick wire, howling and whining in excitement. Len got up from his chair as Clare opened the door and came in with her large back pack. She set it down to let the dogs in.

"I'll let the dogs in," said Len, bending down to get his glass from the side table. He lost his balance and fell back into the chair. Clare let the dogs in. "For chrissake," said Len. "Can't you give me a minute!"

Clare turned her back to him as she hugged the dogs. Then she faced him. "So how have you been?"

"Lousy. What else is new? How was your trip?"

Chapter Fifteen

The Smiling Wolf Gets Around

As promised, Michelle held an exhibition of photographs from their trip to the Arctic, including Clare's photo of the smiling wolf. The gallery was packed with Michelle's friends and Clare's. Michelle's were from a wide range of professions: politicians, writers, doctors from where her father worked, and a number of high-achieving women, all people whose portraits Michelle had taken. She had compiled a book of portraits and bios of 'women of achievement', a coffee table book that had sold well, with part of the proceeds going to the hospital. Clare's friends were her patrons, some retired colleagues of Len's, and her friends from Queen's University days with whom she had re-connected after moving home from Oxford in 1980.

Liz Love, Clare's closest friend from Queen's days, stood out in any crowd. She was unusually tall, with silvery white hair in soft waves to her shoulders. She was Clare's age, turning sixty-five, but it was a time when most women coloured their hair until into their seventies. Liz's hair began to turn white in her twenties. She stopped colouring it in her forties. She also stopped wearing contact lenses and began to sport interestingly framed glasses. She had a beautiful face and a knock-out smile. Liz was widely known for her fundraising and volunteer work, though most of all for her enthusiasm and humour. She had well-known politician and writer friends from organizing the Writers' Trust of Canada's annual fundraiser called Politics and the Pen.

Liz stood for some time in front of Clare's enlarged photo of the smiling wolf, talking with a woman writer. Liz brought her over to meet Clare.

"That's a marvellous shot of a wolf," said the writer. "It's got the smile of a Malamute."

"You know Malamutes?" said Clare.

"I'm getting to. I have one and I'm writing a book about the first woman vet who went to the Klondike Gold Rush to tend them."

"You're kidding," said Clare. "What was her name?"

"Meg Wilkinson. Also known as 'The Dog Doctor of Halifax.'"

"You're kidding!" Clare repeated and laughed. "Meg Wilkinson was my grandmother."

"No!" The writer looked astonished. "Really?!" She smiled and shook her head. "I won't say 'you're kidding!' But are you?"

The following day they met at Liz's house for drinks. Liz lived in a heritage house very near the grounds of Rideau Hall, the Governor General's residence. Liz's house had been the home of a close relative of Susanna Moodie, an early Canadian writer who had immigrated from England with her husband in the early nineteenth century. Her sister Catharine Parr Traill, also a writer, had immigrated at the same time with her husband. Both sisters had established themselves as writers in England but the genteel life they had lived there was lost in their encroaching poverty. There was no hope of prosperity for them in England. In Canada their husbands were given land grants in an area of forest, rivers and small lakes between Toronto and Ottawa. The sisters lived within a long walk of each other, both in rough log houses heated by only a fireplace. Their husbands went off to work in the army.

Catharine embraced the life, hard work as it was. She appreciated the forest, did a collection of botanical drawings, naming plants. She enjoyed the beauty of the river and lakes, was hospitable to the Indigenous people who came by, and was interested in every Canadian animal she saw: raccoons, chipmunks, beavers. Skunks and bears she learned to steer clear of. Catharine loved the sound of loons calling on the lake, and held her breath at the sonorous, haunting sound of wolves howling in the distance in the evening or on moonlit nights.

Clare admired the attitude and written work of Catharine Parr Trail. "She was a lot like my grandmother," Clare said to the writer who wanted to be called by her nickname, Molly. "Susanna Moodie was *not*. Not at all like my grandmother."

Molly smiled and glanced at Liz. It was after all a Moodie heritage house they were in. "Don't worry," said Liz smiling. "I know all about Clare's take on Susanna Moodie. I agree with it. Doesn't stop me loving this house."

"Hasn't Liz done a fabulous job of restoring and decorating!" said Clare.

"I would call it masterful," said Molly. "It's what it should be historically and yet it's Liz's colours and warmth and flare."

Liz laughed. "That's writers' talk. I'm going to get us more wine."

Clare noted that Liz was right. Molly talked like a writer. Precision of words. Clare warmed to her. But she couldn't be sure what Molly would do with her grandmother's life. "My grandmother Meg lived to exactly the same age as Catharine Parr Traill, ninety-eight."

"I know," said Molly. "I've done a lot of investigating and research on her. What a long productive life. But I'm only writing about her early years. Stopping at her life in the Klondike up to when she re-united with the Irish cop Mick O'Mara."

"My grandfather," said Clare. "I never met him. He died before I was five years old. I have no memory of him except for what my parents and Gramma Meg told me about him. He died in the line of duty. My grandmother never married again. She was just in her early sixties when he died. She led an active life, always. Men asked her to marry. But she said no one measured up to her Mick. And she was never going to be some guy's housekeeper. Not *my* grandmother."

"That's also my take on her," said Molly. "I'd like to hear your take on Susanna Moodie."

"Why?"

"I think it could help me to see what your grandmother was not like."

Clare laughed. "Clever! OK." Clare leaned forward onto the verandah table they were sitting round. "Susanna Moodie got more literary attention over time. But I've read Charlotte Gray's *Sisters in the Wilderness* and I see Susanna as a selfish snob and complainer, compared to Catharine. Instead of respecting and exploring the wilderness and culture of Canada, Susanna tried to impose her own attitudes and standards upon it. She hired some poor young woman to live in their rough log cabin … it had been a cow shed, I think. Probably one room with a curtain around Susanna's bed section. The girl was to do cleaning, cooking, gathering of wood, gardening, set the table and do the dishes, haul the water in … everything! And Susanna never allowed her to sit down to the table with Susanna and family. This is because the poor girl was regarded as a servant, a lesser class of human beings according to Susanna's English standards. Susanna could hear the girl crying herself to sleep at night and never made any move to comfort her.

"Susanna was busy feeling sorry for herself because she missed the society she had enjoyed in England, had to tend her children, and didn't have enough time and comfort to write complaining essays and whining poetry. Meanwhile that poor girl was probably crying over the baby she had to give up at birth because she was unwed. And because she had to endure the snobbery and heartless treatment of Susanna Moodie."

"Well!" Molly raised her eyebrows and smiled, looking around at the house and garden. "Too bad Susanna never got to see what a nice home her offspring ended up in."

"Some writers," said Liz, "think readers want to have stories and poetry about the dark side of life. Books about how we're all going to hell in a hand basket are very popular."

"What about your books?" said Clare. "I'll get them. But how would you describe them?"

"There aren't many," said Molly. "I'm not prolific. They're different from one another. But all realistic fiction, based on real people and situations. So they aren't dark or light. Life is full of both. But don't worry, Clare, I'm not out to trash your grandmother. Just love to hear what you have to say about her. But I do have to catch the 7:30 train."

"I'm not sure what to think of her," said Clare to Liz after delivering Molly to the train station.

"I've known her a long time," said Liz. "She's a serious writer. It's dogged her since she was a kid. But she leads a full life and does a lot in the writing community. She was seriously stalled after her last book. But when I started talking to her about your grandmother, she got really interested."

Clare looked at Liz and suddenly figured it out. The coincidence of meeting Molly at the exhibit of Arctic photographs.

"Liz!" Clare shouted. "You set us up!"

Liz smiled and looked straight ahead.

Clare's work life flourished during the next five years. Her photo of the smiling wolf gradually gained some fame. It didn't win contests but it had popularity. She made a modest amount of money from the sales of various sized prints of the smiling wolf. She got work with *Canadian Geographic* and Photo News. Michelle Valberg's career soared with her return trips to the Arctic, taking emotive photos of animals, people and landscapes. Michelle was hired by Adventure Canada as their official photographer on northern expeditions. Eventually she had a grand exhibition of her work in the Museum of Nature. Some of her photographs were bought by the government to be displayed in major airports.

Michelle's was a spectacular career success story compared to Clare's but Clare wasn't given to comparing and competing. She enjoyed Michelle's friendship and being herself a respected part of Canada's thousands of aspiring and flourishing photographers. She was elected to the executive of the Canadian Wildlife Photography Association. Clare knew she lacked Michelle's entrepreneurial drive and ease with digital equipment. But she hadn't stopped learning and exploring. She got an iPhone and mastered most of its mysteries. It became indispensable to her. Being able to connect with her daughters and friends by phone and email from almost anywhere seemed like the best magic. She took courses in the new camera equipment but was never at ease with it the way young photographers were.

In retirement, Len learned new financial programs on his desktop computer but he didn't want the 'hassle' of learning to use a cell phone. He absorbed himself in keeping detailed household accounts and doing online stock investing. He enjoyed the lack of responsibility to anyone but himself with his investments. He would not admit even to himself that he missed the authority and prestige of being on the executive of a large respected corporation, of having the help and admiration of a secretary and people working for him. Clare thought he also missed the company of colleagues and the adrenalin rush of meeting the bank's financial goals and deadlines.

"No way!" Len said. "I like working for myself. And I'm damn good at it. My stocks are up nearly ten thousand today. 'Course they could plunge as much tomorrow and Christ knows why. That's enough of an adrenalin rush for me. And if it isn't, I'll have a rush of scotch."

"You could play golf at the club. Get away from your desk for a while."

"Why don't you get off my back! I'm doing what I want to do."

Clare walked away.

Molly phoned nearly three years after meeting with Clare. There was excitement and relief in her voice. "Clare, the final revision has been approved! I didn't like what they were asking me to do, but I found a way of doing it that I really like. It adds a whole new dimension to the story, a sense of spirit forces that I've come to believe in. I think you will like it too. Even though you don't like the title."

"I didn't say that."

"No, but I could tell. I think you'll find the title is true to the book. It's realistic historical fiction. My gawd, did I do research! But the wolves run through it and the spirits are of real people. I've come to be most fond of them, the spirits of Ike and Piji. Though the wolves run neck and neck with them. Yukon Sally always in the lead."

"Jazuz, Molly! It sounds like a mad fantasy."

Molly laughed. "Don't worry. You'll see when you read it. I'm posting you the manuscript. I'm phoning now because I need to talk to you about the cover."

"OK. Shoot."

"You know your fabulous photo of the smiling wolf…"

"Yes." Clare knew what was coming.

"Best cover for a book, ever!"

Clare gave Molly permission to use the photo without charge.

When Clare received the manuscript, she began reading and found it absorbed and amazed her. "Molly's got it!" Clare exclaimed out loud. "She's captured her character. My grandmother had to be just like this when she was young. She was like this when she was old. Not quite so adventurous physically, but in her thinking she was everywhere. How I loved her. Still do."

The novel made Clare think of her own life in comparison to her grandmother's. I have to do better, she told herself. I'm living submerged. I'm damaged.

Len looked at the book. Its title was *City Wolves*. "Sounds like it's about the Wall Street boys," he said. "The merchant bankers."

"Not at all," said Clare.

Len didn't normally read novels. Occasionally he read non-fiction books. But he was fascinated by *City Wolves*. "It's a good yarn," he commented when reading it. "A damn good yarn. I wish I had met your grandmother. There's a lot of you in her."

Not half enough, Clare said to herself.

"Don't you have anything to say?" Len put the book on the table beside him. "I just gave you a compliment."

"Yes," she said. "That is a compliment." And it's about as good as I'll ever get from you, she said to herself.

"I know what you're thinking," said Len as he watched Clare leave the room. She stopped and turned to him. "You're thinking that's about as good as you get from me these days."

Clare said nothing.

"Well, you're wrong. I provide everything for you. All you have to do is laundry and some cooking."

Clare turned her back, got her coat and went outside with the dogs. Len came to the door and yelled at her. "I'm turning eighty. I can't give you what you need." He slammed the door. Clare was grateful the neighbouring cottages were vacated for the season.

CHAPTER SIXTEEN

Financial Crash

In the autumn of 2008, there was a financial collapse that sent what Len called the Wall Street boys tumbling down like Humpty Dumpty. 'Humpty Dumpty sat on the wall', Clare recalled the nursery rhyme. 'Humpty Dumpty had a great fall. All the king's horses and all the king's men couldn't put Humpty Dumpty together again.'

The stock market crash hit the American market and reverberated in Canada, Europe, and throughout the industrial world. Bank stocks were hit first and hardest. Len became tensely silent. He would not answer Clare's questions about how his investments were doing, other than with, "Those dickheads on Wall Street are a bunch of crooks."

At the end of winter, he drove Clare to the airport to visit Ali in Vancouver. He parked and before she got out of the car, Len burst out. "You're going to have to sell Paws à Terre. We're $800,000 in debt."

"What!?"

"You heard me. We're $800,000 in debt. I've been borrowing to invest. All my bank stocks have crashed and I have margin calls to pay. We have to sell Paws à Terre."

"We won't get that much from selling Paws."

"We can work out the rest."

"What's all this 'we'? I haven't been borrowing to invest. How long has this been going on? What have you been borrowing against?"

"Our property. You co-signed the loan."

"When? I don't remember signing any loan against our property."

"About seven years ago. Don't worry about it. Just sell Paws. I'll take care of the rest. Now don't miss your plane. All those grandsons await you."

Clare had a long plane ride to think it over. She thought back to that tense time after Len had finished his year of counselling. She had become very wary of his anger but she had never had reason to distrust his handling of money. He had always been extremely conservative with investing. Blue chip stocks only. A heavy dominance of bank stocks. She would never have imagined Len would do something so risky as borrowing to invest. She did recall him saying way back, that he wanted to consolidate some bills with a temporary loan. Not a big one. She couldn't remember the amount. She was then so ignorant of investing and financial management, she did not question going to the bank with him and signing a document which she thought was about obtaining a small, one-time loan to consolidate some bills. She assumed that if more money were to be borrowed she would be informed and required to sign something for further borrowing.

She discussed with Ali and Ari what Len had said to her. Ari was an astute business man. After further thought and discussion, they advised Clare to get a good financial adviser and that probably she should consult with a lawyer.

That sounded extreme to Clare. But she did end up having to do both. Len was cooperative once she agreed to sell Paws. He never could see marriage as a partnership of equal ownership between two people. He kept seeing their marriage as provider and facilitator but he did believe the facilitator should be well rewarded. They got a good but not great price for their Paws à Terre. In 2010 when the stock market had begun to improve, Len sold enough stocks to pull them out of debt. Mr. Cane, the lawyer, advised that they draw up an agreement whereby the remaining stocks were divided equally between them and neither could borrow against the value of their property. Loghaven would be secure and was jointly owned by Len and Clare.

Clare missed the advantage of having a little dwelling in town to go to and do her photography business and stay over for social and cultural events. The camera and photography shop she worked in part time had a small store room where she put a futon bed and there was a washroom she could use. The shop owner charged her a pittance for having this as her occasional overnight pad. She had been fond of Paws à Terre and having the dogs stay there with her, but she refused to be heartbroken over the loss of material things. The most upsetting and disturbing thing was learning that Len kept important financial information from her and would continue to borrow to invest. After the agreement was signed he borrowed against his own investments and life insurance. Clare saw it as a kind of gambling addiction. Her financial adviser said it was what a few investors did and some successfully, but it takes a certain steely personality to do that over the long term. Oh well, Clare concluded, Len will do it for as long as he likes, or can. As long as Loghaven can't be taken away, I'm OK.

Clare found happiness from the company of her dogs, from her friendships and most from seeing her children and grand children thriving. She had the comfort and beauty of living in Loghaven on the lake, even though the company of Len was increasingly belligerent and abusive. She could avoid him except at dinner.

Then in 2011, Megan came home for a holiday with Nate and their two children, Aurora and Wilf who were six and four years old. On the Saturday, Megan invited some friends from high school days with their young children for a party at Loghaven. They were to spend the night, filling the guest rooms, the recreation room, and a couple of tents outside. Tory and Hettie next door housed some in their guest room. The children were to be put to bed before the adults gathered for dinner at Loghaven. Disinterested in the crowd of young people, Len sat in the rec room from noon onwards, drinking scotch as he watched Wimbledon tennis on television. In the evening, Clare asked him to come into the living-dining room so children could be put to bed in the rec room.

There was a small TV over the kitchen counter where Clare sometimes watched the news while preparing dinner. She turned it on for

Len to continue watching tennis. He began yelling at his favourite player to do better. "Oh for chrissake! Another God damn unforced error. Jesus Christ! You can do better than that dick head on the other side of the God damn net."

Parents began to gather their children to get them out of ear shot.

"Len," Clare tried to divert him. "We need to set up some nesting tables for us and Tory and Hettie in the living room."

"Why the hell aren't we eating at the table?"

"The young people are eating there. I thought it would be better…"

"Jesus Christ! This is *my* house. I eat at the head of the table in my own house, for fuck sake!" Len was yelling at his loudest. The children were taken out of the room. Clare walked quickly round the counter and looked angrily into Len's face. "Len!" she spoke fiercely. "You have to stop yelling. And swearing. You're being disgusting … shameful!"

Len raised his hand. Nate stepped forward and Megan from another direction. Len lowered his hand. Leaned on the counter for balance. He reached for his glass of scotch, managed to take a gulp then set it down heavily. He looked towards his chair by the fireplace.

"Let me take your arm," said Clare.

He turned on her. "I don't need God damn *help*!" He staggered to his chair gripping onto furniture for support.

Tory and Hettie arrived. Tory assessed the situation, the tension in the air, the strain on young people's faces as they busily set to finishing dinner preparations. "Anything we can help with?" he asked Megan, who was clearly head chef.

"No, thanks. Nate will get you and Hettie drinks. We'll eat soon. Mom is just setting up tables for you four over there."

"Let me do that," said Tory, taking the nest of tables from Clare. "Len, can we get you something? Sure smells good in here."

Tory got Len his scotch and managed to ease him into civility.

Loin of lamb with rice and ratatouille were served. Len could eat only a spoonful, then excused himself and staggered off to bed. Tory and Hettie diverted Clare by telling her of their recent decision. She was not happy to hear it. Tory and Hettie were going to sell their cottage and move into a new bungalow home in Ottawa. Hettie had not recovered well from a fall on the stairs in the cottage.

"It's become too much upkeep for people our age," said Hettie. "I'll be eighty-five in the autumn. Tory's eighty-six."

Clare was genuinely astounded. Tory was so fit and carried himself so well, she thought he was younger than Len. He was six years older. But Clare was far too upset by Len's behaviour to dwell on anything but what she was to do about it.

That night, she was to sleep with Len in their bedroom for the sake of appearances and space. Len had fallen into a deep sleep. Clare lay awake thinking about the repercussions of Len's behaviour. No one would want to bring their children to Loghaven again with Len present. Including Megan and Nate.

Clare could barely bring herself to speak to Len next day. "Do you recall your behaviour yesterday?" she asked when he got up in the morning.

"I watched Wimbledon, didn't I?"

Clare just glared at him.

"I'm sure you'll remind me of anything else," he said and turned his back on her to go into the bathroom.

All the friends departed after brunch. Megan and Nate were to fly back to St. John's the following day.

"Come with us to St. John's," Megan said to Clare. "You've got to get away from that man. He's become dangerous. We saw him raise his hand to you. Has he hit you again?"

"No. Not since he was brought before the judge."

"Drinking makes him crazy. He's got to stop. And you have to get away from him."

"I'm thinking it over."

Clare confronted Len in his office. His pushed back his chair from his desk as she sat down in the chair opposite him.

"Shoot," said Len. "Tell me what I did last night."

"You can't remember?"

"Just tell me your version."

He always does this, thought Clare. He can't remember so he gets the other person to tell him what he did. She told him: "You got roaring drunk. Cursed and swore in front of the children and Megan's friends. The children had to be rushed away. You frightened everyone. Created a pall over the whole evening. Refused to let the young people have the dining table. Yelling that this is *your* house and *you* sit at the head of the table. You staggered around until you fell into the armchair. Tory managed to calm you down. Then you staggered up to bed just after we all sat down."

"So I left the party early."

"No one will want to come here again."

"That's their problem."

"Len! You're driving my kids and grandkids away. I can't live without my kids and grandkids."

"You can always visit them."

"This *my* home too. Are you trying to drive me away as well?"

"No. I want you here. You're my wife."

"Oh for God's sake!" Clare got up exasperated. "You think marriage is a licence to abuse." She walked out of the room.

Once again, Clare considered her options. She concluded that if she divorced she would have to give up Loghaven. Len would never willingly leave it. Where could she afford to live with her dogs? They were not city dogs. Her children loved Loghaven. They had grown up with it as a rough log cabin. A large part of the plan of turning it into a big comfortable country home was that it would accommodate children and grandchildren. It was a place they would enjoy visiting. It was a vacation place, a family resort.

Clare recalled what a strain it was, visiting her mother when she became feeble and had to move into a retirement residence living in a bed-sitting room. Vi was not happy having to move from her spacious apartment where she could smoke at will. But she was legally blind from macular degeneration and her knee gave out. She had to use a walker. Clare or sometimes Len visited her every day and took her outside where she could sit on her walker and have a cigarette.

As she sat there huddled in her winter down coat, hanging onto one handle of the walker in the midst of snow, puffing quickly on her cigarette with her other hand, Clare felt painfully sorry for her. "Momkin," she said. "You should take up drinking. At least you could do that in your room."

"Haven't you had enough drinkers in your life?" Vi shot back. Then she reached for Clare's hand. "Sorry, Clarey. I shouldn't have said that. But Len is a changed man. You won't complain to me. But Megan and Ali are worried about it. So is Julie." She took another puff of her cigarette. Then looked perceptively at Clare. "Don't worry about me. Smoking doesn't kill brain cells."

"I can see that Mom. I hope I'm sharp as you if I get to be your age."

"Who says you've ever been sharp as me!" Vi laughed and coughed.

She died at eighty-nine of emphysema. Clare was able to call Julie in time for her to come and sit with Clare on either side of their mother's bed, each holding her hand for many hours until her body gave out.

After Len's frightening behaviour at the party, Clare spent a week with Megan and family in St. John's. When she came home to Loghaven, she said to Len, "Will you stop drinking?"

"No," he said firmly. "It's my preservative."

"Will you stop getting roaring drunk?"

"Maybe. I could give it a try."

"I've decided I'm going to get a lawyer to draw up a kind of separation agreement that allows me to have my kids and grandkids visit without you being here."

"What! You think you can kick me out of my own house?"

"Why can't you just leave, for short periods? You could take mini-vacations."

"Tell you what I will do. I'll write an apology for bad behaviour on my part to all the parents who were here that night."

"Really!?"

"You compose the apology and I'll sign it. Just a short email to all of them."

Clare drew it up.

"Len has asked me to apologize to you on his behalf, for his bad behaviour on that Saturday night. Please explain to your children that he is sorry for shouting and swearing and did not mean to frighten anyone."

Len signed it, "Mea culpa, Len."

No one replied to the email. They made their decisions quietly amongst themselves about exposing their children to further scenes with Len at Loghaven.

Life at home did not improve. Len continued his pattern of general silence throughout the day as he went over accounts and investing, staying in his office until between 2 and 3 p.m. when, if she were home, Clare would hear him putting ice cubes in his glass and pouring scotch from his jug bottle in the kitchen. He would return to his office and emerge after 5 p.m. when Clare came home from working in Ottawa or from outside hiking with the dogs. Len used to busy himself outside doing work on the property, getting exercise maintaining the trails. From his mid-seventies, the most he did outside was use the riding mower to cut the grass. If Clare arranged doubles tennis, Len would take his place on the court but could not do more than a step in any direction.

He liked it when Clare organized and did the work for dinner parties. He would start a fire in the fireplace but when they sat down to dinner he had already had too much to drink to participate actively in the conversations. He staggered up to bed as soon as guests departed. One night he excused himself early. The guests took that as a signal for them to depart. As they gathered at the door, a heavy thump was heard from the bedroom above. Clare went upstairs to find Len getting himself up from falling on the floor. He wasn't injured. Clare came back downstairs to assure every one and say goodbye. Mitch, their new neighbour, lingered behind. "Are you going to be alright?" he asked Clare. "I can stay longer if there's going to be any trouble."

"Thank you. But no need. Len just stumbled getting into bed."

"Just call if you ever need any help." Mitch looked kindly at her.

He and his wife Cora were nice, a few years younger than Clare. It was good to know she could turn to them. But she missed the stimulating company of Tory and Hettie. She had never known a man so knowledgable and interesting on almost any subject as Tory. He and Hettie went south in winter. Clare invited them to lunch in the summer. It was a rare occasion when Len was relatively sober and participated well in conversation. Then Clare realized that that was because Tory had a talent for drawing good conversation out of people.

When Clare was alone with Len at dinner, the pattern continued. Len would become antagonistic as she prepared dinner but she would not engage with him. When he sat down to the table, he would lift his wine glass joining in "cheers," then launch into complaints about the inexplicable stock market or brag about having made some thousands of dollars that day. If Clare raised a question about what he might do with all that money, he would get angry, yelling, "Reinvest, for chrissake! Make it make more. Don't you know anything!"

"Len. Stop yelling. I'm just taking an interest in what you're doing."

"I'm providing you with a hell of a high standard of living."

"I'm not disputing that. But I do have work of my own."

"Taking pictures is not everyone's idea of work." He took a large gulp of wine and sat back in a smirk.

Infuriated, Clare stood up, picked up her wine glass and pitched wine onto his face. She refilled her glass and left the room. She went down and sat on the dock with the dogs.

When she came back into the house, Len had gone to bed. Clare locked her bedroom door before getting into bed. She had become afraid of his unpredictability, of what he harboured in silence.

Chapter Seventeen

A Good News Story

Clare's work was going well. In 2013 she was elected president of the Canadian Wildlife Photography Association. It was a one-year term, involving a lot of her time, but being elected president was a significant honour from her colleagues.

Clare had been unwell in the winter before she took office. She kept getting bouts of what she thought was the current winter flu. Even Queen Elizabeth was taken briefly to hospital with it that winter. "The Queen and I…." Clare liked to joke. When Clare became so weak from diarrhea and vomiting that it was a struggle to get around, she got Len to take her to the doctor. The doctor arranged for her to have a colonoscopy. She expected no dire results. When two doctors came in to talk to her after the procedure, she thought they were being friendly professionals. When she heard the surgeon speak of a 'mass' on her colon, then use the words 'tumour' and 'malignant', she lay in disbelief. When he asked her if she had children, she thought he was being friendly, at last.

"Yes." she smiled proudly at him. "I have two grown-up daughters, and five grandkids."

"Your daughters will have to be tested," he said. "Colon cancer can be hereditary."

The other doctor said, "You have an irregular heartbeat."

Clare didn't care at all about that, an irregular heartbeat. It was 'cancer', 'my daughters' echoing in her mind. She got dressed, thinking, how do I deal with this? Len drove her home in silence. While she made herself a poached egg which she couldn't eat, Len said to her, "You are brave." But he kept his distance from her, didn't embrace or touch her. Didn't know what to do or say to comfort her.

Clare was put through further tests. She would be given the results after she attended the annual general meeting of the Wildlife Photography Association where she was required to make an acceptance speech. Clare recalled how she had managed to write her exams the week after her father died of cancer. She rallied herself to make a good speech. She was living on green tea with honey and Greek yogurt with maple syrup. The association's staff knew of her illness. They were so kind and supportive, Clare felt buoyed up by them.

Megan and Ali flew in to accompany Clare when she got the results from her surgeon, Dr. Lisi. Len could not be relied on to remember facts or be helpful in the situation, and he didn't want to participate anyway. Megan was an expert listener and recalled every relevant point. Ali was herself an excellent doctor. Dr. Lisi said the cancer had not spread beyond the colon and could be surgically removed at this stage, if all went well. She was fast tracked to be operated on within a week.

Dr. Lisi was pleased with how the surgery went. He had removed one-third of her colon without complications. Clare had to stay in hospital some extra days because of tests on her heart, but she was home within the week and able to carry on with her duties as president of the association. It would be two weeks before full results of the operation would be known and what further treatment might be required. Julie came to help the day Clare came home from hospital. She stayed only a few days because Clare was well enough to do everything necessary.

Julie was angry at Len's behaviour. "He's a drunk and doesn't help you with a thing. Never says anything nice to you," Julie said before departing. "You shouldn't put up with it. You hold way too much within, Clare. Stress-related illnesses come from living with someone like that. It's affecting your digestive system and your heart."

Dr. Lisi phoned Clare when he had the results. She held her breath at the sound of his voice. "It's good news," he said. "The tumour was successfully removed. There's no trace of remaining cancer."

"Oh *thank you*, Dr. Lisi. Thank you for your expert work." She could picture him smiling.

"There's no need for further treatment," he said.

"No chemo? No radiation? Nothing?!"

"Well, you'll have to go for tests on a regular basis for five years."

"They can test me all they want." Oh God, thought Clare, that was stupid. "Sorry. What a stupid thing to say. I'm just so grateful to you. And so lucky. I can't quite believe it. But I won't take up more of your time now. Others need you. Thank you for phoning. Thank you for … my life."

Dr. Lisi laughed gently. "You're welcome. Just doing my job."

Clare hung up and called out to Len. "I'm a good news story." Len came into the room. "Dr. Lisi got it all," she told him. "Removed the cancer surgically. No need for further treatment. No chemo. No radiation. I'm cancer-free."

"I'm glad," said Len. "Damn glad." He smiled and hugged her.

Clare obeyed all the follow-up rules diligently, knowing how lucky she was to have her cancer surgically removed. Tests showed her heart had a wonky beat but it seemed strong enough. Dr. Goode, the lead cardiologist, was extremely thorough in his testing. He summoned her to his clinic for semiannual testing. Clare was able to complete her term as president without further medical issues.

The annual meeting where she would make her final speech and hand over the gavel was held in St. John's, Newfoundland. Spouses usually attended the banquet and dance and the final session when the departing president was applauded. Len wasn't interested in attending and Clare was glad of that. She didn't want to have to deal with his drunken or hungover behaviour. She was proud to have her daughter and Nate attend the final session when all the photographers rose to their feet in applause after her speech. A standing ovation was usual for the departing president. But the wolf howl they all broke into as the staff flashed Clare's photo of the smiling wolf on the overhead screen and the incoming president, with whom Clare had worked especially well, leading the audience in a wolf howl—that was unique to Clare's tenure.

Clare had dinner that night at Megan and Nate's with her lively grandchildren. It was a happy ending to her challenging and productive year as president of the association. But when she went back to her hotel room and got into bed alone, she sank into the peculiar loneliness of a wife who did not want to go home to her husband. It was only Loghaven and the Malamutes Clare wanted to return to.

CHAPTER EIGHTEEN

In Fort McMurray 2014

In July of 2014, Clare received an invitation to visit Fort McMurray. The notorious Fort McMurray, city of the vilified oil companies where a flock of ducks had suffered a terrible death by drowning in an oil waste tailings pond. Photos of that and of smoke-spewing oil sands processing facilities went round the world on social media. Canada became the nation that was told by extreme environmentalists to keep its oil in the ground. Russia, Iran, the Arab states, other much larger producers of oil carried on generally uncriticised for oil production, as did the US and the UK. Even Norway, well known to be environmentally conscientious, produced oil at good profit.

But Canada, though a model for diversity and large-scale conservation of parklands, tends to be very self-critical. There was a strong and growing international movement as the twenty-first century moved into its second decade, to combat climate change by reducing or eventually eliminating the use of fossil fuels. The big oil companies around Fort McMurray, producing oil from oil sands, became a prime target for the 'ban the use of fossil fuels' movement.

I'm not even sure what 'fossil fuels' really means, Clare admitted to herself. And the issue of climate change is complex. I'm too unscientifically trained to know if global warming is caused by the natural movement of the planet and the sun or if human polluting of the environment is the major cause. Pollution is bad. That she knew for sure. Pollution has to be mitigated as much as possible.

Clare wanted to have more conversation with Tory Sanderson about climate change and pollution and why there was a need for these large tailings ponds, the size of lakes. He was a scientist, a geophysicist, whose long and distinguished career had to do with locating mineral mines throughout the world. He invented instruments to locate an area rich in reserves, before any digging began. He headed his own international company for locating valuable areas for mining operations. In semi-retirement, he was a consultant and became the go-to person for the United Nations, CIDA, the World Bank and the International Monetary Fund for locating mining areas in developing countries. All this Clare had learned from conversation with Tory's wife, Hettie, at lunch, when Tory had gone to Toronto to attend a geophysicists' conference.

Hettie had herself become a practising scientist at the University of Toronto after raising their four children. She was made a senior associate researcher in environmental chemistry. Her job had been to study the effects of toxic chemicals in the environment. She could calculate how much mercury in a river would poison how many fish.

"You should go to Fort McMurray instead of me," Clare said to Hettie. "You'd have plenty to study there."

"The effects of oil sands processing and tailings ponds are all too obvious," said Hettie. "As I understand it, oil companies now are developing new technologies and meeting higher standards of environmental regulations. And a lot of that work is voluntary, not required by government regulations. But I'm turning eighty-eight and glad to be long retired. Tory's the one to talk to. He's still in the game. Writing complex papers on climate change from a geophysicist's point of view. His is not the popular view but it's supported by a lot of highly respected scientists."

"Wish I could understand it." Clare sat back in her chair. "But I'm even confused about the role of CO_2. Big mining industries produce it, but so do plants. I want to go to Fort McMurray just to see the life there. I've been asked to photograph the wildlife." She laughed. "Meaning animals. I'm sure there's lots of human wildlife. All kinds of people from all across Canada going there for work … all of them pretty young. And me pushing seventy. I think I'll just keep quiet about that."

"Seventy seems so young," said Hettie.

The invitation for Clare to visit Fort McMurray came on social media from a complete stranger. There had been a conversation on Facebook about the novel *City Wolves*. A few people had read and loved the book, recommending it to one Lisa Schaldemose who lived in northern Alberta. Lisa said she was eager to read it before she went in the Yukon Quest sled dog race, assisting a musher friend as his sled-dog handler. Then Clare read on Facebook that Lisa had to cancel out of the Yukon Quest because of some looming surgical operation. Worried that Lisa was going to have serious, maybe life-threatening surgery, Clare contacted Molly to send a signed copy of the book to Lisa. On Facebook conversations Lisa raved about the novel. She auctioned it at a fundraiser for sled dog rescues and got an astoundingly high bid for it. Then Lisa invited Molly to visit her. Molly said she was sorry she couldn't, but recommended Clare, the photographer of the front-cover wolf photo, to visit in her stead.

"Where do you live?" asked Clare when she received a phone call from Lisa.

"Fort McMurray."

Clare was surprised and excited at that. She had long thought of Fort McMurray as the capital of the oil industry in Canada and the discovery of oil there as comparable to the discovery of gold in the Klondike in the late 1880s. She thought of the development of Fort McMurray as similar to the development of Dawson City in the 1890s, with people rushing there from all over North America and some from Europe, to make their fortune. Or like her grandmother, Meg Wilkinson, a pioneering female veterinarian who went to Dawson City, seeking adventure and an interesting application of her profession.

Am I following in my grandmother's footsteps? asked Clare of herself, smiling wryly. At last? Julie has been doing that, very successfully, all her adult life. But my grandmother was in her twenties when she went to the Klondike gold rush. I'm nearly seventy. That brought the comparison in her mind to a halt.

Lisa's voice on the phone sounded young. Clare imagined Lisa's life. Lisa is an animal lover. She works for a shelter. She's probably not well off. Visiting her probably means sleeping on the floor. I'm too old for that, Clare quickly decided. Clare replied to Lisa that she could come in September. She'd stay for a few days, in a hotel.

"No," said Lisa. "You must stay with me. It's just me and my mom who came up from Manitoba to live with me. We have a guest suite in the basement. Stay for a week. I want you to take photos of my friend's wolf dogs. Do you want to fly over the oil sands? Catch some wildlife shots up river?"

"Would love to, but I'm afraid I can't really afford to hire a plane to fly me around."

"You wouldn't have to. I have just the right person in mind who will take you."

It turned out Lisa was a mover and shaker in Fort McMurray. The animal shelter was just some of her volunteer work. She was an environmental scientist and her job was to negotiate agreements between oil companies and the Indigenous communities around Fort McMurray. Lisa had friends in the oil companies, in the Indigenous communities, in the media, the municipal government, and the cultural centre. Before Clare landed in Fort Mac, as they called it, Lisa had worked out a full week's busy schedule for Clare.

On the plane to Fort Mac, Clare sat beside a nice-looking man, casually dressed in jeans, a light sweater and peaked cap which he did not remove. The plane was full of men dressed similarly to him, everyone well under fifty. Clare was one of three or four women passengers. And by far the oldest. The man sitting beside her was reluctant to converse. Clare sensed a general tight-lipped, low spirit on board. This was not a plane load of people bound for a holiday. They were men returning to work, hard work.

Clare let the man know she had been invited to Fort Mac to photograph wolf dogs. That piqued his interest. Clare knew that mentioning she photographed wolves usually opened up conversation with people. But she didn't want to spend the time discussing wolves.

"I'll also be looking for bear." She smiled as she looked to see if he knew the expression 'looking for bear' meaning looking for trouble.

"Seriously?" he asked. "You know there's a lot of people come to Fort Mac looking for trouble. Are you one of those?"

"No," she said. "I'm a wildlife photographer. And I'm not one of those who say Canada should leave its oil in the ground."

"That's a break," he said. "I'm a foreman for Suncor. Worked with them for over ten years. I support my young daughters in Napanee with the money I earn in Fort Mac. Can send them to university if they want. There's been a lot of improvements in oil extraction in recent years." He went on to explain the processes to Clare and described to her the shift-work system which allowed him to visit his daughters or take them on vacation for two-week stretches. He and his wife were divorced but amicable. Clare shook his hand when they parted getting off the plane.

In the line-up for luggage retrieval, Clare noticed that people saw her camera equipment and then did not regard her in an open or friendly manner. They assumed she was there to troubleshoot. I understand that, thought Clare. They are defensive about their city, their workplace. I get that. They can see I'm no rock star or movie star looking for photo ops as an environmentalist. I'll just have to also show that I'm not aiming at bad press for them.

It was a new, efficient airport. As Clare came down the escalator she saw a slim, younger, probably in her forties, woman with straight blonde hair. She smiled and waved. "Hi Clare." She grabbed for Clare's suitcase. "I'm Lisa. Welcome to Fort Mac."

Lisa hustled Clare out to her big SUV. Lisa was warm and talkative, not one to linger or evade. "Sorry about the dog hair on the front seat," she said. "My dogs like to be up front. The driver's seat is their favourite."

Clare laughed. "Just like my Malamutes."

"Mine are northern mixed breeds. Rescues," said Lisa. "But I have one that's mainly Malamute. And my mom has a Westie."

On the dashboard, Clare noticed a soft stuffy-toy sled dog and a dream catcher hanging down from the rear view mirror. "Your mascot?" Clare asked of the stuffy-toy.

"Oh that's just one of many." Lisa started the engine. "People give them to me. You'll see them all over the house. Some I've bought myself. Other women have kids. I have dogs and stuffed toys."

Clare knew that being childless was a sensitive topic. She did not pry. She often thought there was a tyranny of parents. Parents assuming everyone has children or never wanted any. She patted the stuffy toy. "Hi there," she said to it.

"Her name is Piji," said Lisa, looking pleased by Clare's gesture, "after one of my favourite characters in *City Wolves*."

Clare smiled at Lisa. She liked her very much. They drove through central Fort Mac. It was not a beautiful city. Wide dusty streets lined by shopping malls with large parking areas in front of them. Many pickup trucks and SUVs, few cars. The buildings were mainly flat-roofed rectangles. None of the creative shapes and skyscrapers of Calgary. This looked like a quickly built, functional city, one easy to drive around in. Not a city of parks and promenades. It was a cool, sunny day, the second week in September. Clare figured she had got it right by wearing jeans, running shoes, and her red wool autumn jacket.

People on the street corner, crossing over to the mall, were wearing light coats and jackets. She saw a woman in a hijab. Clare had read newspaper articles about the influx of workers in the population of Fort Mac and the extreme housing shortage it created. Many people were accommodated in trailer homes. But not Lisa. They drove into a small suburb of modest houses built before 2000, mainly to accommodate oil sands workers and their families. They were well taken care of, with small front lawns and back yards.

Clare could hear a Malamute's brief howl from the back yard when Lisa got out and slammed the door of her SUV. "Hi, Spirit," Lisa called out. Inside the house they were greeted by a small white Terrier and two more medium-sized Husky-like sled dogs "My pack of rescues." Lisa smiled, holding her hand towards them. "You've met

Spirit. This is Abbee, Maggie and Snow. And my wonderful mother, Annette. Mom, this is Clare."

Annette was a tall, quiet, kindly woman with poor eyesight, who nevertheless was tuned into CNN on a large-screen television, all her waking hours it seemed to Clare. Lisa and her mom looked after each other like an old loving couple. Their house was comfortable and cluttered. They each drank a lot of coffee from a small Keurig coffee maker and smoked cigarettes, but not in front of Clare. "I don't mind if you want to smoke," said Clare. "This is your house."

"We're both trying to quit," said Lisa. "We never smoke in front of people, so you're good for us."

Lisa let Spirit inside and began to show Clare around the house. Spirit greeted Clare and after sufficient attention, pawed the back door to be let out into the cool air again. The main floor was spacious with kitchen, living-dining room, an office, Annette's bedroom, and a large addition for Lisa's bedroom and ensuite. On the basement level was a utility room and the guest suite. Lisa opened the door into it for Clare.

"Oh my gawd!" Clare couldn't help exclaiming with a laugh. "I love it! I've never seen such a collection of wolves."

There were stuffed toy wolves on the bookshelves which ran the length of two walls around the double bed. In the sitting area were more wolves, some as statuettes and soapstone carvings on the side tables and coffee table. The room was tidy, spacious, and bright with two pale blue walls and two white ones. The furniture was golden pine and blonde upholstered arm chairs. The bed had a wolf blanket covering. It was neatly made with a long pillow at the head with a white case saying, 'Dog Tired. Let Me Sleep'. In front of that was a bright red heart-shaped pillow. On the shelfless walls were various framed prints of wolves and sled dogs.

"One could never feel lonely in this room," said Clare. "It's a fortress of friendly wildlife."

Annette stayed home by preference while Clare took Lisa out to dinner. Lisa chose a large modern bar where food was served at the bar or on high tables with chairs one had to hoist oneself up onto. The décor was shiny black with blue strobe-like lighting. There were many big-screen TVs so that anyone anywhere had a view of several, all of them showing team sports. The menu was burgers and steaks, shrimps and fried chicken with fries, mushrooms, Caesar or green salads. Unlike restaurants in the Yukon and Arctic, here there was an abundance of food. And pitchers of cold beer. There were no empty tables.

"Most popular bar in town," said Lisa.

Clare looked around. It was a mainly male crowd, busy with their food, watching the TV screens when they drank from their glasses. Clare noticed a young woman with a man's haircut, drinking red wine and eating hungrily at the end of the table where Clare and Lisa sat. She seemed to be on her own but exchanged remarks with people further along the table.

"Do you know her?" Clare asked Lisa.

"No. Haven't seen her before. She looks strong. Maybe works in the mines."

When the other people at the table finished and left, Clare invited the woman to join them. She quickly sized up Clare, who was old enough to be her mother and therefore harmless. And Lisa seemed OK. She moved to sit across from them. "I'm Catherine," she said. "From Saskatchewan." The waitress brought Catherine dessert. Clare ordered more wine.

"I'm flying out tomorrow for six days in Vancouver," Catherine told them.

"Why Vancouver if you're from Saskatchewan?"

"My woman's in Vancouver."

"Gotcha," said Clare, thinking that was smart. It got things clarified right away. I like that. "You work here in Fort Mac?"

"Yeah, I drive the big equipment. Came here in February, four years ago, right after I got my licence for driving the big ones."

"Wow!" said Lisa. "That's impressive. Not a lot of people come here in mid-winter, let alone come to drive the big equipment."

"It pays good," said Catherine. "I'm sticking this out for five years. Then Lynn and I should have enough to buy a little farm in Ontario. Lynn wants to raise Icelandic sheep."

"Icelandic sheep. Why Icelandic?"

"Lynn's father is Icelandic. And they're freakin' hardy. Said to be the oldest sheep breed in the world."

"There's some lousy farmland near Ottawa, where I live," said Clare. "A lot of rocks. Could be good for sheep. Should be cheap. But I'm not sure it is."

"We could look into that," said Catherine. "I'll be leaving here next March."

"I'll give you my card." Clare rummaged in her purse. "I know a good real estate agent in Ottawa who could put you onto a farmland agent." She handed Catherine her card. "So what's it like, driving the big equipment?"

Catherine scrutinized the card then scrutinized Lisa and asked her, "You also a photographer?"

"No," Lisa smiled. "I'm just an agreement negotiator. You can say what you want in front of me."

Catherine considered this, then replied to Clare. "If you really want to know what driving big equipment's like … it's not for sissies. Nor addicts."

"I guess not!"

"First thing they check if you have an accident is for booze or drugs in your system. The union doesn't allow random testing, but they can if you get into any trouble. A lot of young guys come to Mac and wreck themselves on drugs. We do twelve-hour shifts. The night shift, 8 p.m. to 8 a.m., is the tough one. Get a twenty-minute break every three hours. I keep the windows open and crunch on sunflower seeds to keep myself awake. Sometimes use the break to power nap. Twenty minutes isn't always enough for me to climb off and on the truck, eat my sandwich and have a pee. So I wound up in the office getting a reprimand for asking for too many washrooms breaks, beyond the regular twenty-minute breaks. They gave me shit for having nine in one year. But I don't get fired because I'm too damn good on the job. After a couple of years, I got to operate the 797s."

"What's that?"

"Biggest fuckin' trucks in the world." Catherine went on describing the equipment and her work. "The trucks are thirty feet off the ground. You climb up sixteen double-size steps to get into the cab. Getting into the cab of a shovel truck is like climbing up into a small, glass high-rise condo. The excavator trucks are similarly enormous.

"There has to be near perfect synchronization of the movement and work of the trucks. They have to begin and end the three-hour shifts and breaks simultaneously. They have to follow in line at similar speed. One monster truck colliding with another can make a fatal calamity. An accident can be a disaster of stupendous expense. Every group of trucks and drivers has a supervisor overseeing them at all times, even on the breaks. Behaviour does not go unobserved.

"If you get stuck in the muck, the supervisor comes to your rescue. Fast! Other trucks are brought to a halt. Then begin again on command.

"You get bussed to your equipment, everyone in buses that stop and go with continuous precision. Once at your truck, you have five minutes to inspect it for any leaks, flat tire etc., climb up into it, start engine and drive ahead.

"It's like being in the fuckin' army," said Catherine. "Except you're not supposed to kill people." She smiled. "I like the work. Enjoy drivin' those big suckers around. But five years is enough. Couldn't take life in the barracks any longer than that."

Catherine described the large modules with women's accommodation in one wing, men's in others. Everyone gets their own room and shower. There's a cafeteria and store to get provisions for making your own packed lunch. There used to be pubs but they led to 'unacceptable behaviour' so were closed. After three months in the camp, you were to find your own accommodation in town. Accommodations in town weren't likely an improvement, but Catherine liked to get away from the cafeteria life and do her own cooking when she wanted. After a couple of years, Catherine developed sinus problems and got silica in her lungs. She had sinus surgery that improved her breathing ability, though nosebleeds happened frequently.

"Life on a sheep farm sounds good," she concluded. "I'll find more equipment to drive if I get bored. Without the smell of fumes and dust up my nose."

Chapter Nineteen

Fort Mac People and Pets

Next morning, Lisa drove Clare to the outskirts of Fort Mac where her friend Randy had large kennels for wolf dogs. He also boarded a few exotic pets for people working in the oil industry. A parrot, an iguana, dogs. Further away on a dog lot, he kept his team of sled dogs, each chained to their own dog house. Lisa was his volunteer helper. Randy's office for his various enterprises was in a large trailer. His wife, a very attractive Nordic woman with large blue eyes, was a real estate agent.

A young local photographer, Tracey Holland, was invited to join them. Lisa explained that Randy made some money to keep the wolf dogs by training the tamest ones to have their picture taken with tourists or townspeople who wanted to have a photo taken in the woods with a 'wolf'.

Randy led the way to the spacious kennels. Each one had a dog house, a bone-shaped wading pool of water sunken into the ground, and stairs leading up to a platform where the wolf dogs could have a lookout similar to being on a hill top or cliff. Each kennel held three or four large wolf-like dogs.

"They're better called 'hybrid wolves', not wolf dogs," said Randy. "The percentage of wolf in each is obviously high but you never know exactly how high. Crazy people do crazy things with animals. Wolves, by nature, don't choose to mate with dogs and vice versa. They have to be captured, tied up, and forced to mate, at just the right time."

"Sounds like hard porn movie stuff to me," said Clare.

"You got it," said Randy. "Twisted stuff. Not funny. Look at what comes of it. Abandoned animals, because of their unpredictability. Not safe for human homes and no longer fit for the wilderness."

Clare stood still at the wire kennel fence intently observing the hybrid wolves, all the size of Malamutes, but with differing colours of fur coats. There was a completely white wolf named Sage, ones with various shades of sable coats like Koyuk and Lyra, and a large black wolf, Talon, who paced the back of the kennel while the others moved cautiously closer to the fence where Randy stood with Lisa and Tracey. Randy opened the door of that first kennel where the white wolf, Sage, was with two others. All three came over to Randy in a friendly, eager manner, sniffing him. They seemed almost as friendly as Malamutes as they followed Randy around the kennel. Sage and Koyuk followed Randy up the stairs to the platform where he reassured them by ruffling them at their shoulders from behind their heads.

"He really knows how to handle them," said Clare as she watched him interact with the wolves. "They trust him."

"For sure," said Lisa. "But the hybrid wolves at this kennel are the friendliest, the most tame. These are the ones Randy has trained for Tracey to do photographs with people."

Clare kept her camera hung behind her back as she moved over to the kennel with the black wolf. She wanted to have the wolves approach seeing her empty-handed. She was most intrigued by the black one. She stood still with her hand held out slightly, palm down, at the fence. One of the sable wolves approached and sniffed her hand, stood for a moment, then walked a small distance away to observe her. Another sable wolf did similarly.

"The black one, Talon, won't do that," Randy told Clare as he came down from the platform. "He keeps his distance."

Clare kept watching Talon, the black wolf. She thought him most regal and discerning. She felt the most sympathy for him being captive and fenced in. He stared back at Clare. Then, while Randy tethered Sage and Lyra, Talon, the large black hybrid wolf, walked straight across the kennel towards Clare. Everyone stared in silence as Talon stopped a couple of metres from Clare, who kept still. Then

Talon moved right up to her at the fence, to sniff her hand. He sniffed twice, then walked away, sat down and stared at all of them.

Randy burst out laughing. "Guess Talon just told me off. Made a liar out of me."

"I got it!" Tracey said triumphantly. "I got the shot of him sniffing your hand, Clare."

Clare smiled. She felt she had been honoured by Talon.

Randy brought Sage, the white wolf, and the sable, Lyra, out of the kennel on leashes. He and Lisa led them down the dirt road to an area of woods with mature trees. Clare took some souvenir shots of the hybrid wolves, but she felt uncomfortable with the staging of wolf dogs as wolves. This was not true wildlife photography. But then when she saw how these animals enjoyed being in the woods and sporting with people, she joined in with them. She knelt with her knees on the ground and her back against a tree trunk so she was more on a level with the dogs.

Sage came over and sat politely in front of her, looking happily expectant and gave a couple of howl notes. Clare answered in imitative tones. Sage rolled over on her back for a belly rub. Clare complied. Then Sage got up and licked Clare's chin, her nose touching Clare's cheek. Clare laughed and ruffled behind the dog's ears. "You are a friendly wolf," she said. "And an excellent performer!"

Randy laughed and Sage went over to him for another ear rub. Lyra, the sable dog, went to Clare and did a short howl, which Clare joined in on. Then Lyra leaned up against her and stood with his front paws on her knee on the ground. Clare laughed at his playfulness, his sense of triumph in standing on Clare, his moment of lording it over her.

The photos Tracey took of Clare's romp with the hybrid wolves gave Clare smiles for years afterwards. But when they returned to the kennels and Clare stood at Talon's fence to say farewell to him, she was haunted by his loneliness, or was it his helplessness? Certainly it was everything pent up inside him. He paced the back fence, then came near, but not close enough to sniff her hand again. He sat down and stared at her. She wanted to promise him she would help him but she knew she could not. She remained haunted by that scene with Talon. Clare left, knowing Randy would do the best he could for each one of the hybrid wolves. But she felt they were doomed. Had been doomed from birth, to a life of imprisonment, like wolves in a zoo. And yet Randy had rescued them from being killed and provided them with sanctuary and forms of companionship.

Late morning of the next day, Lisa drove Clare to the area of the airport where there were hangars for private planes. Lisa's friend David Bouchier was to fly them over the oil sands mines around Fort Mac in one of his three private airplanes. Clare watched from Lisa's vehicle while Lisa went to a hangar, where David Bouchier emerged. He was a tall, early middle-aged man with dark hair, wearing jeans, a white fleece jacket, and a cap he never removed. Clare was sure from their glances towards her and their brief conferring, that David was asking Lisa if she was sure Clare was not someone coming to trash Fort McMurray. He gave a look that expressed 'OK. I'll have to trust your judgement.'

They got into David's four-seater plane which had wheels, as well as pontoons for landing on water. David and his young pilot sat in the front two seats, Lisa and Clare in the seats behind them. David also had a two-seater plane and a much larger one that could fly him and his wife plus four children and guests to their third home in Kelowna, British Columbia. They had a home in the Indigenous community of Fort McKay adjacent to Fort Mac and a cottage on a lake north of the city, Moose Lake. To the community of Fort McKay, Moose Lake was a cultural area of their traditional homelands, still relatively untouched by industrial development.

David did not give out information readily. He was watchful and careful about what he said. Clare instinctively respected his reticence and asked few questions, allowing him to say only what he wished to say. Lisa was a natural and experienced facilitator and negotiator of various situations. She put people at ease.

Tom, the young pilot in jeans, brown plaid shirt, and baseball cap, took directions from David. They flew up over the city, seeing that it was built near the wide Athabasca River at the junction of the much smaller Clearwater River. There was a golf course on the city outskirts along the bank of the river. Flying higher and further, Clare could see large areas of bare beige earth where surface oil sands mining had been and was taking place. Clare pictured Catherine driving the big equipment to scoop up the oil-drenched sands and dump it into enormous trucks to be taken to processing plants where the oil would be extracted to be transported to faraway destinations. Now those acres of mined earth were being reconstructed to be eventually replanted with natural foliage to restore the land to what it looked like before oil was extracted. That reforestation would take a long time and it was still unknown as to what would become of the multiple tailings ponds.

Newer areas of mining looked smaller and more neatly laid out, with dense green forest growing up to the very edge of the mine site. There were also below-surface drilled mines, which took up comparatively small spaces with pads not much more than an acre. According to the new rules of mining, once the drilled mines were finished, the surface was relatively quickly reclaimed with planted trees, following the motto 'leave as found'.

Clare had brought along her small digital camera and took some, not many, photos of the landscape. She noted David kept a watchful eye on her use of her camera. Clare was careful to ask him to explain what she was seeing before she took a photo. His answers were clear and brief. She let him know she was in need of basic understanding of mining processes. She told him she had come to Fort Mac mainly to photograph animals, but as a Canadian she was interested in the life and work around Fort Mac. David grew more at ease with her and said she and Lisa could, if they wanted to, continue on further north to his cottage on Moose Lake where he had a couple of errands to run.

Clare and Lisa looked at each other. "Yes, please!" they said, almost in unison.

They flew north beyond the oil mines to a landscape of the wide Athabasca and dense forest, then over what looked like small lakes and wetlands with shrubs and sparse forest. Tom landed the plane expertly at the end of a narrow dock on the lake in front of a new log cottage, two storeys high with an A-frame roof and floor-to-ceiling front windows. It was set amongst silver birch trees. The leaves were still green but beginning to turn golden.

Clare tried not to show how cold she felt in the more northern air as they walked up to the cottage. She also tried to tone down her remarks as she entered and was struck with admiration for the design and décor of this grand new round-log cottage. It was light and bright, with log walls and pine floor still blonde and shining. The front wall onto the lake was almost all window glass, bringing in all the light of day and reflecting the sparkle of the lake. There was a big soft black leather sofa by the wood-burning stove, which David immediately started filling with logs and set alight. He had more spring in his step and warmth in his eyes as he set about making the fire in his cottage and getting the coffee maker going.

Clare took in the good quality furnishings and fixtures. There were black bear and moose motifs in the sofa cushions and the upholstery of the black leather armchairs, also in the border of the beige floor rug under the coffee table. Not too much to make it silly, just enough to make it fun and quietly striking. Antique snowshoes decorated the top of the smaller side windows.

"I live in a lakefront log cottage, which I pretty much designed and we had built about ten years ago," Clare told David. "But yours makes mine look like hodgepodge. Who designed and decorated this place? It's absolutely splendid. Totally tasteful Canadian."

David laughed. "My wife and I," he said. "It's just us. Mostly her. She did hire a decorator for our house in Kelowna but let her go after a while."

David invited Clare and Lisa to look upstairs if they wished. He and Tom took care of the firewood supply and the coffee making. The upstairs had a master bedroom with pine log bedstead, side tables and chest of drawers. A large fur throw covered the bed. The single beds in the kids' room had Hudson's Bay blankets neatly folded on top of the beds along with white quilts. Every room in the cottage was tidy and clean, ready for occupancy, like a well run inn.

As they sat by the fire drinking coffee, David opened up about his background, but concisely. His father was a trapper, as was his grandfather. His father died young and David was raised by his grandparents. "You can't make a living as a trapper anymore, even if you wanted to. There's not enough money in it. That way of life is gone. I went to high school and became a fireman. Saved up enough to buy some machinery, then some more and started a business with that equipment to service the oil industry."

He talked more personally about his first wife dying of cancer when their children were very young. It was an almost unbearably sad time which was hard to pull through. But there was some incident at the hospital which led him to connect much later with his second wife. Clare was confused about it. It had something to do with coincidental dates that portended his second wife, whom he was clearly very proud of. They worked in partnership together.

"She's a real powerhouse," Lisa explained later. "She's also active in cultural and political circles. She and David do a lot for the community. They're generous and quiet about it."

"He's certainly generous in the time and expense of fuel he's given to us, especially me. I don't know what I have to give back to him."

"He's a very smart, hard-working businessman," said Lisa. "But he's not someone always looking for payback. Sometimes he just likes being a good ambassador for his people and our community."

Clare was left pondering about the character and life of David Bouchier in the years to come. How did he fare in the downturn and disaster that were soon to befall Fort McMurray? There was so much she wanted to ask him. But her experience was that asking too many questions of guarded people made them less forthcoming with you. Still, she kicked herself that she had neglected to ask him about the black bearskin hanging over the beam on the stairs to the bedroom.

There had to be a story behind that bear.

David did a couple of quick chores in the workshop beside the cottage while Clare and Lisa put the coffee things away. Clare snapped some photos of the cottage and property then they got back in the plane for the return trip. David instructed Tom to land at a small dock near a modest cottage en route. There were no other cottages in sight that compared in size and grandeur to David's. With some dexterity, David handed a package to a man in a small motor boat at the dock. The man lived with David's mother. The package was a carton of cigarettes for her.

They flew back over the lakes and wet lands, along the Athabasca and seemingly endless forest on flat land. What a lot of havens for ducks, thought Clare. How shockingly unfortunate that that flock chose to land in a tailings pond when the alarm system warning them to stay away from it wasn't working.

David looked at his watch. "Want to see more of the industry?" he asked.

Clare left it to Lisa to answer. "Whatever you have time for," she said to David.

"A brief over all," he instructed Tom.

They were flown over the rivers and forest edging onto several large areas of industrial oil company camps. They were different in size but basically each had a processing plant where columns of white smoke rose up from a few chimneys in what looked like the central factory. There were enormous storage tanks for treated oil waiting to be piped to destinations beyond Fort McMurray. Artificially created, rectangular waste ponds held the waste products. There were numerous and various outer buildings with purposes Clare could not imagine.

Big industry is a complexity I know almost nothing about, she thought. The training and education that goes into inventing and running a complexity like this is ... beyond me and my little camera. She wanted to talk with someone knowledgeable about it. The only person she knew who would have some understanding of such engineering feats was Tory Sanderson. Flying in the compartment of a small plane does not facilitate conversation. It's too noisy and difficult to hear. Clare kept concentrating on what she could see from the window.

She could discern at the end of roads leading to and from the several large oil company plants, unadorned metal fabricated buildings which looked like the barracks and recreation buildings Catherine had described for the men and few women who ran all the equipment of the oil companies. Catherine said the facilities inside were comfortable enough, with private bedroom and baths plus communal rooms and cafeteria. But the atmosphere was heavy with a sense of hard work, regimentation, and fatigue. "Unless you're lucky enough to be in a unit with a lot of Newfoundlanders," Catherine had said. "They know how to lighten things up."

Tom swooped the plane back towards the hangar. Fort Mac itself came back into view.

Clare felt she had indeed been given the "brief over all," the uncensored brief tour over the notorious oil sands of Fort McMurray. She wondered how it compared to the oil fields in other countries, like Russia, Saudi Arabia, the USA.

The gift, she felt, the special advantage and privilege, was seeing it from the private plane, from the perspective, of David Bouchier. Indigenous, born and raised on the land his ancestors had inhabited since human beings first trod there. The son of a trapper, he became a fireman and then an entrepreneur in the oil industry arising on his native land. He acquired wealth which he used to benefit his family, community, and society. She couldn't have had more of an insider tour guide.

It was hard to believe he would take the time out of his busy and important life to show her the industrial and recreational scenes around Fort McMurray. She believed he was doing it mainly as a favour to Lisa, who must have negotiated good agreements for him when she worked for several years in the community of Fort McKay. But Clare also believed Lisa's view that David was proud of working in the oil industry and liked to be an ambassador for his community and people.

As a final favour, Clare asked if she might have a photo with him in front of his biggest plane. "Sorry," he said, "have to get back to my office."

Then Clare realized that a photo of him in front of his biggest private plane was just the sort of photo that could be used against him. 'Oil industry rich guy in front of one of his private planes'. He had probably experienced that kind of 'trashing' before.

Then Lisa stepped up. "Let me take a pic of the two of you in front of the small plane we were in."

Then David laughed. "OK. I'll tell the press it's her plane. She had it flown in from Ottawa, at government expense."

David made a joke of it but it was his final gesture of trust that Clare would not abuse the trust and benefit he had extended to her. An idea of how she might extend her skills as a photographer beyond wildlife animals into the largesse of life as she experienced it, began to grow in her mind.

Lisa had arranged that Clare would give a talk at the library about the photo of the smiling wolf on the front cover of *City Wolves*. With input from Molly, Clare would also talk about the writing of the novel, her own relationship with her grandmother, the first woman veterinarian who went to the Klondike gold rush, and Clare would top it all off with a reading from the novel. Proceeds from sales of the book would go to the Fort Mac animal shelter. Molly warned Clare that book readings could be poorly attended events. Even well-known authors had experience of only one or two people showing up.

But Lisa was in charge of promoting this event. She arranged for a radio interview with Clare. Tracey gave the library a photo of Clare with Lyra, the sable hybrid wolf, nuzzling up to her face. The librarian had a poster made with it to advertise the event. Lisa had a supply of the posters and handed them out around town, introducing Clare everywhere they went, from the grocery and wine stores to the animal shelter.

Lisa had a party at her house an evening before the event. It was not a large party but influential people were there, all friends. Someone from the mayor's office, an administrator from the biggest oil company, a security guard foreman, Randy and his wife, the executive director of the animal shelter, an assistant to the member of Parliament.

Clare was amazed at the quick transformation of Lisa's back deck and yard, from a jumble of stacked outdoor furniture and dog toys into a neat sitting area around a large flagstone coffee table with a wood fire blazing in the centre of it. Clare helped Lisa get all that done within a couple of hours. Her mother, Annette, had spent much of two days preparing an array of appetizers set out attractively on the kitchen table. Beer and wine were available on the kitchen counter top. Lisa walked around with her bottle of beer, making sure everyone was comfortable and introduced to Clare. People kept their jackets on, moving at will from kitchen to the back deck. The relaxed party was over by ten o'clock when guests went home for next day's work. Spirit, who had greeted every guest, went into her dog house.

The Fort McMurray library was a spacious, well-equipped part of a massive new community centre. At the entrance was a brief history of Fort Mac written on the wall with some old photos of the times before oil was discovered. The community centre had sports facilities and meeting rooms as well as the library and offices. The very large parking lot outside had many vehicles, indicating the community centre was in good use that Thursday evening. Sports and gymnasiums are a bigger draw than book talks, so Clare was relieved to find her event had many more than three in attendance. Over ten times that. More thanks owed to Lisa, she thought.

The talk was held in what seemed to Clare a vast, modern, open-plan room. Not cozy. One wall was glass. The others were lined with shelves of books. In the central space, the librarian had arranged a lectern and a table displaying copies of *City Wolves* for sale. In front of these were some rows, not of the usual hard stacking chairs put in meeting rooms, but big, soft upholstered arm chairs.

Lisa introduced Clare with enthusiasm, but then Clare blanked out. She experienced sudden stage fright and a powerful memory of her grandmother that choked her voice. Tears welled up. Clare looked down at the lectern as she held onto each side of it. She looked up at the awaiting audience. "Bear with me," she said.

She swallowed and held her breath. The audience held their breath.

"I'm not the author," she managed to say. "The author could keep you from falling asleep in those big soft armchairs."

Someone laughed. Then others did.

"Seriously," Clare continued. "I'm just a wildlife photographer. And this photo I took of the wolf smiling was a fluke. Most of my best shots are."

The audience laughed or smiled.

"This book is about my grandmother who got called 'The Dog Doctor of Halifax.'"

Some laughter and smiles and eyebrows raised.

"Then she went to the Klondike gold rush. Which will remind you of Fort McMurray. Money to be made. And some pretty crazy characters."

Laughter and some clapping.

Clare just kept saying what came to mind. "What choked me up just now," she told them, "was the memory of my grandmother on her death bed."

No laughter.

"'I've had a wonderful life,' my grandmother Meg said, speaking to us from her death bed. 'I love you all.' Then her eyes closed and she seemed to sink into death. A couple of moments later, she opened her eyes quite wide and said 'What! Am I still alive? Cripes! And I made such a good speech.'"

The audience was laughing again.

"That's what my grandmother was like." Clare choked slightly. "I can't do her justice. She was great. A first woman veterinarian. I would like to be like her. My sister Julie who lives here in Alberta, is quite like her, a great veterinarian. But I'm just a mediocre photographer, who sometimes gets a good fluke shot. Like this one." She held up the book. There was some clapping and murmurs of disagreement with it being a fluke. "I'll tell you now a bit about what a fluke it was in marvellous surroundings. Up in our High Arctic. Then I'll read a little from this book by this author who really got the early life of my grandmother. Dead on. If you're all not dead asleep in those big soft armchairs."

Much encouraging laughter.

Most everyone bought a book. Some bought more than one. The animal shelter received a lot of proceeds from that night.

On Clare's final day in Fort Mac, Lisa took Clare to Randy's dog lot. Clare had seen dogs that looked like Randy's dog team when she and Len went to the Yukon. They weren't at all like Malamutes, the original sled dog teams of the Arctic, whose glory days were at the height of the Klondike gold rush, when a team would sell for the price of a fleet of luxury limousines today. Randy's dog team was short-haired, smaller, generally black and tan, slim, muscular dogs. Smart, fast runners.

But recently, one of Randy's older dogs had produced her last litter. In it were some sable and white pups that looked very much like Malamutes. "Not sure how that happened," said Randy. "Looks like she must have had a fling with Lisa's dog Spirit."

Lisa picked up the pup Randy had given to her. "I've named her Yukon Sally," Lisa said, cuddling her, "after your first Malamute."

As Clare's plane to Ottawa rose up into the sky over Fort McMurray, Clare looked down on the receding landscape of forest edging the city and oil fields. I'm so lucky, she thought. I'm not great like my grandmother. But I do have a wonderful life, with great kids and dogs and friends.

Chapter Twenty

Same Old and Worse

Clare landed back in Ottawa and returned to the usual scene at Loghaven. The dogs leaping up in eagerness, howling and vying for her attention. Len was sitting on the porch overlooking the lake, scotch in hand. He did not get up to greet her. "Come sit here and watch the sunset," he said. "Get yourself a drink. Is Fort McMurray and those oil sands as bad as they say?"

"Just let me unpack," Clare said. "Everything is crushed in my carry-on." She didn't want to sit with him and answer a question she found not just prejudiced and unfair but belligerent. Same old 'drunk and belligerent'. When she had unpacked and saw Len through the window as she got herself a glass of wine, it struck her how old he was, eighty-two. Not bad looking, with thick white hair and sunglasses. But he looked thin and somewhat shrunken. Diminished. She herself would be seventy in a very few weeks.

She had given Len a party at a restaurant for his eightieth. Megan, Ali, even Julie had flown in for it. Clare had managed to locate Len's niece Tanya, who lived in Toronto, and gave her train fare to attend the party. Tanya seemed a sad case to Clare. She was fourteen years old when her father, Len's brother Stefan, committed suicide. His business ventures had gone wrong, he was losing his eyesight from glaucoma, he was estranged from his wife. He shot himself in the head with his hunting rifle. Tanya had found him dead in the garage.

Clare had flown to Winnipeg with Len to attend the funeral. "Poor bugger. He always tried too hard to be a big-shot businessman," was all Len was willing to say about Stefan's death. Len swept his own feelings under the carpet. "Your dad was a good man," he said to Tanya after the funeral. "He taught me how to ride a bike." When Tanya nodded her head and looked tearful, Len turned away in embarrassment and moved to talk with others.

"I'm sorry, Tanya," Clare gave her a hug. "You have our very deep sympathy."

"Thank you," said Tanya with a thoughtful look, then turned away. She was Stefan's only child and Len's only niece. Tanya quarrelled with her mother, quit school as soon as she was sixteen and floundered with petty jobs, then moved to Toronto. She had had a bad marriage, no children, and now worked as a cashier in a pharmacy. She did not keep in much contact with Len but phoned him a couple of times a year, telling him about relatives in Winnipeg with whom he had lost touch. He was polite with Tanya on the phone but thought altogether she was "a loser, not very bright." But she was his "blood relative" and he wasn't going to hang up on her.

Lots of speeches were made for Len at his eightieth birthday party. Clare found Tanya's strangely unreal. It was about what a generous uncle Len was, keeping in close touch with her as his favourite niece over the years. Clare chalked it up to wishful thinking. Tanya did not stay the night after Len's party. She took a late train back to Toronto because she had to work the next day.

What bothered Clare about Len's eightieth birthday party was that Len made no response, other than a nod of thanks, to all the nice speeches made about him.

"Why not?" she asked him. "You could at least have thanked them for coming. That would have been minimal."

"It's stupid to thank people for coming to a party," he said angrily. "They're the beneficiaries."

"Ali and Megan came across the country. You might have mentioned that."

"Get off my back! I just couldn't think of what to say and then everyone started talking amongst themselves."

"I would have called their attention to you, if you stood up to speak."

"Oh for chrissake! It takes me too long to get up out of a chair these days."

To keep up appearances and give more guests room, Clare had slept with Len that night, but they slept far apart on the bed. Len passed out and Clare lay awake in anger and loneliness.

Dr. Lisi called Clare to his office. It was over a year since her cancer was surgically removed. She had six-month checkups and there had been no recurrence. Dr Lisi said he wanted to test to see if she had a cancer gene. Having tests for cancer genes was currently in the news. A famous movie star had breast removal after her mother died of breast cancer and she, the movie star, was found to have that cancer gene. Clare thought that at age seventy she didn't really want to know if she had a cancer gene. She'd soon enough die of something or other. She would face what she had to, when it came. But she trusted Dr. Lisi's advice that preventative measures could be taken if she had the gene and if she did, her daughters should also be tested. It was her daughters Clare worried most about. She agreed to the test.

Two weeks later Dr. Lisi called her in for the results. "I'm not the genetics expert," he began. "This information will be sent to him for assessment and you will have a meeting with him to confirm the results and possible treatments. I have to tell you now, a particular cancer gene has been found…"

The rest of what he said blurred in Clare's mind. The name of the gene sounded something like Brax. Some kind of abdominal or brain tumour might come of it. Clare drove home in a daze with moments of panic. It felt more overwhelming than being told she had a tumour on her colon. There was something that could be done about that. It was done quickly and successfully through surgery. Nothing could be done about a killer gene that lurked in uncertain places.

Clare walked in the front door. Her dogs sensed she was in fear and dread. They did not leap up in greeting. They stood watchfully. Len got up from his armchair. "How did it go?" He could tell it had not gone well.

"I have a cancer gene." Clare put her jacket on the hook and faced Len.

"Oh for Chrissake!" He got angry. "What the hell does that mean?"

"I don't know. I'll probably die of cancer. Down the road." She sat in the middle of the couch.

Len turned his back and went to the cupboard for scotch. The dogs got up on either side of Clare. She put her hand on each of them. Tears dribbled down her cheeks. Len came in with his scotch and sat down in his armchair. "I don't know what the hell to say." He took a big swallow. "Or do."

I know what you'll do, thought Clare. Just what you're doing. Sit in your chair hugging your scotch. The most you do is get angry. You won't look after me. Can't even give me a word of comfort or sympathy. She got up for some tissues to wipe her cheeks and blow her nose. She wanted to get away from Len. Permanently!

She put on her jacket and went to sit on the bench overlooking the lake. It was the first week of October. Darkness was increasing all around her. The dogs lay down near her, also looking out at the lake. She needed to talk to someone. She phoned Lizzie.

"You have to look upon this as a good thing, an advantage," Lizzie told Clare. "Since they found you have that gene, you'll be tested regularly. You'll be put in the front of the line, so to speak."

Lizzie had had lymphatic cancer some years ago. She was expected to die, then ultimately, stem cell treatment pulled her through. Lizzie had always been a positive-thinking person with a delightful sense of humour. It was what everyone loved about her. Having come through a perilous cancer, Lizzie became all the more positive about life. "Negative thinking and negative people can drain your energy," she said to Clare. "Steer clear of them."

Clare, by nature, agreed with Lizzie. Complainers irritated and bored her. But how to steer clear of Len? She concentrated on minimizing fear her daughters might have about her having a cancer gene and them inheriting it. She decided to wait until she had a meeting with the geneticist to give them any further information.

Clare's seventieth birthday was October 28. Not a good time of year on the lake at Loghaven. Rainy and cold. Most of the colourful leaves would have fallen from the trees. Len had their membership in the golf and country club cancelled during the financial crisis of 2008. He told Clare he'd foot the bill if she wanted to have a dinner party at a restaurant in Ottawa. All she had to do was organize it.

Clare kept it small. Family and special friends. Ali and Ari flew in for the weekend from Vancouver. Megan from St. John's. Nate stayed home tending the kids. Julie and Al flew in from Scrag Creek. Lizzie and her husband Jeff, Michelle Valberg and her handsome husband, and Tory and Hettie Sanderson plus a few other Ottawa couples attended. Len did not.

Clare, along with her daughters, had gone into Ottawa for the party early, to tend to last minute details. Len was to arrive in time to greet the guests alongside Clare. He phoned Clare, just minutes before the arrival of the guests, to tell Clare he wasn't coming.

"You're kidding!" She took her phone aside.

"No," he said. "You'll have a better time without me."

"Len, do not do this to me." Clare tried to keep her voice steady and low. "We're all here waiting for you."

"Well, don't!" He started shouting

Ali and Ari came over to Clare.

"I can't *drive*, for chrissake!" Len shouted and hung up.

Megan joined them as Clare turned off her phone. "Len's too drunk to drive," she said in a low exasperated voice.

"Do you want me to go and get him?" Ari offered.

"No," said Clare as Ali put her arm around her. "Thank you."

"We should have seen this coming," said Megan. "Chin up, Mom. Forget about him. We're here for a good time and that's what we'll have. Come on. I'll help greet the guests."

"Me too," said Ali. "Just say Len is indisposed and leave it at that. His drinking problem is no secret."

Everyone made a good time of it. There were witty and heartfelt speeches.

"I get to start them off," Clare announced when everyone was settled in their chairs with their drinks. "The speeches. It's my party." People laughed gently. Some clapped, leading to full applause with a couple of whistles. They had been having drinks and appetizers for a sufficient time. "Now, doesn't *this* feel better than a funeral!" Clare responded.

"You won't get to speak at yours!" a friend chipped in.

"That's right," Clare replied. "So I'm going to take the opportunity here to say, having hit seventy, I'm nothing but grateful. Absolutely no laments. I've had a wonderful ride. And if there's more, I'm up for it. Old people get asked for their secrets to a good life. Sometimes." Clare paused to let people mumble about old people being disregarded or ignored. Though several looked towards Tory Sanderson, the oldest man in the room. He smiled and waved at them.

"I have to set an example here for brevity and to the point. So, I'll say, greetings and welcome from my husband Len, who is temporarily under the weather. But he's the sponsor of this event and we're grateful for that." Clare clapped and everyone followed her cue. "No one has yet asked me, but I am going to tell you the major ingredients of a good life… Friends. Friends, wonderful friends. Thank you all for being here. And thanks to all who can't be. Another ingredient … is animals, pets. In my case, dogs. I couldn't live without my dogs, let alone have a good life. And work. Work that you enjoy and think has some value to society. And for me, the main ingredient, is my kids and grandkids. My kids, Ali and Megan, make my life great. That doesn't work for everyone. I'm just lucky to have such kids. Also I have an understanding, supportive sibling. Dr. Judith Wilkinson-O'Mara. Not many have that. But I have that good fortune." Clare raised her glass. "Here's to a fortunate life. For you all."

Glasses were raised and clinked. Cheers sounded.

After the guests departed, Clare and family gathered in the lounge of the Lord Elgin Hotel where they had arranged to spend the night before departure next day at the airport.

"Good party, Mom," said Megan. "But why the funeral speech?"

Clare had no quick answer.

"It was just a reference," said Ali. "But you shouldn't think of seventy as old age, Mom. These days it's just later middle age. Lots of people live to be one hundred."

"You had to ad lib, didn't you," Julie said to Clare. "You had to change your opening remarks because Len had pulled a no show. That was unforgivable. What's with that guy!"

"He's become unpredictable," remarked Ari. "He really needs professional help."

"He's not open to it," said Clare.

"That's another sign of how much he needs it," said Ali, concurring with her husband.

"Unpredictable means not safe for you, Mom," said Megan firmly. "I speak from case histories. We glossed over his behaviour tonight. But it was a way of hurting you and it can get worse, what he does to hurt you.... We expect it will."

Clare felt sick inside. "Is this why I don't see my grandchildren at Loghaven any more?"

Ali and Megan were uncomfortably, sadly silent.

"It embarrasses and hurts the whole family," said Julie. "Getting too drunk to make it to your big seventieth ... I can't stand him doing that to you. What next? I would call his no show the last straw. I would *make* it the last straw."

Clare recalled nearly forty years ago when she and Len smiled wryly over thinking of the number of last straws there might be in a marriage.

Julie's husband Al stepped in. "It's late at night after a happy celebration," he said. "Let's have this discussion another time."

Julie got up and gave Clare a hug. "I'm sorry, Clarey. That was me stirring things up. I don't want to spoil your birthday."

Clare wouldn't let herself break down. She held onto Julie's hand, squeezed it and let go. "Don't worry about me," she said to everyone. "I'm figuring things out. Bear with me. I won't let things go on as they are."

*****

In November Clare went for her six-month cancer checkup. During the course of questions, Clare told the nurse she had a cancer gene. The nurse looked up from her clipboard very surprised. "What makes you think that?"

"They tested my colon, the part that was surgically removed and found it."

"Have you spoken with the geneticist?"

"Not yet."

The nurse excused herself and returned to say. "Someone will phone you tomorrow."

Next day Clare answered her phone to a kindly voice who asked her questions about any cancer history in her family. All Clare knew of was her father dying of leukemia at age fifty and her mother's older sister was said to have died of breast cancer. But there was no one still living in the family who could verify that. She said proudly her grandmother on her father's side had lived to be ninety-eight.

"That history does not seem to add up to a family cancer gene," said the kindly woman. "But you'll soon hear from the geneticist about a meeting in which he will clarify things for you."

Clare received a letter arranging for a meeting at the hospital in early January.

It was a snowless Christmas at Loghaven with the dogs and Len. On Christmas Eve, Clare made a dinner of tortière and salad. Len came to the table too inebriated to eat more than a couple of bites. He was agitated. "You don't act like someone with cancer," he began. "You're not at all like Karen. She was obviously sick."

"I don't have cancer. I might have a cancer gene. That's all."

"Karen suffered." Len drank some wine. "For months and months."

"I know. I mean I heard about that from my mom. You never talk about it. It must have been awful for you to see."

"You got that right!" Len's eyes welled up. "I couldn't take any more of it. I smothered her. With a pillow. She asked me to. She was trying to do it to herself. I just helped her."

"Len. Stop it. She died of cancer."

"She was dying alright. She'd been given a big dose of morphine that afternoon. I helped her end it."

"Len, are you hallucinating?"

"No. I'm just drunk as a skunk and telling you what I've never been able to tell anyone. No one ever asked me. I was never questioned. I called 911. Said my wife died. She had cancer. The ambulance arrived. The paramedics saw she was dead. They did their job. The doctors and nurses, the palliative team knew she was dying. Nobody ever questioned me. Ever."

"That's because there was no point in questioning you. Even if what you say is true, it was still cancer she died of."

Len poured more wine and gulped it. He got hiccups. Between them he managed to say, "You forgive me, don't you. You forgive too damn much. I coulda been thrown in jail."

"Oh for God's sake, Len. You need to forgive yourself."

He burped and began to stand up. "I'm toast," he said and staggered up to bed.

Clare looked in on him and saw he had managed to discard his shoes and pants and get into bed wearing his sweater and shirt. She went back downstairs to sit by the fire with the dogs and listen to Pavarotti singing "O Holy Night."

Indeed! Clare said to herself as she let the dogs out to sleep in their house in the cold. O Holy Night.

Chapter Twenty-One

The Wake-Up Call

Clare woke around three in the morning on Christmas Day. Not unusual for her to have 'wake and worry hours'. But that night she was feeling unwell. Len's confession had upset her but not all that much. She really felt it was understandable to help your wife end her suffering when she was near death anyway, especially if she pleaded for your help. Len's memory was getting more and more unreliable and confused—from alcohol killing his brain cells, she was sure. She didn't think he had a mental illness like Alzheimer's. He could be confused in his memory of his wife's death. But it didn't matter. She didn't think he had done anything that should be considered criminal. What worried her was that he let the memory fester for decades in his mind. She wondered that he had never told his counsellor, Dr. Bodker, about it. He could have helped Len come to better terms with it.

What bothered Clare was her own situation. Len had driven her grandchildren away and made Loghaven a place her daughters were reluctant to come to. She herself had become hesitant to entertain friends at Loghaven because Len made people feel uneasy with his 'out of it' condition. Though he was not unfriendly or belligerent with them. To become isolated from family and friends and confined to Len's daily demeaning and belligerent comments was not tolerable.

Something on her back and side was bothering her. An itchy ache. She got up and looked at it in the mirror. A rash was developing. Shingles! Bloody hell! she thought. It's Christmas Day. She wouldn't be able to get to a doctor for days. There was some medication which helped relieve it, if taken within the first day or two, maybe three?

She would get herself to Emergency right after Boxing Day.

It turned out she did not have a very severe case of shingles. It dissipated a few days before her appointment with the geneticist. But it made her tally things up. She took it as her final wake-up call. She couldn't go on living with Len. After colon cancer, the cardiologist diagnosed her as having atrial fibrillation. A common enough heart condition in older people. But it was exacerbated by stress. And shingles ... that was definitely connected to stress.

She concluded that living with Len was not just curtailing but shortening her life. Whereas he could go on drinking for years and years and have no serious illness. Maybe, as he said, scotch was his preservative. He amazed his doctor. He had come home from a checkup with his doctor and reported, "Of course she tells me I drink too much. But after seeing my test results and examining me, she said, 'You have an *amazing* constitution.'"

"You do," said Clare. "You really do."

On New Year's Eve, Clare also drank too much. They were sitting by the fire, listening to music, not having anything to say to each other, until Len remarked, "You don't have to worry about that cancer gene."

"Really? Why not?"

"Only the weak die of cancer and you're not weak."

"Jazuz, Len! You can't be serious. Only the weak die of cancer? Tell that to Steve Jobs, Jack Layton, Ted Kennedy, Pierre Trudeau..."

"They were all old."

"Steve Jobs was in his fifties." Clare stood up. "This is too stupid. Completely crazy. I'm going to bed." She finished her drink and went upstairs to her bedroom.

Len stayed slumped in his chair. "Happy New Year," he called weakly after her.

Clare's New Year's resolution was to make an appointment with a family lawyer after she met with the geneticist.

The geneticist had come from the hospital associated with Queen's

University in Kingston. "I have studied your case," he said, looking at papers assembled on the desk and then directly at Clare. "The good news, to put it colloquially, is that, all in all, you do not have an effective cancer gene."

Clare exhaled months of repressed anxiety. She smiled and made a gesture of removing and shaking off sweat from her brow. He smiled.

"You have a combination of genes that does have a potentially cancerous one but it is, shall we say, trumped by a stronger gene which you have." He named the gene. But Clare was so focused on the good news she couldn't memorize it. She left the meeting with a letter that explained it all and a huge feeling of ... once again I've been given another chance to live. I must make the most of it.

She phoned the good news to her daughters.

"So that's what's been bothering you these past few months," said Ali. "I knew there was something."

With Megan she added the news that she wanted to obtain a legal separation from Len and would she, Megan, ask around about a good family law lawyer in Ottawa.

"Of course," said Megan. "But why just a separation?"

"I'm worried about income. I'm afraid being divorced would decrease my rights."

"I can't tell you about that. As you know, I don't do divorce or family law and never want to. But I'll find out who are the best in Ottawa."

"I'll tell Ali about this when I've settled on a good one. And don't worry. I won't involve you kids at all. I'm sorry to have you see me divorce again."

"What we're worried about, Mom, is your safety. Len is unstable. Your lawyer will warn you about the dangers in your situation. Don't discuss this with Len. And don't be anywhere near him around the time he is served papers."

Clare had naturally kept abreast of newspaper stories and magazine articles on domestic violence ever since Len had got violent with her. It was now fifteen years since that second episode when he slugged her in the bathroom. She felt she had learned how to keep the violence at bay, though the psychological and verbal abuse had increased. There was a recent case in Toronto of a neurologist and his wife, a general practitioner, who were touted on social media as an ideal couple with three young children. Then the wife suddenly disappeared and was found a couple of days later, her body cut up in pieces put in a suitcase which was found in a ditch in the countryside where Clare had once lived, just north of Toronto. The husband pleaded not guilty.

He was convicted. The story that then came out in *Toronto Life* magazine told of their marriage gone bad, with the husband being privately abusive and his temper out of control. The wife eventually fell for someone else and sought a divorce. The night after learning that divorce proceedings had begun, the neurologist strangled his wife and cut up her body, putting it in a suitcase he drove north of the city and dumped in a ditch. He showed up at the hospital to perform operations next day and the next, until he was charged with her murder.

In reading the magazine article, Clare found traits in the neurologist that reminded her of Len, particularly the uncontrolled anger. This true story shocked and disturbed many people because it involved what seemed to be a well-matched professional couple with children and a good lifestyle and the husband very much admired for his neurological work. Family law lawyers knew that intimate partner violence was not confined to non-professionals or people on low incomes. But that had been the common perception. Some non-fiction books on highly abusive relationships came out in the years after the tragic story of the general practitioner and her neurologist husband.

Another magazine article and nonfiction book that interested Clare was on the new phenomenon of 'gray divorce'. This was about the growing number of couples deciding to divorce as they broached old age. They were in a marriage that had become abusive or very unhappy and they did not want to spend the rest of their life in that relationship. It used to be that unhappy couples would just endure and wait 'until death did them part'. Men more likely would divorce in older age and take up with someone else, usually younger, because they had the financial means to do so. But many women now had earned the financial means to live independently and chose to do so. Also, divorce laws had developed such that marriage was regarded as a 50/50 partnership, no matter who earned how much. Though prenuptial agreements and other exceptions, plus the ability to hide assets, could undermine the equal partnership concept. One needed to have a very good lawyer.

Out of courtesy and appreciation of his previous legal work for her, Clare asked Mr. Cane for his recommendation of a family law lawyer. He immediately recommended Hannah Judson. She turned out to be the same person Megan came up with. "She's very expensive, Mom. The best are. She knows the law inside out. She's known for her integrity, efficiency, and strategizing. She's said to be majestic in court."

"Sounds like a wolf."

"People up against her have called her the Rottweiler."

"I don't want a Rottweiler attacking Len."

"Mom, she's good. She'll get you the best deal and save you money because she won't let things drag on. Colleagues close to her say she's tough but full of heart."

"How did you get all this info?"

"I have connections, Mom." Megan paused. "Actually, Hannah taught at Dalhousie years ago. I took her course but decided not to practice family law. She might remember me. Probably not. It's a long time ago. She set up her practice in Ottawa because her mother is there, she grew up there."

Mr. Cane referred Clare to Hannah Judson and quite soon Clare was given an appointment. The first half hour was free, to see if Hannah thought the case appropriate for her to take on.

Hannah's office was stunning. Downtown, top floor, large, several rooms, polished slate floor, an interesting display of original contemporary art works on the white walls, including photography. In the waiting room, Clare saw a smaller work of art by the doorway which made her laugh. It was designed to resemble an 8½-by-11 inch notebook page. At the bottom of it was an arrow pointing to the doorway. Above that was printed

SHE'S IN THERE WITH STUPID

Good sense of humour, Clare concluded.

An assistant led Clare into Hannah's office. Hannah stood up to come round her desk and shake Clare's hand. Hannah looked formidable. She was a strikingly handsome woman with shoulder-length thick white hair, pulled back becomingly, and large black-rimmed glasses. She wore a black dress with an artisan necklace. She did not smile but looked discerningly at Clare. She offered Clare a leather chair and went to her own chair behind her desk.

"You resemble the mother of a student of mine at Dalhousie years ago, Megan Stanton."

"Yes," said Clare. "Megan is my daughter. She recommended you to me. She didn't think you would remember her."

"I keep track of my outstanding students. Megan has become a highly respected litigator. At a young age." Hannah smiled fleetingly.

"That's very good to hear, from you." Clare smiled. She couldn't pin down Hannah's age. She had a beautiful, unwrinkled face. Piercing eyes. Clare felt she was in the presence of a power house.

"Tell me why you want a legal separation." Hannah got down to business.

As the half hour neared its end, Hannah said she would take the case on. Then she wanted to talk about Clare's safety. "Your husband has a history of violence," she began.

"But that was fifteen years ago."

"He drinks excessively on a daily basis," Hannah continued, ignoring the interruption, "and has anger management issues. You have concluded you are not the cause of his anger but you have become the target of it. He is at times abusive and belligerent with you. Is there somewhere you can stay until the case is resolved?"

"No," said Clare firmly. "We have two dogs. Malamutes. I can't leave them alone at Loghaven with Len, except for short periods, like when I visit my daughters. They live on either coast."

"Would he harm the dogs?"

"No. He likes them."

"There have been cases of a partner harming a pet in order to hurt the other partner."

Clare thought about it. "Len would never do that," she said. "He does get drunk and oblivious. Might forget to feed them. But the dogs would pester and howl to remind him. He just doesn't pay close attention to them. It's always been me who sees when they're ill. I had to lay to rest our two previous Malamutes when they got cancer."

"You say you have learned to steer clear or walk away when he insults or antagonizes, but what if that changed? What would or what could you do?"

"I would flee to my friend in Ottawa, Lizzie's house."

"What if you were not in condition to drive?"

That's right, thought Clare. These things usually happen at night. Dinner and drinking. "I'd phone the police," Clare answered. "But I get what you're driving at. I need to think about this some more and make arrangements."

After leaving Hannah's office, Clare stopped in at Lizzie's.

Lizzie hugged her. "I'm proud of you," she said. "It takes guts to divorce at our age."

"I just hope I don't end up poor and alone in old age," said Clare.

"Don't worry about that. You've been married for thirty-five years. You've been that guy's *servant* for thirty-five years."

"Laundress." Clare half smiled. "He's been the 'sole provider' and I the 'laundress.'"

"Yeah, well … let him tell that to the judge. The law won't let you be destitute. And you can always shack up with someone. Meanwhile, I'm giving you my house key, so if you need to flee, you can flee here, whether I'm home or not."

"Thanks pal." She hugged Lizzie. "But you know what else I'm trying to do? I'm standing up for women not having to flee from their homes. It's the abuser who should have to leave. Women and children having to flee to shelters … that's wrong and traumatic. Also expensive, to house and feed children with their mothers. It's the abusers who should be taken to shelters, given counselling, and hopefully turn themselves around."

Lizzie perked her head at Clare. "Have you told that to your lawyer?"

"Not yet."

"Good luck with that." Lizzie went to the fridge. "Let's drink to it."

Clare drove home, making plans.

She would not tell Len she had obtained a lawyer until the papers were drawn up and ready to be served. She would bring an old friend and colleague of Len into her confidence. Warren Leduc, with whom Len used to play golf. Papers would be served immediately after Easter Monday. Warren agreed to call Len before that and set up lunch for the following week. Clare would spend two weeks visiting Ali and family in Vancouver over Easter. Ali had a guest room and household help. Blossoms and flowers would be blooming in Vancouver. St. John's would be cold with chilling winds blowing off the Atlantic.

Clare also talked with their parish minister. Len had served on the parish council for years as treasurer. He had helped solicit, and had himself donated, sufficient funds to build a new parish hall. But he withdrew from parish council some years ago when he no longer went out to evening meetings. He continued to attend Sunday morning services with Clare. They now had a new parish minister who listened sympathetically to Clare and said he would offer to visit Len when Clare was away in Vancouver.

Their neighbours, Mitch and his wife Cora, who had bought the Sandersons' cottage, were not in the least surprised when Clare informed them of her basic plan. Mitch had seen Len with scotch in hand early afternoon, many a time, and had turned down offers from Len to join him.

"We won't be here ourselves, over Easter," said Mitch. "Cross country skiing is pretty well over now and Easter is a lot of mud. We probably won't be back until late April. But you have our key. When you get back, you can use it for your own emergency, not just ours."

"Mitch is trying to say"—Cora touched Clare's arm gently—"our cottage can be a refuge if you need one. We have heard Len's yelling at you."

Len's niece, Tanya, happened to call one evening in early March. Before telling Len to pick up the phone, Clare casually informed Tanya that she was going to Vancouver for Easter and Len might appreciate a phone call during that time, even a visit.

Lizzie readily agreed to fetch Clare and take her to the airport and to drive her home on return so that Clare would be accompanied when she returned to Loghaven the week after Len had received the notice of filing for legal separation.

On the day of departure, Clare put her luggage in Lizzie's car then went back into the house where Len was finishing his breakfast.

"Len, I have something serious to tell you."

Len looked at her, then dipped the last of his toast into his coffee and ate it. Then he looked at her again. "Go ahead."

"You won't like this. But it should come as no surprise. You have driven our grandchildren from our home and our daughters are reluctant to visit. I can't live without my children and grandchildren being able to visit. The stress of living with you and the way you treat me has made me ill."

"What bullshit!" Len yelled and banged his fists on the table.

"Len, calm down. You have to listen to this."

He listened.

"I've done everything I can think of to help you, but you turned to scotch in retirement. You've become an abusive, frightening alcoholic. I've obtained a lawyer and you will be served with papers. I'm seeking a legal separation. I'm sorry it's come to this."

"Nice speech," he said, pushing back his breakfast dishes and folding his arms onto the table. It reminded Clare of him sitting at his desk in his office. He was maintaining control. "Well planned. With Lizzie waiting in the car."

The Malamutes scratched at the door. Clare let them into the kitchen. She patted each of them. "I'm going now," she said to them. "I'll be back. Be good dogs."

She went into the front hall and opened the door.

"If you think you can get me kicked out of my own house," Len called after her, "you're dead wrong."

As Clare got into the car with Lizzie, they could hear Len call out from the front door, "Have a nice time in Vancouver."

"Did it go *that* well?" asked Lizzie, incredulously.

"I think that was for you to hear," said Clare, feeling sick inside. "And sarcasm aimed at me."

CHAPTER TWENTY-TWO

Reflections When Fleeing to Vancouver

Both Clare and Len read the national newspaper, the *Globe*, every day. Len drove to the local general store every morning to get it. He also subscribed to a weekly national and international news magazine. They had been following the news of the fall in oil prices, which began shortly after Clare's visit to Fort McMurray. She did not establish or maintain correspondence with Lisa beyond thank-you notes because Lisa did not have time for social emails. She posted on Facebook or used the telephone. Clare had a Facebook page and website for her photography, but Clare fell off using Facebook because she didn't find it informative for what she was interested in and she never became sufficiently familiar with its technology. Also her illnesses and private-life turmoil became too consuming.

She did keep up friendship with the Sandersons and had had an enlightening discussion with Tory after she returned from Fort McMurray. Oil prices were dropping fast. Oil companies were having to cut costs and postpone or cancel expansion. Next, employees would be let go. Clare wondered how David Bouchier's company was doing.

The issue of creating more pipelines to transport the oil to the United States and to Europe became hotly debated. Extreme environmentalists opposed oil being taken out of the ground, let alone being transported across the country. Some Indigenous communities opposed pipelines on their hunting and fishing lands. Other Indigenous communities welcomed the economic benefits and used them to improve their facilities and standard of living. And of course there were disagreements within the communities.

As a geophysicist who had worked internationally locating mineral deposits and establishing mines in developing countries, as well as in Canada, Tory took interest in what was happening with the oil mining industry around Fort McMurray.

"Do you think they have a future?" Clare asked Tory. "The oil companies around Fort Mac?

Tory smiled at her earnestness. She had obviously come back with a strong liking for the people of Fort McMurray. "Oil is too valuable to be left in the ground," he assured her. "They will have to develop cleaner methods of extracting it and processing it to make it liquid enough to transport to refineries. But they are doing that already and they will do more of it. Most people who oppose the oil industry just don't realize its many uses. Right now less than fifty percent of oil is turned into gasoline. If and when electric cars replace gas-fueled ones, that percentage will drop drastically. But oil is used for many other valuable things."

"Such as?" Clare enjoyed discussions with Tory. He made her think harder and she learned so much. He was good at clarifying complex issues. "Plastics. I know oil is used in plastics. But what else?"

"Pharmaceuticals, building products, clothing, roads, and components of vehicles." Tory saw her trying to imagine those things. "Am I being too general?"

"Yes. Pharmaceuticals covers a lot."

He took out his cell phone. "I'm going to Google this for you," he said.

Clare observed him. She never Googled for information. She didn't actually know how to. She had thought it offered unreliable information which led to trouble. Like looking up illnesses and making a wrong self-diagnosis.

Tory had retired from being a consultant just a few years ago. Clare knew he had worked far beyond the normal retirement age of sixty-five. He was now in his late eighties. He had written his memoirs and was now working on a short mystery novel. What a remarkable man, she thought. And a nice one, it seemed.

"Here are some interesting specifics," Tory looked up from his cell phone. "Heart valves, anesthetics, artificial limbs, Aspirin, deodorant, vitamin capsules. And car battery cases, not to mention car seats, tires, and paint. They'll need the oil industry for those electric cars." He smiled at Clare.

"You're awfully good with that cell phone," Clare remarked.

"An old engineer has to learn how to use new gadgets." Tony smiled.

Flying over Alberta, on her way to visit Ali at Easter, Clare wondered how long the downturn in oil prices would last. But worse news was soon to come to Fort McMurray.

When she returned from Vancouver, Lizzie met Clare at the airport and accompanied her into Loghaven. It was early evening and they had brought mild Indian take-out curries for dinner. Lizzie was going to stay the night on the pretext that she wanted wine with dinner and didn't want to drive home afterwards.

Len had not had as much as usual to drink. He was tense but surprisingly benign.

"It was good seeing Warren again," he said. "We had three good lunches together. He still plays golf and has found a nice woman he sees a lot of since his wife died. I'd go golfing with him, if I could get myself walking again."

"You could start by walking around the property here. Increase your distance gradually."

"To hell with that. I hung up my hiking boots along with my tennis racket. As long as I can walk to the Jeep and around the booze store, I'm OK."

Clare and Lizzie looked at each other. Lizzie shrugged gently and raised her eyebrows. Clare shook her head and smiled wryly.

"I thought that would get a rise out of you." Len swallowed some scotch and looked satisfied. "And as for those papers your dickhead lawyer served me, they'll get you nowhere. No judge is going to kick me out of my own house. Worst case scenario is the house gets sold and the proceeds are split between us. Neither of us wants that. Of course I could buy you out. You don't have the means to buy me out."

"Len…" Clare started to speak.

"That's all I have to say tonight." Len got up out of his chair. Finished off his drink and started slowly upstairs to bed. "Good night, ladies."

Next day, after Lizzie had returned to Ottawa, Len told Clare that his niece, Tanya, had come with her boyfriend at Easter and stayed two nights.

"Really!" Clare was surprised. "What did you do with them all that time?"

"Nothing. They just wandered around looking at stuff, making a lot of compliments about everything. They went into town and got steaks and chicken. The guy likes to barbecue. Tanya took over the kitchen."

"What's he like, the guy?"

"Typical middle-aged pothead. Long hair, balding, the works. Of course Tanya's not much of a catch either."

"What did you talk about?"

"You know how Tanya runs off at the mouth. She had a lot to say about you. She thinks you're the wicked witch of the west."

"You told her about us? The legal proceedings?"

"She pried it out of me. She's good at that. 'Course we'd all had a few drinks."

Clare pictured the scene. Tanya sympathizing and siding with her 'favourite uncle'.

It did not surprise Clare that Tanya began phoning Len two or three times a week. Sometimes Len cut her short or said he was busy. Other times, he was in need of being supported and told that Clare had no right to the property, hadn't a leg to stand on legally, she was just out to rob him. The property belonged in the Rekai family.

Len obtained a lawyer who cost little and did little. His main tactic was obstructing proceedings.

It was legally established that they were living separately within the same household at the beginning of April 2015. Len and Clare both avoided discussing their legal situation and what their lawyers were doing. They ate dinner together with Clare doing the shopping, cooking, and clearing up as she had always done, except for the years long ago when Ali and Megan were at home and old enough to do the clearing up. Dinner conversation continued much as it had since Len retired, worsening over time. Now there was the added taboo on discussing their legal situation. Clare felt that often Len came to the table resolved to talk about pleasantries, which were to him television tennis and the movement of the stock market. But soon something would overcome him and he would say something insulting to Clare. She would remain silent and he would harp on it. It ended with Clare having to leave the table. Same old.

Clare took safety precautions. She kept her cell phone with her and a lock on her bedroom door, though she knew Len could use the house key to open it. She had a baseball bat under the bed. When she discovered Len had been moving papers around on her desk, she got a separate lock for her office door and kept the key on her key chain with her purse in her office. Their computer help person let Clare know Len had asked for her password one day when Clare was not home. Len told the computer helper that Clare had wanted him to look something up in her computer for her. The computer helper simply said she could not give passwords to anyone at any time, and then informed Clare of Len's request.

Clare confronted Len about this.

"Oh for chrissakes!" Len dismissed it. "That was just some stupid suggestion of Tanya's. I should have known better. Let's just say our computer help passed the test. She didn't give out the password."

Clare realized Tanya was having a stronger influence on Len than she expected. Clare continued taking precautions but she did not think Len was in a frame of mind to hurt her physically. Still, she knew that could change. He could unexpectedly 'snap', as he did when he got violent years ago.

Legal proceedings moved slowly in that spring of 2015, as Len's lawyer stalled and resisted. Len adopted an attitude of not taking things seriously. His lawyer informed Hannah that this was a case where the wife really just wanted independence of income and the husband was willing to give that. Clare was left wondering if Len had convinced his lawyer of that or if the lawyer was just trying it on. Hannah reiterated that this was a case seeking full legal separation of residence and income.

In late May, Clare went to Kingston to attend a reunion at Queen's University of the *Queen's Journal* staff. Darcy McGee, who had been the *Journal* editor when she did some photography for the *Journal*, was also there. She remembered him as a multitalented, good humoured guy who was taking Commerce. He would graduate a year ahead of her. They dated in the autumn of Clare's third year. Clare's father had died at the end of her second year. Darcy gave Clare his Commerce pin. He was her first lover. As Christmas holidays approached, he asked her to marry him. She said yes. But then a panic began to grow within her. She wasn't ready for marriage. She didn't want to be one of those couples married as undergraduates. It was the thought of washing a man's dirty socks that kept coming into her mind and making her want to flee in panic. She laughed at the triviality of that, but the panic remained strong. After just five days of this, Clare told Darcy she didn't want to marry. He should find someone else.

He didn't accept her change of mind. He sent letters of appeal to her at home. He sought psychological counselling. He was dignified and did not plead. Eventually he wrote her a letter explaining that he understood from counselling that the relationship needed time to develop or fade of its own accord. If she changed her mind or wanted to see him again, she could let him know.

"What a decent guy!" said Lizzie, who roomed with her at the time, in an apartment with other girls. Clare fully agreed but she knew she wasn't ready for marriage and she never wanted to dally with a guy's feelings. Keeping anyone on a string seemed cruel to her.

She avoided Darcy in the *Journal* office and lost contact with him after that third year at Queen's.

Her grief for her father left her questioning purpose and meaning in life more intently. She found that the philosophy course in existentialism appealed to her deeply. Disillusion, 'God is dead', life is meaningless, one has to create one's own purpose in life and be responsible for one's moral behaviour … were all concepts that made profound sense to her. And in that course on existentialism she became intrigued with the top student, Stan Stanton. He was not smart-looking in any preppy sense. But they were well into the sixties. Preppy was out. Stan slopped around in sandals, a plaid shirt, anything but a Queen's jacket. He had been the Queen's scholar at St. Andrew's the previous year. He seemed enamoured of the culture at St. Andrew's and kept his St. Andrew's red robe in his room at Queen's.

He laughed at the work of some existentialist philosophers such as Heidegger, but he respected Jean Paul Sartre. Stan talked about the British linguistic analysts and Wittgenstein. Clare couldn't agree with his approval of the English class system and claiming the working class were happy in their lower-class position.

"If they are," Clare argued, "they shouldn't be."

Stan laughed at that so much he cackled. Clare loved his cackle. She fell in love with his intellect, his adventurous attitude, and with him. Stan would never speak of being in love. He planned never to marry. But he showed no interest in anyone else as he moved on to an American graduate school for his M.A. and then to Oxford to do his D. Phil. By then, Clare had completed the course work for her M.A. at Queen's. She thought about her future. A life without children, living in academia as Stan planned to do. He would teach philosophy. She could aspire to teach literature. She was doing her thesis on Iris Murdoch, a philosophy don and novelist at Oxford. It would be interesting, quite fabulous, to live in Oxford with Stan while he finished his D. Phil., then come home to a good position, which was likely for Stan at a major university in Canada. But a life without children ... no! And not being married.... Clare didn't mind the feeling of that as young, 'liberated' students. But a lifetime of that.... The question of why he wouldn't marry her bothered her increasingly. She had already begun to not like it.

There was a new young professor at Queen's who had taken a serious interest in her. He wasn't against marriage or having children at all. Clare felt comfortable talking with him and began to see a comfortable future ... with children. After three years of feeling she had to follow along with Stan's sense of being free of the bourgeois life, Clare decided the time had come to make it clear that she wanted to have children sometime and for her that meant marriage first. She wrote to Stan in Oxford explaining that and sincerely wishing him well in his career as a philosopher. She believed he would become as famous as Wittgenstein.

Stan called her from a phone booth in Oxford at dawn, saying he had thought and walked around all night after reading her letter. He concluded, "I want you to marry me. Having a couple of kids sometime isn't such a bad idea."

Clare talked it over with her roommates, Lizzie and Shirley.

"It's about time!" said Lizzie. She had doubts about Stan. She recalled Darcy McGee, how certain and eager he was about wanting to marry Clare. Stan and Clare had been seeing each other exclusively for three years and no plans about their future had been forthcoming.

"You'll have an interesting life with Stan," said Shirley.

"The Chinese curse," said Clare, smiling. "May you have an interesting life."

She recalled that exchange often over the years and reminded Shirley of it when she was invited to attend Shirley's installation as the first female president of Princeton University in 2001. Shirley had become famous as a scientist after discovering crucial things about cloning. She retired in 2013 after twelve years as a productive, progressive president of Princeton.

Chapter Twenty-Three

Len's Threat

It's time I got my life going again, Clare thought as she drove into Kingston in 2015, recalling her time at Queen's, rooming with Lizzie and Shirley, her brief engagement to Darcy McGee, then her long relationship leading to marriage with Stan in Oxford. Now I'm divorcing again. Not an admirable life. But I have my kids and grandkids and dogs. I'm going to get productive again. I could make a small income doing portraits of families, pets included. Maybe I could specialize in that. Seventy is not too old to take a new tack. Taking family portraits is easier then lying in the grass or snow, for days and days, waiting for a good focus on wildlife.

Clare paused at the entrance to the *Queen's Journal* reception room. She spotted Darcy McGee talking to a couple of people whom she couldn't quite remember. He was still over six feet tall, broad shoulders, not paunchy, his blonde hair gone white. He still tossed his head back in laughter. Clare walked toward him. The other two went to the bar as Darcy turned to greet Clare.

"I was hoping to see you here," he said with a big smile and held his arms out for a hug.

"Likewise." She moved in to hug him. "What have you been doing all these years?"

He looked carefully at her. "You're looking good. No worse for the wear."

"You too. A bit thinner," she smiled, "in the hair."

"Ha!" He laughed. "Ever honest."

"You haven't told me what you've been up to all these years."

"What would you expect? Newspaper guy. Kept myself poor running the *Peterborough Standard* and then editor of the *Kingston Examiner*. Waited a long time to marry. Had nice stepkids. Now divorced. I keep in touch with my grown-up stepkids. What about you? I know you're a hell of a good wildlife photographer."

"What a nice thing to say!" She beamed. "Thank you. But I myself am a scandal. Twice married. Now in the throes of legal separation. But I have two great kids and lots of grandkids. And beautiful dogs."

"Let's get a drink," said Darcy. "We have a lot of years to catch up on."

They spent as much of the reunion together as they could without neglecting others. Clare drove home feeling there was a new future in the making, or at least possible. She noted Darcy drank only wine and mostly white. She also noted he wore socks with sandals. Not cool, she laughed at herself. And not important. Socks!

Clare visited Darcy in Kingston a few times over the summer. He lived in a condominium overlooking the lake and Wolf Island. It was not clean or tidy, though it was well arranged with furnishings and art Clare liked and walls of bookshelves.

"We bought this condo when I got the editor job at the *Kingston Examiner*," Darcy said. "Neither I nor Tilly like gardening. She's a musician, a talented singer, but it's not easy to get gigs. Tilly would fall into depressions and we'd both drink too much. Then her parents died and she came into an inheritance, including their house in west Vancouver. She lives there now, married to someone else. Younger than her, but she made a prenuptial agreement, at my urging."

"Do you keep in touch a lot?"

"No. But we're not acrimonious."

As a newspaper man, Darcy had been used to long hours with odd meal times. He never learned to cook. He had lived on fast food, take-out, and occasional meals in a good restaurant. Tilly cooked for him but their marriage lasted less than ten years. He had been on his own for the past decade, retired from his work on the newspaper for two years. He had women and men friends, which gave him a social life.

"Retired and living alone," he said. "It's a colossal bore."

"You're a good writer," said Clare. "Why not write a book?"

"I've thought of it," he said. "Not sure I have the brain cells for it anymore."

"You can't know if you don't try." Clare felt lightness of being, a release of anchors and tensions as she chatted with Darcy while preparing dinner and then sat down with him, sharing interests and quips and opinions, learning about his life and responding to questions about hers. They cleared up and did the dishes together. They danced to some old favourites from the sixties. And went to bed.

"I've lost my prowess," Darcy said into the darkness, turning onto his back. "Viagra doesn't work for me. Maybe if I stop drinking…"

"It's OK," said Clare. "I've been used to nothing, for years and years. I'm happy now to have affection."

"Gotta hope you mean that." Darcy turned to kiss her.

Clare had told Len she was visiting an old friend from Queen's days she had encountered at the Queen's Journal Reunion. Len thought it over.

"I guess that's what a separation is for," he said.

No, that was not my goal, Clare wanted to say, but didn't. It would not be a constructive conversation. She knew it was not good for her case and situation to have a relationship with another man at this time. But it felt good in her heart, it gave her hope for a better future. She would be as quiet and discreet about it as she could. She and Darcy phoned each other daily on their cell phones when Len was not in sight or in hearing distance.

Len spent his days in his office working on accounts and the stock market, scotch at hand. When the markets closed, he drank and read by the fireplace. He sat on the bench overlooking the lake after dinner, watching the sunset. Heading back into the house, he stumbled and fell on the path but did not injure himself … until he fell on the stone step of the porch. There was a small gash on his forehead, which bled until Clare bandaged it. His hand was sore from breaking his fall.

"Guess I'll stick to the house," he said, and ceased to sit outside.

Len told Clare that their car insurance company was offering a significant discount if they put a device on their cars which tracked their speed. If the device showed they stuck regularly to the speed limit, their insurance would cost less. Len put the device on his car because he didn't drive long distances and wasn't tempted to go over the speed limit. Clare thought about it and decided she did not want the device because she did drive long distances and often needed to speed up to pass slow vehicles or wanted to drive a little over the speed limit when traffic conditions warranted it, particularly between Ottawa and Kingston.

Then one day, mid-summer, she looked out into the yard where her car was parked and saw Len doing something under the steering wheel. She went out and confronted him.

"Len, what are you doing?"

He stood up, surprised, then answered honestly. "Just adjusting the tracking device for you."

"I told you I didn't want that thing."

"It saves a lot of money."

"Len, you put that on my car without my knowledge or permission. Remove it. Please."

"Remove it yourself." Len turned his back and walked into the house.

Clare seethed. She felt around under the steering wheel and touched the device. She wasn't sure how to remove it. She got her purse from the house and drove straight to the office of their car and house insurance company in Ottawa. She asked to speak with their agent. She was soon invited into his, Jim's, office. He was a pleasant man whom they had dealt with for years.

Clare explained to him in confidence that she and Len were in the process of legal separation and she did not want to have the speed-tracking device. Len had installed it without her permission. She didn't know how it worked or how to remove it properly. Jim looked alarmed.

"It was installed without your knowledge? You don't know that the device connects to a computer and can be used to track your speed and where your car is at any given time?"

"No, I did not know that." Clare felt a fear and chill.

"Our apologies, Clare. I did not know your situation. I'm sorry to hear it. You've been married a long time. Len led me to believe you had asked him to pick up the device and install it for you."

The device was removed. Clare phoned Darcy to tell him about it. He became irate. "That guy is dangerous!" he exclaimed. "Whacko. Crazy creepy. Following you around on his computer! You have to get away from him. I've covered stories like this. The woman usually ends up dead. Murdered. Come and live with me. You have to. For your own safety."

The thought of leaving her own beautiful home and dogs on the lake, moving into a condominium… No, no and *no*! Clare said to herself. "Sorry," she tried to put it gently to Darcy. "I can't do that. I'm fighting for the right to stay in my own home."

"So is your crazy husband. And you just can't tell what he'll do next."

"I'll report this to Hannah."

"Of course you must. That's minimal."

At home, Clare went to Len in his office and told him, "I know you were tracking my whereabouts with that device. You lied to the insurance company. They have taken back the device." Len leaned back in his chair with his hands clasped together on his desk, thinking of a response. Clare turned and walked away.

Clare reported it to Hannah's assistant. Next day, Clare received a copy of the formal letter Hannah sent to Len's lawyer, pointing out the illegality of what Len had done and requesting that Len be informed of his wife's right to privacy and freedom of movement.

"Safety is the real issue," reiterated Darcy. He became more demanding that Clare leave Loghaven and move in with him. Clare reacted by talking to him less often and saying she couldn't visit him until things settled down.

"I'm not waiting forever," he said. "Not this time."

She phoned Darcy one early afternoon and he remarked that he was still in his dressing gown.

"Are you not well?"

"Just didn't feel like getting dressed. Why should I? Nothing to do around here."

"You could go golfing."

"Don't feel like it."

"I'll phone you tomorrow," said Clare. "The dogs are pestering me for a hike. Then friends are coming over for tennis and a swim."

"Take a hike then." He hung up.

He sounded drunk, thought Clare. He sounded slow and slightly slurring. She phoned him around the same time next day and he apologized, saying he had been feeling down and under the weather yesterday. He was dressed now and on his way out to "get provisions." It looked like rain today but he planned to golf tomorrow.

The legal proceedings carried on into September, which was not a long time for matrimonial cases. But Hannah Judson did not let her clients linger in limbo. She called Clare to her office. "This case needs to be resolved," she said. "We've tolerated enough obstructions. I think it's time to draw up our affidavit and take it to court. A lot will depend on the judge. If we get some regressive old.... But that's always the risk. Mahalia," Hannah turned to her assistant, "can you draw up the affidavit with Clare next Friday? Then I'll work on it over the weekend."

Clare had submitted all the history of violence and abuse in written reports along with the journals she had kept sporadically over the past seventeen years. She thought it fair to warn Len that she had an appointment on the Friday to draw up her affidavit. He spent most of Thursday in his office with the door closed. Preparing for his own affidavit, Clare assumed. That evening at dinner he exuded a solemn confidence, or was it resolve, that worried Clare.

"Is this a good mood I'm seeing?" asked Clare.

"You're the only one who gets into bad moods," Len put down his fork.

I'll just let that go, thought Clare. Let it sink into all the other polluted water under the bridge. She cleared up and sat outside with the dogs until dark. She noted that her neighbours' lights were on. She put their house key in her housecoat pocket. She quietly locked her bedroom door and put her charged cell phone under her pillow. Len's bedroom light had long been turned off. She had heard his snore as she passed his bedroom door. She had had an extra glass of wine and fell quite quickly to sleep.

Nothing happened that night.

Her appointment was at 9:30 a.m. She rose at 6:30 a.m. to give herself plenty of time to get to Ottawa and Hannah's office. She fed the dogs, had her green tea with honey, yogurt and toast, was opening the door to depart when Len yelled from upstairs, "Wait! Clare, wait!"

She turned in alarm. He had something in his hand. It was not a weapon. She exhaled in relief. It was an envelope. He came down the stairs and thrust it at Clare. "Show this to your dickhead lawyer."

Wanting to get away from him, Clare took it to her car to read.

It was dated September 16, 2015.

> Dear Clare,
> Knowing the history of suicide in my family, you must take this absolutely seriously. My brother Stefan shot himself in the head. My cousin hung himself in the basement. My sister in law gassed herself in the car in an enclosed garage. We have an enclosed garage. That will be my method of choice, if you do not allow me to live out my life at Loghaven, preferably with you there too.
> My life is in your hands.
> Absolutely seriously and sincerely,
> *Len*
> Leonard G. Rekai

'Len' was written with a pen. The rest was typed on a computer. Clare felt sick in her stomach, her heart beating fast. She breathed out to calm herself, several times. She read the letter three times but knew on first reading that Len would carry through on his threat. She started the car and drove carefully to Ottawa. She figured out what she thought had to be done.

She would ask Hannah to work out a separation agreement that allowed her and Len to continue living separately within the same household. But when her family and occasional friends came to visit, Len had to go elsewhere. This could be done for limited times per year, with due prior notice. It had to allow Ali and Megan to visit with their kids twice a year and faraway friends once a year. The daily abuse had to be curtailed. Clare pictured Len choosing one of the many modest hotels in Ottawa to stay in on a regular basis where he could recreate a social life in the city with old friends and colleagues like Warren. He could have his meals in the hotel and take taxis so there would be no drinking and driving.

Clare showed Mahalia Len's letter first thing at their meeting and told her of her plan to ask Hannah to draw up an unusual, creative separation agreement. Mahalia left the office to speak directly with Hannah. It was a half hour before Hannah could join with Clare and Mahalia. Hannah looked piercingly at Clare then read the letter. She lay it down on the table and leaned on her forearms, her hands clasped firmly together on top of the letter. It was a desktop gesture like Len's. Hannah looked harshly at Clare. "You understand this letter is further evidence of this man's controlling, coercive, violent nature."

Clare had not seen it that way. She thought it was a desperate ploy. A form of blackmail. Selfish in the extreme, as Len had become. And ultimately a desperate plea. But she could also see Hannah's experienced professional interpretation.

"I understand," she said to Hannah, "that your professional advice is not to cater to this threat. You're probably right. Time will tell. But right now, I need to ask you to do something different. I realize it might not be legally possible to draw up the kind of agreement I'm picturing. I guess it's never been done before."

Hannah looked harsher. Clare sensed that Hannah thought maybe Clare was trying to challenge her. No such ploys would work with Hannah Judson. Hannah had been planning this morning to prepare a difficult courtroom case for Clare. Now she was being asked to completely back down and bow to a threat of suicide. Clare thought all had come to naught. Len had her over a barrel. She would have to go home and live with him on his terms. Things would get worse.

It was as though Hannah could tell what Clare was thinking. She considered Clare's position and request.

"I'll look into it," Hannah concluded. She stood up, not pleased, but able to change gears and direction at her client's heartfelt request. "I'll draft something up." She left the room abruptly.

"She has another meeting," Mahalia explained.

"She's amazing," said Clare. "She has a lot of compassion."

"Yes," said Mahalia. "She can read people's needs."

Len opened the front door when Clare parked in their driveway. He left the door open for her and went to sit down in his chair by the fireplace. "Well....?" he said. "What's the verdict?"

Clare brought the dogs in with her. She hung up her jacket and sat on the couch. Ikey then Yukitu got up on the couch beside her.

"So what's the verdict?" Len repeated.

"Hannah is looking into drawing up a separation agreement that allows us to live separately within the same household."

"Thank you," Len said flatly.

"But when my family and occasional friends come to visit, you have to go elsewhere."

"Elsewhere. What the hell does that mean?"

"You could go to a nice hotel in Ottawa, renew some friendships. Or take a trip somewhere."

"You mean I have to bugger off. Down the road." He got up to get a drink. It wasn't yet noon. "OK," he said with his back to her. "No sweat. I can do that."

Chapter Twenty-Four

An Unusual Legal Separation

Hannah drew up a highly professional, airtight separation agreement that covered all the bases. Income was split 50/50, investments and life insurance remained separate, though Clare had no life insurance. They became tenants in common, which meant each owned half the value of the property and neither could make loans against it. They shared maintenance, taxes, and insurance costs for the house and property. When one person predeceased the other, the remaining person could continue living in the home as long as they wished, then it could be sold, with half the proceeds going to the estate of each.

An arbitrator was agreed upon. Should either party violate the terms of the agreement, the case would be brought before the arbitrator. An essential term of the agreement was that there be no abuse causing psychological or physical harm to the other party.

The agreement was ready to be signed mid-October. Neither Len nor Clare had any complaint about the agreement. Len said his lawyer had no specific complaint about the agreement but was going deer hunting when it was to be signed. They delayed for two weeks. Then Len's lawyer arranged for his assistant to deal with the signing in his absence. The papers were signed. Len's lawyer returned to his office and sent a letter to Hannah, saying that since he was absent when the agreement was signed, he washed his hands of it.

"A lawyer can't wash his hands of an agreement he was part of and was legally signed," said Clare. "Can he?"

"Washing his hands of his own work," said Hannah. "Very strange. It's not a legal term."

* * * * *

The legal fees, which Clare paid out of her investments, were very much higher than Len's. "Of course my legal fees were much higher," said Clare to her sister Julie over the phone. "And I feel nothing but gratitude and admiration. I've been able to work with … The Best."

"Sounds like it," said Julie. "But you caved in to Len's threat and tied her hands." Julie paused. "I'm sorry, Sis. But this is not the end. It's not a good life ahead of you. Len has been spiralling downward for years. Resorting to a threat like that. That's got to be the bottom of the barrel. But I'm afraid it isn't. Damn it, Clare! If our parents knew what you've had to put up with… Having to keep a baseball bat in your bedroom! If our grandmother, Meg … and our grandfather, Mick … a police chief!"

"Julie, I don't have the worst life. I'm independent now. Thanks to Hannah. I live in a beautiful place, of my own design. With my Malamutes. And my wonderful kids and grandkids and friends can visit, with the Dark Cloud out of sight, out of range. I don't have cancer. Our entire family is healthy. Lucky us."

"OK, Clare. I'll back off. Be healthy. Be safe."

Clare and Len carried on at Loghaven for another five years. Len tried to be more civil, at first. Then old patterns returned with his sarcasm and alcoholic belligerence. In summer he got on the mower and mowed grass and weeds for a few hours a week. But his mobility and strength kept decreasing from lack of exercise. His legs were weak and he couldn't stand up for more than a few moments. He had had a hip replacement some years ago but his hip still bothered him.

Instead of going to a nice hotel when kids and grandkids visited, he drove to a cheap motel on the outskirts of Ottawa. It had a coffee shop which provided sandwiches and muffins. He called Warren on the phone when he wanted some conversation. Tanya called as often as Len would allow once the separation agreement was signed. If Clare picked up the landline at Loghaven when Tanya called, Tanya would hang up or rudely demand to speak to Len. Clare made sure relevant people had her cell phone number and then ceased to use the landline. She let it be Len's phone.

"I get fed up with Tanya," said Len to Clare, "listening to her rants about you. But she doesn't get the message. Not the sharpest knife in the drawer, that one. Quitting school at sixteen did not improve her brains."

"You could just tell her not to call, period," said Clare.

"She's the only niece I have," Len responded. "My other brothers have adopted kids. You know that."

"There's nothing wrong with adopting kids," said Clare, and nothing wrong with stepkids she thought, but didn't say it. "They should be treated equally."

"Blood is thicker than water," said Len, not for the first time.

"Oh, for God's sake Len! There are duds in every family. And how about merit?"

"How about it indeed. Do you think you merit all that you have? Are you the one who earned my pension?"

Clare left the room. She went to her office. She had no one to talk to. Julie would be at work. Lizzie was dead. Died of pancreatic cancer. So quickly. And so magnificently. Outward and comforting others to the end. Her three sons gathered round her, her husband brought from his assisted living quarters, Clare herself, the last friend invited to visit. She had held Lizzie's hand and kissed her goodbye on the forehead. How she missed Lizzie. They were sympatico friends since university days. Roommates. Separated during Clare's Oxford years but back in closer and closer touch after that.

Lizzie had thought Clare's renewed relationship with Darcy McGee was a fabulous piece of fortune, a reward for Clare. But it didn't last. Fizzled out within months. Darcy expected Clare would spend most of her time with him after the separation agreement was signed. It was impractical as winter weather set in and Clare spent Christmas with Megan and Nate and grandkids Aurora and Wilf in St. John's. Nate's work as an architect of Indigenous-inspired buildings was doing very well. He won prizes for his designs in

Newfoundland and Labrador. They had a large winterized cottage near Happy Valley–Goose Bay in Labrador. A dogsledding company run by another Métis man, Scott Hudson, was nearby. Clare loved going for rides as much as the kids did. Nate's parents came to Christmas dinner.

Stan had retired from teaching in Oxford. He and Marta came back to Canada and bought a house in Victoria, British Columbia. They spent Christmas with Ali and family. The following year would be Clare's turn to spend Christmas with Ali, Ari, and family.

Darcy's parents were long dead. He was invited to Christmas dinner with friends. Darcy spent New Year's alone. He planned to come to Ottawa by train in mid-January and spend a couple of nights in a hotel with Clare. He phoned the night before to say he had fallen on ice, sprained his wrist and couldn't make it. He said he would come a couple of weeks later. Since Clare had prepared to go to Ottawa to be with Darcy, she decided instead to take the train to Kingston and surprise him.

Darcy came to the door of his condo late afternoon in his bathrobe. He was swaying. He had to go to the couch and fall back into it. "Sorry." He slurred. "Missed you too much. Bit of a binge. I'll get over it." He lay down on the couch. Clare lifted his feet up onto it. She saw his bandaged wrist. She looked around. The place was a mess. Kitchen counter littered with dirty dishes, pizza boxes. There were several empty vodka bottles dropped in the kitchen, living room, his bedroom.

Drinking out of the bottle! "Bloody hell!" said Clare. I've never seen anything like this, she thought. This is binge drinking, is it? Completely disgusting.

She set about picking up bottles. Using a dustpan to pick up a broken mug swept into the corner of the kitchen tile floor. Why am I doing this, she thought. What's with me? Do I have a big 'A' tattooed on my forehead? Not the 'A' for adultery of early American stories. But 'A' for alcoholics, 'come to me. I'm a sucker for you. A total magnet.' She kept tidying up, by instinct and habit. She heated up a piece of pizza from the box. She found a beer in the fridge. Clean sheets in the cupboard.

The shower curtain had been pulled from its hooks. She pictured him staggering for it. She brushed her teeth, washed her face, and applied some cream. Got into bed and thought and thought. Should I just get on the train in the morning? Or give him another chance?

Darcy came to his bedroom before dawn, went into his bathroom, ran the tap for water to drink and to brush his teeth. He lay down on his back beside her on the bed.

"You awake?" He spoke into the darkness.

"Yes."

"You have to forgive this. It's an old newspaper man's regression. Binge drinking. I'm too lonely without you. I'll stop drinking. I've done that before. Gone for years without drinking. At least none of the hard stuff. I'll start today. You'll see. Just give me another chance."

Clare had the feeling he had said these things before. To his wife? Maybe others.

"I can't answer you now, Darcy. I'm too upset. I've never seen anything like this. You must feel horribly ill."

"Yep. But I'll get over it." He reached for her hand. "Trust me."

"Let's just get some sleep." She rolled over with her back to him, but did not sleep.

In the morning he had the shakes. He couldn't eat. Clare went out and bought him nourishment drinks and soup, crackers, bread, and other food she imagined he could work up to eating. She got food for herself. A bottle of wine and a lasagne for the evening. He needed more sleep. He was grateful and affectionate. She tried to hide how hopeless and sad she felt, how hard it was to swallow food and wine in front of him slurping soup. She wished she had not agreed to stay another night but she didn't want to arrive home unexpectedly early. And why pay for a hotel?

Before she got into bed with him, she brought herself to say, "Darcy, I'm truly sorry, but I don't think I'm up to dealing with another alcoholic."

"I'm not an alcoholic, Clare. I just went on a bender being away from you for so long, over Christmas. People do crazy things over Christmas. You must know that. Give me another chance and I'll show you. Don't you think you owe it to me?"

"OK, Darcy," she thought it best to say. "But I had no sleep last night. I need to sleep now. I'm feeling pretty bad."

"I get it." He put his arm gently around her. "We both need sleep."

She pretended to fall asleep … for hours.

It was good to be back home with her dogs, hiking around on snowshoes. Len had told her right away. "I had visitors. The guest room needs making up."

"Who was here?"

"Tanya and Carson. That's his name. Easy to remember, once he explains it. He's a car mechanic. He said he decided that would be a good trade, ever since his dad kidded him, saying 'So you want a car, son.' Carson's not a bad guy. Likes to joke around."

"Did you invite them to come while I was away?"

"No. But when Tanya learned you were going to be away, she invited herself. It was OK. Only one night. That's about right for me. And they had to get back to work. They had called in sick."

"Really! She sure is determined to build a relationship with you."

"Why not? She is my niece. How was your rendezvous?"

"Not very nice. I discovered he has a drinking problem."

"You think everyone has a drinking problem. Drinking isn't a problem if you enjoy it."

"He doesn't enjoy it."

"Too bad. He looked like a pheasant plucker to me."

"When did you ever see him?"

"I looked him up in your Queen's University yearbook. You met him when you worked on the *Journal* in third year, right?"

"Jeez, Len. You remember some things very well."

"I remember things I write down. You forget I keep a daily journal."

It was not a good feeling, discovering the tabs Len kept on her.

Days passed and then Clare received an email from Darcy saying:

I've recovered. Much thanks to you. I will not go on a binge again. After a year from your separation date, you can get a divorce. It's just a matter of paper work. Will you marry me then? I won't ask you a third time.

Clare declined, as kindly as she could. Several months later, Clare received another email from Darcy saying:

It was a good idea of yours that I should write a book. It's a mystery, solved by a newspaper reporter. Good fun. More importantly, I have married Cheryl Madill. Remember her from the *Queen's Journal*? She was at the reunion. Her husband died a few years ago. We live in her old stone house on Bagot Street. She likes to garden. I'm enjoying short visits from grandkids. It's a good life. I hope you find one for yourself.

CHAPTER TWENTY-FIVE

Laying To Rest

Fort McMurray's economic downturn continued into 2016 with the decline of oil prices. The city was still regarded by many as the engine or boiler room of industry in Canada. It was also a cosmopolitan city, a model of diversity. When this diversity was celebrated, the flags of seventy-six nations connected to the various citizens of Fort McMurray were raised. Every country, from Australia to Chile, Ethiopia, Germany, Saudi Arabia, Ukraine, Indonesia, Finland, and others, was represented. With so many diverse cultures, quick unified action would not be expected.

But this was Canada, where history has been made through surprising, peaceful actions. In 1995, when a referendum was called which would allow the province of Quebec to secede, suddenly over 150,000 Canadians, from coast to coast to coast, got into cars, trains, planes, and showed up all together in central Montreal. It was a united massive throng, making a peaceful plea for Quebec to stay in Canada. Quebec then voted to stay.

In 2016, the diverse population of Fort McMurray was suddenly required to act immediately, in unison, to evacuate the city. A ferocious wildfire had sprung up upon it. Fort McMurray is surrounded by forest, dry forest. Wildfires appear in northern wilderness areas every year. They are usually brought under control by expert fire teams within relatively short times. The spring of that year was record-breaking dry and warm. Dryer than it had been in seventy-two years. The month of May began with high winds and a high temperature. A spark from somewhere turned into flames that raged towards the city of Fort McMurray, exploding high through trees, over moats, and to most everyone's surprise, across the mile-wide Athabasca River.

Evacuation was then ordered. Immediate evacuation. The firefighters had moved in to save as much of the city as they could. The citizens rallied fast to get into vehicles, forming an astonishingly orderly convoy of trucks and cars moving down Highway 63 towards Edmonton, sparks and flames hounding and surrounding them. Homes and possessions, sometimes frightened pets had to be left behind. People who got onto airplanes were allowed to hold their cats or dogs on their laps. Police had permits to break into houses to get dogs and cats rounded up for the shelter volunteers. Eighty-eight thousand people were evacuated from the city. Only one young couple died en route.

Clare later learned from Facebook that Lisa Schaldemose was among the shelter volunteers. Then Lisa, some other volunteers, and her mother escaped in her van down the highway to a motel outside of Edmonton. Lisa's own immediate neighbourhood in Fort Mac was spared from the ravaging fire.

The neighbourhood of Beacon Hill was burned to ashes. But the firefighters performed heroic and miraculous deeds. They saved eighty-five percent of the city structures. People across Canada saw the valour and the horror on TV and in the newspapers. They rallied to help the people of Fort McMurray. Water, food, beds and bedding were sent to the shelters opened to the evacuated citizens. Donations of money and goods came from all parts of the country, from the Arctic, the east and west coasts, from communities in all the provinces. A fire brigade from South Africa flew in to help, as payback for help given to them from Canada in the past.

Seeing on TV the fire brigades being cheered by Fort Mac residents standing on the main city bridge after the fire had been brought under control, made Clare have to wipe her eyes. She wished she could be there with them.

Of course there were some remarks on social media suggesting the terror and the destruction of the fire in Fort McMurray was the city's 'karma' or God's punishment for being the 'villain' of the oil industry. But mainstream media and the population showed sympathy and support for the people and the enduring city of Fort McMurray.

One year later, a lot of news coverage showed the post-traumatic effects on the residents, but also their resilience and determination to rebuild their city with its cosmopolitan culture and industry. It would take a very long time to rebuild and restore. The oil industry itself would keep undergoing change as it adapted to more environmental restrictions and concerns. Fossil fuels would diminish in importance as electric vehicles and machines increased in number. The question of more pipelines to transport oil east, west, south, and to other countries remained unresolved. Oil products would be needed as long as one could imagine. Clare recalled Tory saying oil was too valuable to be left in the ground.

A year following the fire, Fort McMurray had a flood. This had happened only once in a hundred years in Fort Mac. But once again, many residents had to evacuate their homes. And again many lost their homes and businesses. Clare learned that Lisa had to evacuate because of the flood. Lisa packed her dogs into the same SUV that had transported Clare from the airport years before and had saved their lives from the fire in 2016. But her mother Annette was not with them at the time of the flood. She had died that summer, at age 84, when illness befell her while happily working in their garden. When Lisa returned to her home after the flood and found it amazingly spared again from damage, she couldn't feel much joy. She felt her mother's absence.

Now in her early seventies, Clare had to struggle for her own resilience. 'Living separately in the same house' with Len was too far from stress-free. She had to be hospitalized with Afib four times in three years. With the first attack she didn't know what was happening to her. For two days before it happened, she had been scurrying around entertaining women photographer friends who had come for the weekend. Then she had to clean up and pack for a week in Vancouver with Ali and family. She got out of breath just hosing and sweeping the garage floor where the dogs bedded for the night and Ikey had left a big poop. Doing other chores and packing up, Clare got so out of breath she had to sit down and catch her breath frequently.

"I don't know what's wrong with me," Clare said to Len at supper.

"You're just having panic attacks," he said. "You get too excited when you travel."

"That's ridiculous," said Clare. "I'm not given to panic attacks. And I don't fear flying"

Len shrugged his shoulders.

The breathlessness worsened. It eased when she lay down after going up to her bedroom. But she couldn't sleep well. Next morning, carrying her suitcase downstairs wasn't easy but it had wheels and she got it into the car, drove to the airport, parked and made her way slowly to check in. Was she having a mild stroke? She couldn't let Ali and the boys down. She hadn't seen them in a year. She relaxed on the plane. When it landed, she retrieved her suitcase and wheeled it slowly to arrivals. A limo driver was holding up her name. He drove her to Ali and Ari's house. The two older boys were at camp. Todd and the nanny were there until Ali got home from her shift at hospital.

Clare read stories to Todd so she could rest sitting down. She stood up and walked to hug Ali when she came in the front door.

"Sorry, I'm feeling a bit weird," she explained when Ali asked why she moved so slowly. Ali asked her symptoms. She felt her pulse than got a stethoscope.

"God, Mom! You're in serious Afib. And you got on an airplane!"

Ali rushed her to hospital. They were able to bring her heart rate down through drugs over the course of three days. She was prescribed stronger heart medication. Back in Ottawa, Clare's cardiologist adjusted her prescription and lectured her appropriately on never getting on a plane when she had an increased heart rate. The plane might have to do an emergency landing to take her to hospital. Clare learned more about Afib and bought a wrist device to measure her heart rate.

It happened three more times under stress and tension with Len. But the third and fourth hospitalization involved cardioversion, which Clare felt weakened her heart. She kept on with her sports of swimming, tennis, snowshoeing, and skiing, but she did them very slowly and had to pause frequently to catch her breath. She couldn't run. Stairs and going up hill required rests to catch her breath. She had to play tennis with a good partner who did the running. "I'm living like a sloth," she said repeatedly, "but I'm living." More dear friends died of cancer.

Why am I still standing? she asked herself. She knew there was no special reason. Life is unfair. She could not believe in a beneficent God, certainly not a God the Father who cared for some people and not others. But she maintained a belief in goodness. God as absolute goodness. She tried to live on the side of goodness. There was so much to love about life and living. Clare thought about that every summer morning as she took her green tea with honey onto the porch, put her feet up onto the sofa, her dogs lying close by, and looked out over the grass and wild flowers edging the lake, the rocks sloping into the water, calm and sparkling in sunlight. Winter, spring, and autumn have their own beauty, which Clare also appreciated. She had even come to like days in April, which could be cruelly cold, and the month of November, which could be bleak. Living at Loghaven she could feel the beauty and goodness of life and living, so much more than she ever could in the city.

And yet it was her dogs and family and friends that Clare loved most about living and watching what happened in the world. She didn't feel she could contribute much to the world any more. She had done her bit with wildlife photography. She could always take a photo when inspired by something. But trying to run a portrait business, renting small quarters in Ottawa, commuting weekdays in winter darkness and poor driving conditions, was dangerous and stressful. It was not sufficiently profitable.

She considered setting up a studio at Loghaven. People would not want to drive from Ottawa in bad weather. And there was the Len factor. He showed almost no respect for her working hours. He would come into her office interrupting her with trivial self-focused questions at any time. "Where's the newspaper? When are you getting the mail? Did you put instant coffee on the shopping list?" He would yell and swear if she didn't give a satisfactory answer immediately. Their home was too full of tension and unpredictable outbursts.

Clare sold her small business in Ottawa but could not get a business going in her home. She sank into involuntary retirement, working disheartenedly on collecting her photographs into albums. To get out of the house and away from Len, she took some classes on sketching, which she had always been quite good at.

Keeping in touch with Tory and Hettie, she learned that there were afternoon classes in painting and sketching in an art complex in Ottawa that wasn't difficult to drive to. Tory took classes there. Painting and sketching were amongst his several hobbies. His mother had been a talented artist and illustrator.

Clare took the class on Tuesday afternoons in the autumn of 2017. Afterwards some of the students gathered in the coffee shop. They were interesting older people, Tory the oldest and most interesting. He was ninety-one. He never sought to dominate the conversation. He asked questions of others but when he spoke everyone listened. His good humour put people at ease. He excused himself to leave early. Hettie wasn't well. Their house was up for sale. They were planning to move into a retirement residence where Hettie could have as much care as needed. She had recently turned ninety-one.

New Year's of 2018 Clare spent with Megan and Nate, Aurora and Wilf at their winter cottage in Happy Valley–Goose Bay. Aurora had become a pretty teenager with lustrous black hair and almond-shaped dark eyes. She had solemnity and was a good athlete. She told Clare she'd like to ski in the Laurentians and maybe she could stay at Loghaven and do that sometime with one or two of her friends.

"How about next Christmas?" Clare said, eager to have her grandchildren stay with her anytime.

"Me too," said Wilf. "Not fair if I can't come."

Megan and Nate gave a tentative OK to Aurora.

It was no surprise that Tanya had visited Len over the holidays. Nor that she left her bed unchanged and the kitchen disorderly. Clare tried not to be annoyed by her stealthy visits. Clare focused instead on the eager welcome of the dogs. Yukitu was turning thirteen, which was old for a Malamute. She was healthy and could run well when she wanted to. Ikey, turning seven, was bouncy as ever.

Len was noticeably weaker. He had a scab on his forehead.

"Fell into the fucking coffee table," he said. "Must have passed out briefly since I can't remember falling. Just came to on the floor."

"Was Tanya here?"

"No. I did it all by myself."

Clare had to smile and shake her head at his humour, but she worried that Len should not be left alone for long. And he was too old and weak to be holing up in a crummy motel. He really should be in a retirement home, she concluded, not for the first time. When she suggested this to him, he got angry and raised his voice at her.

"No fucking way! Over my dead body."

Clare visited Ali and family over Easter. She phoned every day to make sure Len was not lying on the floor. He told her Tanya was doing the same, phoning every day, and she had visited him. "I'd rather you called than her," Len said to Clare. "She has nothing interesting to say. And she doesn't take no for an answer." Clare started to say goodbye when he interrupted. "Wait! There's something I wanted to tell you. Just can't remember what it is."

He called her later to say, "Hettie Sanderson died. Stomach cancer. A day or so before they were to move into the the Bradgate. Their house is sold so Tory has to move in there by himself. Poor bugger. The funeral is next week. Warren said it'll be a big one. The Sandersons have a lot of friends."

"What day next week?"

"How the hell should I know!" Len was shouting, angry because he couldn't remember. "OK. I'll find out and call you back, for chrissake."

Hettie's funeral was two days before Clare's return. She felt sorry for Tory. Hettie was a nice, smart woman. They had a long good marriage. And four smart adult kids, grandkids and a great-grandkid. Two lived on either coast like her daughters, Another son lived in Toronto, another ran a lodge in the Caribbean. Would Tory move away to be close to one of them?

She phoned before visiting him in the Bradgate a couple of weeks later. No, he had no plans to move. He had a nice three-room suite in the Bradgate. He liked having no chores, no housekeeping, or shopping and cooking to do.

"You did all those things?" Clare was incredulous.

"Of course." He smiled at Clare's surprise. "Hettie and I shared the work. We had a housecleaner. Hettie had to do it all when I was off in the field and we had four young kids. But after that I pitched in as much as I could. There was a lot to do when Hettie was ill." He looked away. "It's good to be free of that now."

He was currently working on a book about the history of geophysicists in Canada during the heyday of the 1970s, a book Hettie had been urging him to do for years. His eyes welled up when he spoke of her. But he wasn't one to sit around mourning or sink into depression. He showed Clare the "Lives Lived" article he was drafting on Hettie for the *Globe and Mail*. It was well written and gave Hettie her full due as an achieving woman who got back in the work force at age fifty and became a highly respected environmental scientist. Clare had never seen another example of a husband able to give his wife her full due in her career. Her role as wife, mother, grandmother usually overshadowed her other achievements.

When Tory walked Clare from his suite to the entrance of the Bradgate, she noted that he was already popular amongst the residents and staff. He greeted and was greeted by everyone. A whole phalanx of women heading for the dining room stopped to smile and make remarks to him. A free-standing, tall, well-groomed man with all his marbles was appreciated, if not coveted, in a retirement residence. Tory had the advantage of driving a car which he often filled with ladies going out for a drive or lunch in the countryside, their walkers piled in the trunk.

She told Len how much Tory was enjoying the Bradgate.

"Good for him," said Len. "He's a nice guy. He's welcome to it."

Clare noticed on returning from Vancouver that Ikey was limping slightly on his forepaw. She examined the paw but could find nothing wrong. Sometimes he limped and sometimes he did not. Clare wasn't sure if it was the left or right leg that bothered him. When the warm weather came he seemed to have no trouble getting up on the teak dining table on the porch as he liked to do. The air coming up through the slots must have cooled him a little. He took up half the table and rested his head near the pot of red geraniums. Ikey was good at endearing poses. Clare took photos of him. Visitors smiled and laughed at him. Everyone loved to cuddle him.

"Not a lot of people keep a big longhaired Malamute on their dining table," Ali responded to the emailed photo.

Tory visited with his golf buddy, Buck Rogers. Ikey got up on the table. Buck roared with laughter. Tory leaned down to cuddle Ike's big head. "Pure cuddle monster," he dubbed him.

One morning, Ike lingered on his bed rather than rushing to his food bowl. He squawked in some pain as he got up, limped, then walked normally, though slower, to his food dish. Clare made an appointment at the vet's.

Dr. Ardiel examined him through touch. Ike seemed to have sensitive spots. "I want to do some blood work," she said solemnly. But then she usually was solemn. "Leave him with me so I can do some tests. X rays may be necessary. Is that OK? We'll have to keep him overnight for an anaesthetic."

"Do whatever you have to do," said Clare. She was afraid to ask what Dr. Ardiel suspected might be wrong with Ike. She had not expected the appointment to be so serious. She knew that Malamutes were stoic in the extreme and it was hard to tell when they were hurting. She drove home to Yukitu with a sense of dread but reprimanded herself for it. Do not anticipate bad news was her rule. It will come soon enough. Yukitu did not like her coming home without Ike.

Len questioned her about the appointment and got angry that she had no results because he too was suddenly worried.

Late the next day, Dr Ardiel phoned. Her voice was at its most solemn. "Clare. This is not good news. I have to tell you, the tests show that Ike has bone cancer. It is not early stage, Clare. There is no cure. You can give him injections to relieve pain … for a while. Days. A week or two. Clare, we won't let him suffer long. You can come for him now. We'll show you how to do the injections."

"Thank you," was all Clare could say, before she broke down crying. Len got up from his chair and put his arms around her. She blurted out the basics to him. He sat down in silence.

Clare brought Ikey home. She gave him his injections and gave him meals of the human food he loved. Beef, chicken, pork, spaghetti bolognaise. He stood up for these. He walked on the grass and looked at the lake. But more and more he lay down. Yukitu watched and kept a respectful distance as Malamutes do when another dog is in pain. Dr. Ardiel's assistants called every few days. Until Clare said, "I think he's in too much pain. He lay down before finishing his supper yesterday and before his breakfast today. He's restless but can't stay up on his feet."

The assistant phoned back to say that Dr. Ardiel would be there tomorrow morning at 8 a.m. She came to Loghaven with her assistant. Ikey was the third Malamute of Clare and Len's that Dr. Ardiel laid to rest on a blanket in Clare's arms. She had named their first and second Malamutes, Yukon Sally and Jake.

They had built an Inukshuk in the meadow at Loghaven where they buried the Malamutes' ashes. Less than a month after they had the burial ceremony for Ike, they had to do the same for Yukitu. She died of stress and heartbreak.

Chapter Twenty-Six

Life without Malamutes

I can't live without a dog, Clare knew that. My beautiful Malamutes made living with Len in this wretched situation tolerable. She considered her age. She was seventy-four, almost seventy-five. And the weakness of her heart. The friends she knew with serious Afib didn't live far into their eighties. Clare was OK with that likelihood for herself. She had had a wonderful life. She planned to die with some grace and a sense of gratitude. If she got another Malamute, it was likely to outlive her. Her daughters didn't want to take on a Malamute. They are too difficult and big. They need people who understand them and have a home where they can live outside and have running space. Clare concluded she needed to get another kind of dog, medium-sized. Loghaven was such a paradise for dogs with its ten acres enclosed by an invisible electric fence, custom made to contain Malamutes.

Considering other Canadian breeds, she thought a Nova Scotia Duck Toller would appreciate the space of Loghaven and the lake for swimming. Her daughters agreed. They would take on a Duck Toller if need be. Then Clare found that the breed was so popular yet scarce, that no breeder could offer her one until about a year hence. Clare considered fostering dogs until then. She went to the local pet shelter to discuss that. She came out of the meeting knowing she couldn't bear to give a dog back after the allotted time. She asked to see the dog that had come into the shelter that day. It was a northern rescue dog.

The dog was brought into the waiting room on a leash. She was wearing a tee shirt to deter her from touching where stitches had been removed from her recent spaying operation. She sat down in front of Clare, looked up with her Beagle-like brown eyes as if to say, "Just get me out of here, please." Then she went towards the door and sat down looking back at Clare and her handler. Are either of you going to get me out of here?

She was four years old. Rescued fully pregnant. Brought to a nice local fostering family. At eight weeks, all of her pups were quickly adopted and then she was brought in for adoption. Clare observed that she didn't cower, had good manners, and assessed situations like a strategizing Malamute. Clare smiled at her. My mutt from Nunavut, she decided.

Clare phoned Len from her car. "She's not stupid or cowering. Eyes like a Beagle's, looks like a small Boxer, colouring of a German Shepherd, chest like a bulldog, and ears like no other's. She's survived four years as 'a stray' in Nunavut, probably pregnant twice a year. I saw the lives of feral dogs when Julie took me on her No Name Dogs project in Alberta. Not a good life and usually not a long one. This dog had to be super good at everything."

"Sounds like a winner. Did you sign up for her?"

"I want to."

"Then do it. Dogs don't cost much from a shelter. They go fast."

Clare was well known at the shelter. She had donated some of her wildlife photographs for their fundraising auctions over the years. They were glad to see the dog go home with her. Clare immediately named her mutt from Nunavut Piji, after an Inuit character in City Wolves.

She grew to love Piji, though she often told her, "You're not beautiful like my Malamutes. But you are as fast a runner, almost as smart, and altogether a lucky find."

Len could not agree. Piji growled, barked and lunged at him when he came down the stairs and stood at the entrance to Clare's office. Some instinct and previous experience made Piji extremely protective of Clare and hostile to Len approaching Clare in her office. Len was frightened by Piji and jabbed at her with the cane he now sometimes used. That made Piji attack more and she snapped at Len, tearing a hole in the sleeve of his sweater and piercing his skin a little bit. Len learned to accept Piji as Clare's guard dog.

Tory phoned Clare after he heard she had had to lay her Malamutes to rest. He expressed his sympathy and asked if she was coping alright. She was touched by his concern and told him about Piji. Not long after that, Tory paid a visit and brought a toy for Piji. Piji tended to growl at men who came to the door. Women she welcomed and made an affectionate fuss over. "That's in case she gets kicked out, as has no doubt happened too often to her," Clare explained to the women. "If it comes to that, she wants you to want to take her in."

Piji did not growl at Tory. He was good with dogs, held out his hand for Piji to sniff. Piji loved toys. She grabbed and tossed them around wanting to impress with how high she could toss and grab and shake her toy. She suckered Tory into a game of chasing her around the room for the toy he had brought her. Len sat in his chair with a scotch and enjoyed the show.

The Ottawa cinema club that ran over the winter months and was attended by mostly retired people at 4 p.m. weekly, was where Clare met up with friends, including Tory and friends he brought from the Bradgate. Sometimes she sat with them in the cinema and enjoyed discussing the movie afterwards, particularly with Tory who often invited friends to drinks in his suite before dinner.

The year 2019 ambled along. Clare was fearing what would happen at Christmas when Aurora and her friend were due to come skiing for a week after Boxing Day. Clare didn't think she could send Len "elsewhere" in winter now when he was so old and weak.

The dilemma was suddenly resolved when, at the end of October, Len staggered up to his bedroom very drunk as usual. When Clare went up to her bedroom, she saw Len sitting in his chair still dressed. She asked if he was OK.

"'Course I am," he yelled. "Get off my back."

She surmised he was too drunk to get undressed and get himself into bed. She got into her own bed. She was wakened in the night hearing Len yelling for her. Piji came barking up the stairs from Clare's office where she slept. Clare got up and found Len face down on the floor, moaning something about his hip. He couldn't get himself up. Clare knew she couldn't and shouldn't try, to lift him. She called 911. The paramedics took him to hospital.

Len's replaced left hip was dislocated by the fall. The orthopedic surgeon said it would be months before Len could put any weight on that hip. He was laid up in hospital for weeks and then would be taken to a rehabilitation centre to be taught how to walk with a walker, then possibly with a cane. On heavy painkillers and going through alcohol withdrawal made him a sorry sight for Clare to see. He was at times delirious, trembling, couldn't say what day or year it was, though he had been told. He looked blankly at her and turned his head away. Gradually, he became more conscious of where he was and why.

Clare couldn't help thinking … what a dignified man he used to be before he retired and turned to scotch. I tried to help him in every way I could think of. Nothing worked. He brought this on himself. But she also couldn't help feeling sorry for him and bringing anything he requested. He never requested scotch. Her visits were very short. He had nothing of interest to say to her and never asked how she or Megan or Ali and their families were, or what they were doing.

He had a cell phone to be used for emergencies when he was driving. Clare brought it to him in hospital and taught him again how to use it. She put Tanya's and Warren's numbers in for him to have contact with them.

Clare felt peace in her home. The tenseness and tension were gone. She could sleep in the master bedroom again with the ensuite, and she could dress there where her clothes were kept and not have to wait until Len was up and out of the way. She could invite people over without fear of a scene with Len. She had a couple of dinner parties before the snow flew in December. She went out to dinner with Tory after the cinema club and attended Buck's ninetieth birthday party at Buck's ski club with Tory. She discovered what a good dancer he was. The party had a 1950s dance hall theme. Clare had a full skirt indigo taffeta dress which fit the theme. She had stopped colouring her hair after age seventy and found that naturally she was silver white and the texture was softer with more gentle waves.

"What a doll!" Tory commented in fifties lingo when she met him at the Bradgate in her indigo dress. Tory wore a suit, striped shirt, and bow tie. Being trained in the military when he was young and a good athlete all his life, he stood straight and tall, resembling Prince Philip. "What a dapper guy!" Clare complimented him in the same lingo. There was eighteen years between them but she felt they were the same age on the dance floor.

Watch it! she told herself driving home alone, you can't get emotionally involved with an eighteen-year age gap. The twelve years between Len and her turned out badly enough. But then so did marrying someone her own age. I don't approve of myself, she concluded. I'm a no-good role model for marriage. But she felt some happiness and hope for having a few years with a marvellous man friend. A really nice man, she thought of Tory, good humoured and even tempered. No wonder everyone likes him.

She was unafraid living alone with Piji at Loghaven. That November, usually a bleak month, brought unexpected peace and freedom from tension for Clare and there were good times with friends. But the dark cloud of Len and the near future loomed.

She met with Dr. Maria Bartelli, who had been her and Len's general practitioner for more than fifteen years. Dr. Bartelli knew Len's medical and addiction problems well. Len now had a medical team: his orthopedic surgeon, Dr. Bartelli, physical therapists, and social workers. They had found a good rehabilitation centre, which Len could get into at the end of November. His surgeon assessed his condition and said Len needed to live in a one-level dwelling and should use a walker. He also said to Clare that he noticed more dementia confusion and recommended that Len be given the simple memory test that a GP can give in her office. Clare took him from rehab for the test in Dr. Bartelli's office. Dr. Bartelli concluded that Len did have memory loss but could still function well enough and was in sufficient command of his faculties. He could certainly make his own decisions.

When Clare met later, on her own with Dr. Bartelli, she told Clare that Len would need a good amount of home care when he finished the course at rehab. Was Clare willing to be his caregiver wherever Len went after rehab?

Clare answered with a firm no. They were legally separated. She was unqualified to be a professional caregiver. And Len had shown himself to be incapable of accepting care from her in a civil manner. He would likely be civil and polite with a professional caregiver. He would have to be!

Dr. Bartelli nodded in understanding and agreement.

Clare investigated retirement homes where Len could live on one level, make friends with people of similar professional backgrounds, have a nice suite of his own, enjoy the dining room and activities, and have any amount of care he needed. There were two very good retirement homes with vacancies. Clare took their brochures to Len and tried to persuade him to consider them seriously.

"You're wasting your breath," Len said to Clare and put the brochures facedown on the table.

Clare took Len to the meeting called by his medical team. The surgeon could not attend. Dr. Bartelli was flanked by the social worker and physiotherapist. Dr. Bartelli informed Len that he should live on one level and would need professional care giving.

"No thanks," said Len. "I'm going back home, to Loghaven."

"It's impossible," said Clare driving him back to rehab. "You'll fall on the stairs. There are fourteen stairs between levels at Loghaven. There is no full bathroom on the main floor. Just a toilet and sink."

"I'll do stairs again," said Len.

"I'm not going to be your caregiver," said Clare. "You treat me too badly."

"I don't need any god damn caregiver."

Len was due to complete his rehab course mid-January. Clare arranged to spend Christmas with Megan and Nate, then bring Aurora and her friend back to Loghaven for a ski holiday. Len phoned Clare from his rehab saying the new physio program was going well. He had been taught to go up three stairs that day using a cane. "Well done," was what she said, but thought, Get real, Len. That was with a physio team at hand. It's nowhere near fourteen steps and it would never be safe.

A couple of days later, Len informed her that Tanya planned to visit him on Christmas Day. She and Carson would have dinner with him in the rehab dining room. Alright if they spent the night at Loghaven?

How can I refuse, thought Clare, it's Christmas. Len needs a visit from some form of family. But she didn't like the prospect of Tanya and Carson in her home by themselves. Not at all! They had visited Len one weekend in the summer when Clare was visiting friends at a cottage on another lake. She came home unexpectedly early and as she got out of the car could see her office window. Tanya was in her office along with Carson. Clare always locked her office when she left Loghaven. Her legal correspondence, journals, and documents she didn't want Len or anyone rummaging through were in there. She ran into the house with Piji barking ahead of her. Tanya was emerging from her office, Carson behind her.

"What were you doing in there?" Clare said angrily.

"The door was unlocked and the lights left on. Just turning them off for you," was Tanya's quick answer.

"I always lock my office when I go away. And I never leave the lights on."

"Guess you just forgot this time," said Carson as he passed in front of Clare.

"Carson and I are leaving now," said Tanya, walking past Clare to the front entrance.

Len had watched in silence from the hallway. He said goodbye to Tanya and Carson. Then sat in his chair with a drink. Clare had checked and found her office door unlocked. Clever brat! she thought. She's used to lying and covering her tracks. So is that rude Carson. I've never been introduced to him and he treats me like that. What a pair of burglars!

Len went along with Tanya's story. Clare was determined to get to the bottom of it. She talked it over with Julie.

"Skullduggery," said Julie. "There's skullduggery afoot, as our mother would say." She laughed, then she raised interesting questions. "It's pretty obvious that niece is after an inheritance. But why is she trying so hard to make you look bad?"

"Maybe it's that fool psychology that putting me down raises her up."

"It never works in the long run. But she doesn't sound farsighted. Quick with lies though. Where do you keep your keys?"

"On my key chain. By my purse."

"Which you leave in sight of Len when you're outside, swimming, playing tennis?"

"Yes. Oh spit! I do."

"Maybe Len got a copy of your key. Maybe he's had it for sometime. Maybe Tanya suggested he do that."

"I bet Len could think that one up all by himself."

One night after a lot to drink, Len responded to Clare's nudging him about copying her key. "Sure," he said. "Why not? Tanya was right in saying it's my house. I shouldn't be locked out of any part of it."

Clare reported the incident to her lawyer, Hannah who directed her to report it to the police. The police came and talked with Len. He willingly gave them his copied key. The police warned Clare that Len could have made more than one copy. She should change the lock to be used with a key that cannot be copied. Clare did so immediately.

The prospect of having Tanya and Carson in her home by themselves over Christmas night gave Clare the creeps, as she used to say as a child. Now a well-aged adult, she did what she thought was the right thing. She made arrangements for a neighbour to give them the house key and she laid in a frozen lasagne supper for them. She was already prepared to accommodate and feed Aurora and her friend Chantelle when she returned with them on December 27.

Tory left to spend Christmas with his daughter in Vancouver. He would return after New Year's. It seemed way too long to have no chance to see and talk with him.

Clare dropped Piji off at a good kennel en route to the airport. "Don't worry, Piji," she assured her. "I'll be back in eight days. For sure. That's a promise." Piji wet the floor, something she had never done at Loghaven. But then, she put her mind to surviving what lay ahead, jumped up eagerly at the attendants, making a fuss over them. Piji knew them from coming for checkups and vaccinations. She had to hope they would take her home or to another good home. She had never known anything anywhere near as good as Loghaven with Clare.

CHAPTER TWENTY-SEVEN

The Last Straw

Clare arrived back at Loghaven on December 27 with Piji, Aurora, and friend Chantelle. She was shocked to see Len's car in the garage. They went into the house. There was Len in his chair, a cane at his side. He was smiling. "Tanya and Carson brought me home," he announced. He had no glass of scotch. "Hello, girls. I'm Len. Who are you?"

"Grampa. I'm Aurora, your granddaughter. This is my friend, Chantelle."

"Did you have Christmas dinner with Tanya at the rehab?" Clare asked, trying to contain her anger and exasperation.

"No. They got me out of there as fast as we could gather up my stuff. I signed myself out. We had steaks back here. They brought them."

"All according to plan?"

"You got it."

"They just left you here on your own?'

"They stayed until yesterday."

"You managed the stairs on your own?"

"There's a knack to it, with a cane. But I slept on the couch last night. Hey, would you mind getting me a drink. I think I've earned it. Just one."

Clare quickly thought it over. "No," she said. "I'm going to show the girls to their room. Let's haul our stuff upstairs, shall we? Aurora. Chantelle."

Piji was racing around the room so happy to be back at Loghaven. She raced upstairs ahead of everyone. Len got up and used his cane to get to the cupboard with the scotch. He did have only one drink.

Clare wanted to just sit down and cry in anger and hopelessness, like a normal person. Maybe throw hysterics like a madwoman. Release the tension that had come back in spades. But she carried on to the top of the stairs, leading Aurora and Chantelle to the guest room with single beds. She was out of breath from the stairs, carrying a small suitcase, and tension. "Sorry, girls," she said. "I need to sit down for a moment."

The girls looked at each other and sat on the bed.

"I've been taken by complete surprise," said Clare. "Len is supposed to be in rehab. He was to have another two or three weeks there."

"It's OK, Grammy," said Aurora. "I know the basic story. Mom doesn't like to talk about it. But I get it. I remember Grampa Len from when I was little. Chantelle, I've told you about this, haven't I."

"Yeah. Don't worry, Clare. I have a relative in a rehab for addictions. I get it. Happens a lot."

"Your parents aren't going to like this. I'll have to tell them."

"Why?" said Aurora. "We can tell them when we get home. We're sixteen, Grammy. Not children. We can just keep out of his way. We're here to ski."

"You girls…" Clare choked with emotion. She got up and hugged each of them. She wiped her eyes. "You're so grown up!"

Clare took her suitcase to the master bedroom to unpack it. The bed and armchair had plastic bags of Len's clothes thrown upon them. His bag of disposables was thrown in the closet. His toiletry kit was in the downstairs washroom.

Tanya and Carson had used the double-bed guest room closest to the guest bathroom, leaving the sheets piled on the floor. Clare picked them up, wanting to hold her nose as she took them to drop down the laundry chute, wanting to hold her nose of Tanya and Carson period. It was the bedroom she had used since sleeping separately from Len. She did not want to go back to it. Certainly not the night after its occupation by Tanya and Carson. She took her night clothes to the smaller guest room down the down the hall. I'm not going back to square one with Len, she told herself. They have dumped him on me, trusting I'll be his caregiver. I won't. I just won't.

But she couldn't resolve the situation at the expense of her granddaughter and friend come for their first ski holiday at Loghaven. Clare made dinner for all. Len sat at the head of the table. They made strained conversation. Len drank a glass of water as did the girls. After dinner, Len announced he was going to climb the stairs to bed. Clare gasped inwardly. The girls looked at her.

"I'll follow you up," said Clare.

"We'll do the dishes," said Aurora, giving Clare a look that said, we're at hand.

"I can do it myself," said Len.

"OK." Clare got up from the table. "I'd just like to see it."

"So would we," Chantelle said quietly. Len couldn't hear her.

He limped with his cane to the stairs. With remarkable exertion, determination and some dexterity, Len grabbed the railing with his left hand, put his good leg firmly on the step, gripped his cane tightly and set his left foot minimally on the next step, then his right foot strongly on the step above, hoisting himself up step by step. Clare followed two steps behind. The girls watched from the bottom.

"Get off my heels!" Len yelled. "I can do this myself."

"Don't yell at me, Len. I'm doing what needs to be done."

"Oh for chrissake!" Len muttered, continuing on. He rested on the landing after the seventh step, then continued to the top. He went into the bedroom and headed for the arm chair. Clare quickly removed the bag of clothes before he sat down. The girls came to the top of the stairs. "Everything alright, Grammy?"

"Yes. I'm just going to quickly put these clothes away."

"OK if we watch some TV after the dishes?"

"Of course."

They got up early next morning to go skiing in the Gatineau Hills. Len was having a scotch or two when they got home around 5 p.m. Dinner conversation was less strained as the girls laughed, recounting their first day on higher runs than they'd ever skied before. Clare followed Len up the stairs less closely.

"For chrissake don't dog me!" he yelled. "Piji did enough of that today. I got down the stairs without you and I'll get up them."

He stumbled onto the landing but managed to grab the window sill and the next railing without hitting the floor.

New Year's Eve, Len was slumped in the armchair when they got home just after 4 p.m. His scotch glass was emptied. He opened his eyes and sat more upright. "Don't need any supper," he slurred.

The girls went up to shower and change. Clare changed, then came down to have a glass of wine and get the fire going in the TV room. She came into the kitchen to set out a charcuterie board.

"I'm toast," said Len, getting himself up. "Heading for bed."

Clare stood at the bottom as he gripped his way upstairs. He stumbled and fell, gripping the rail with both hands.

"Aurora! Help!" Clare yelled as she moved up to catch Len. Aurora and Chantelle came running. Len started sliding down the steps with his face to the stairs. He slid to the bottom, managing to protect his face with his hands and arms. Clare gripped his ankles on the bottom step. Aurora and Chantelle got hold of each of his shoulders. Len struggled to roll himself onto his back. The girls helped him. He seemed oblivious of his bumpy ride, his body pliantly relaxed.

Thoughts raced through Clare's mind. This had to be the last straw. She pulled her phone from her pocket and took a photo of the girls holding Len. They would not have to bear witness. The photo would do it.

They eased him onto the floor. He tried to get up but hadn't any strength. He showed no sign of injury. He was actually smiling slightly as though it were amusing.

"I should call 911," said Clare.

"But there's no sign of injury," said Aurora.

"He's conscious," said Chantelle. "Hasn't hit his head. I've seen a drunk like this before. He just needs to sleep it off."

"It's New Year's Eve, Grammy. Not a good time to take a drunk to hospital. It will be full of them. Let's get him up onto the couch and just keep an eye on him."

The girls pulled his pliant body to the couch. Clare took his feet and they lifted him onto the couch. It wasn't long before he was snoring. They had New Year's Eve dinner in the TV room. Clare went to bed right after watching midnight on Times Square in New York, as did the girls. They wanted to get a good morning's ski on their last day. Len snored on.

He was sitting up on the couch when they came down in the morning. "I'm going up to shave," he said. "And I don't want anyone following me."

"Nice. Thank you," said Chantelle, quietly sarcastic as they heard him make it to the landing.

"He has no memory of what went on last night," Clare explained.

Clare did not ski with the girls that morning. She used the time to phone Megan and tell her what had gone on with Len.

"Tomorrow," Clare said, "I'm writing to Hannah to ask her to proceed to arbitration and divorce."

"It's time, Mom. Beyond time. He'll threaten suicide again. Are you prepared for that?"

"I will be," said Clare.

Chapter Twenty-Eight

Arbitration Begins

As soon as the holidays were over, Clare emailed Hannah and a meeting was arranged with her to proceed to arbitration. The agreed-upon arbitrator was contacted and willing to take on the case within the next few months. Hannah began having the papers drawn up.

"We can't go on sharing Loghaven," Clare said to Len before he started drinking that day. "We have to go through arbitration. You need to go into a residence where you can have a good life, live safely on one level, have friends and as much care as you need."

"You're wasting your breath. Again! I'm staying right here. With you. I can manage the stairs easily now."

He could manage the stairs. Not easily. But he had become better at it and no longer used a cane on the stairs. After the fall at New Year's he drank somewhat less and slept on the couch when he got super drunk.

"You have violated our agreement repeatedly, getting drunk and belligerent and abusive. The scene you have left in my granddaughter and her friend's mind is shameful and harmful. The way you live and treat me is damaging and has been for years."

"Poor dears. Count yourselves lucky if that's the worst you have to bear."

Clare seethed. "Get yourself a better lawyer. Papers will be served next week." She left the room.

Len took outwardly a more cavalier attitude to the legal proceedings than he did the first time. At least outwardly. Clare never could tell what was going on in Len's mind. He did obtain a better lawyer, a woman called Sadie Pitblado.

The arbitration papers were delivered to Len at an unexpected time in early evening. Clare was preparing dinner in the kitchen. She received the envelope at the door and gave it to Len, not knowing what it contained. He was sitting in his chair. He put down his glass, opened the envelope, read the enclosed papers then scoffed at them. "These will get you nowhere, unless out of here," Len said, waving them at Clare, then putting them down on the table beside him with his scotch. "And you don't want *that*."

Clare kept quiet and her cell phone close at all times. Len did not raise the subject again and spent more time in his office over the next days.

It was Valentine's Day, no less, when Len came down in the morning and sat across from Clare having her tea on the couch. He looked very seriously at her.

"Are you sufficiently aware," he spoke slowly, solemnly, "that if I have to commit suicide, everyone will know it's your fault? They will blame you."

Clare thought he had come to say something nice to her, on Valentine's Day. She felt sick in the pit of her stomach. But she had prepared her answer to this threat. "Len, if you commit suicide that will be your responsibility. It is something you yourself decide to do. It is not my doing. You are aware that suicide is something you do to other people. It can cause irreparable psychological harm. Think of your niece Tanya. Think of how her father's suicide affected her. You have been stepfather to Megan and Ali for forty years. Why would you want to hurt them? They have been nothing but good to you. They have done you proud. And the grandchildren … completely innocent. Why would you want to give them such a family history?" Clare got up and took her tea to her office.

The nausea subsided. She was to attend a Valentine's dinner dance fundraiser that night with Tory. She phoned him. He was good to talk things over with. He was understanding and calming. "What bothers me most," she told him, "is his wanting to see me blamed for the rest of my life. He wants me *punished*. That's the motivation of men who kill their wife and then themselves."

Tory was quiet, then replied. "I don't think he's going to do it. It's a threat that worked before and he's trying it again. Inform your lawyer and let her deal with it professionally."

"You're right. I'll do that now. I won't tie her hands this time."

"Good! Can you come fetch me a little early at the Bradgate? We can have a drink in my suite before we go out."

Hannah took serious note of Clare's report. She advised Clare to also report it to the police. "It's a threat of violence," she said. "They should be on the alert to Len."

Two days later, a cruiser arrived at Loghaven with two police women. One talked with Len in his office, the other talked with Clare in hers. "He needs counselling," the officer concluded to Clare. "You need to get this arbitration done with. This is not a good or very safe situation."

The other officer was more reassured by talking with Len. She came into Clare's office and said to her colleague and Clare, "He doesn't exhibit a lot of anger. He comes off as pretty benign. But he could do with some counselling. He said he'd at least think about it."

After they left, Len was in a softened mood. "Nice young woman," he said. "Wants me to get some counselling. I said I'd think about it."

"But you won't do it."

"I've had enough counselling."

The eve of the Valentine's fundraiser, Clare stepped into Tory's suite wearing a red satin floor-length skirt and a white bustier with some red sequins on it.

Tory whistled. "What a knockout!"

"I shop in my closet," said Clare. "This is from years ago. You're pretty sharp yourself in that suit and tie."

"Maybe I should sport my war medals to add some sparkle like you." He was joking. No way would he wear his medals except on Remembrance Day.

Tory had set out wine and a cheese plate. He sat down in the armchair. Clare sat on the couch. They were into their second glass of wine when Tory changed the subject. "There's something I have to tell you."

"Oh?" Clare looked at him with interest.

"I'm afraid I've fallen in love with you. I missed you so much when I was away over Christmas. And today … the thought of anything happening to you … I'm sorry." He reached out his hand on the arm of the chair. Clare moved over to lay her hand on his. "Love is a serious thing," he began. "It has different parts. There's love from the head." He touched his head. "There's love from the heart." He touched his heart. "And there's love from the groin. But that part's over and done with."

Clare laughed. She held his hand with both her hands and laughed again. "Groin love. That's hilarious. Good thing that's over with. Who wants groin love!" She hoped she hadn't offended him. "I feel the same," she said seriously. "I fell for you quite a while ago but never expected to let you know. I don't approve of the age gap. I advise people against big age gaps. But then, having no age gap didn't work for me either. But love is a good thing. Depends on what you do with it."

"We could go on discussing this," Tory finished his wine and stood up. "But we have to go dancing. People are expecting us."

Clare stood up. They embraced. They went dancing.

When the dance was over, snow was blanketing Clare's car and still falling. Not a good night for driving back to Loghaven.

"You could stay at the Bradgate," said Tory, "and go home in the morning. There is a guest suite, though I'm not sure if it's available. The couch in my office is a pullout. We could call that a guest suite."

"And maybe not bother to use it," said Clare.

Tory raised his eyebrows. "You have been warned."

"About groin love?" Clare laughed. "There'll be none of that."

She phoned Len and told him she was staying in the guest suite at the Bradgate. "Stay wherever the hell you want," said Len. "Just don't drive home in a snowstorm."

Chapter Twenty-Nine

In the Pandemic

Mid-March 2020, Covid pandemic rules were announced and enforced in Canada. The Bradgate was put into lockdown. No visitors allowed in, no residents allowed out, except for medical purposes. Meals were brought to the residents' rooms. Yellow police strips were wrapped around outdoor benches to warn people away. Residents with dementia had to be closely watched to prevent them from wandering out emergency exit doors. Schools, churches, sports facilities, bars and restaurants were closed. People had to line up six feet apart outside grocery and other essential supplies stores so only a limited number of people shopped inside at a time. Masks became obligatory.

Most people believed it would be many years before an effective vaccine would be created. Many elderly in long term care homes and people with compromised immune systems who couldn't keep isolated, died. Many fell seriously ill, many had minor illness. Frontline workers in hospitals, long term care homes and essential services were the overworked heroes of the pandemic. People in every country became all too familiar with the pandemic effects.

Computer companies thrived. Children and university students had to have online classes, business was conducted online, Zoom conferences became the way of having meetings. Creative social people had Zoom dinner parties and Zoom Happy Hour drinks with friends. Clare had to buy and learn how to work a new laptop that facilitated Zoom. She had bought a laptop for Len when he was in rehab so he could do his stock investing, but he wouldn't, or couldn't, learn how to work it. He wanted the familiarity of his old desktop.

*****

Their legal case was carried on mainly by computer with limited in-person meetings. Sadie Pitblado worked up a case for Len, presenting him as a man of achievement and discipline who had a daily drink after 5 p.m. when the stock market was closed and a glass or two of wine with his wife at dinner. She drank much more wine than he did. Clare was described as a dependent, uncontrolled woman, given to angry tantrums and hysterical behaviour, often throwing her wine in Len's face. At other times she showed affection for him, sitting watching the sunset with him, getting into bed with him oftentimes at night. Len was a husband who provided well for her and his stepchildren in a long marriage of emotional interdependence. Len's good nature and Clare's instability were described in a sworn affidavit from Len and corroborated in a sworn affidavit by his niece Tanya.

The final day of arbitration was to be carried on by Zoom conferencing in offices set up by the arbitrator, Mr. Whalen. Tanya was the only witness called. Clare said she did not want to involve friends or family and Hannah respected that. She called no witnesses on behalf of Clare.

Clare and Len were able to live sharing Loghaven until a few weeks before the arbitration day in late May. The procedure was to gather all affidavits and then to have Clare and Len each have a private session with Mr. Whalen in which he could meet and make some assessments of them and their relationship. Physical safety was a major focus. Cases had occurred of one partner assaulting or murdering the other in an elevator or parking lot immediately after a mediation, arbitration, or court case. Rules were made to keep partners separated at crucial times.

The weekend before Clare was to meet with Mr. Whalen on the Monday, was gruelling for Clare. Len sat up late on the Saturday night listening to old CDs of songs they had liked and danced to in the first two decades of their marriage when they were quite happy. Len had been insulting to her at dinner and yet retreated to listening to their old songs afterwards. She cleared up, watched some TV, and went to bed. Len slept on the couch and had left her a message on the pad of paper on the kitchen counter. It was a line from the John Denver and Placido Domingo song: "My memories of love will be of you."

Sunday afternoon he asked Clare to come and talk to him in his chair by the fireplace. He began to go on about suicide. "If I'm going to be kicked out of here, I'll kill myself first. Here in this house. You won't be able to live here with the memory of the scene."

It made her feel sick again. And angry, disgusted. She stood up. Piji stood up in alarm. "You mean you wouldn't have the decency to walk off into the woods like a dignified animal or considerate person." Clare left the room and went for a long walk with Piji.

She phoned her friend Nesta in Ottawa. Nesta was another friend from university days. They had met when Clare was outgoing secretary of International Club and Nesta was incoming secretary. Nesta was a stunningly attractive black Jamaican from a wealthy family. They became close friends when Nesta went to Oxford with her husband, who did a law degree. Nesta had her first baby shortly after Clare had her twins. They kept in touch when Nesta went into the foreign service with her husband and eventually became qualified herself and had an illustrious career there. Clare had visited Nesta on some of her foreign postings. Nesta was twice divorced and now retired in her house in Ottawa.

"Nesta, I've had another crap time with Len. I have to be in Ottawa early tomorrow. Could I stay the night at your place?"

"Of course. You know you can."

"You can visit me too," said Tory when she phoned him. "Tomorrow they're allowing us to have visitors, if we sit outside in the cold."

Wow! Something to look forward to, said Clare to herself. At last!

"The way I see it," said Nesta to Clare over a light, nicely served supper, "is … why wouldn't Len try everything, to stay where he has everything he wants? A beautiful home, the woman he loves keeping it perfect, doing his meals and his laundry for him."

"He doesn't love me. Not in any good way. He can't, just can't, be nice to me. That's all he has to do. But he can't. It's twisted. Twisted and sick how he treats me."

"Some people are sick. And twisted. They enjoy going at someone. All they need is someone who'll take it."

"I won't anymore. I'm done with it."

Nesta put two thumbs up. Clare smiled with her.

Clare met with Mr. Whalen at the end of a long table in his law offices. Masks off. She found him easy to talk to, understanding and very attentive. She got choked up when she talked about Len's threats but she didn't let tears come to her eyes. He saw her distress and said something she hoped was true.

"There are always exceptions," he said, "but generally speaking, partners who threaten suicide in these situations don't do it. Those who are quietly suffering may just do it."

Clare believed Mr. Whalen was fair minded. She liked him. And felt some reassurance in what he said. But the thought that Len wanted her to be punished, wanted her to be condemned by other people and be haunted by a scene of his suicide in Loghaven … those things made her shudder inside and fear more than she had before. There were no guns in the house. But there were knives in the drawer and axes by the wood pile. When she got home she would hide the axes. Len wouldn't notice since he had stopped making fires in the fireplace long ago.

She thought of where she and Piji might go to feel safer. She thought of Catherine and Lynn's place. A few years after Clare had returned from her visit to Fort McMurray, Clare received an email from Catherine, who had driven the big equipment in the oil sands.

Hi Clare,

How are you doing? Thanks for giving me your card. Lynn and I got married. We want to see that cheap farmland around Ottawa. Lynn has this crazy idea of raising Icelandic sheep.

She also has a couple of riding horses. But we'll keep our day jobs!

We think it'd be cool to farm around Command Central, as you called it. Can you put us in touch with that real estate friend of yours?

Might see you around, eh 🙂

Catherine

Catherine and Lynn bought fifty acres not far from Loghaven. Catherine got a job in construction in summer and grooming ski runs in winter. Lynn was a part-time accountant. They sometimes came for a swim at Loghaven. Their sheep farm and the wool products Lynn sold got written up in a magazine and popularized on social media. It became an attraction for city dwellers. Before the pandemic closed down small accommodations, they made extra money from renting out a small cottage on their sheep farm.

On the way home from her meeting with Mr. Whalen, Clare dropped in on Catherine and Lynn. They knew about Clare's situation and that the arbitration day was coming up. They had told her to call on them for any help at any time. Clare asked if she could stay in their cottage for a couple of weeks.

"Sure thing, man," said Catherine.

"Rent free," said Lynn.

Clare notified Hannah of her plan to move to the cottage the day Len was to have his session with Mr. Whalen.

"How far away is this cottage?" asked Hannah.

"About a half-hour drive."

"Is Len familiar with it?"

"No. He knows Catherine and Lynn from their visits to Loghaven. But he's never been to their place."

"Great!" said Hannah. "Still, keep your doors locked. You should have gone there long ago."

Len came home from meeting with Mr. Whalen in a good mood. "He's a nice guy," Len said to Clare. "I liked him. Found him easy to talk to. He wanted to know if I think I'm depressed. I said, 'Would you believe out of my mind! But I cope well enough, with some scotch.' Can't say for sure. But I think he's fair minded."

Len seemed only mildly surprised when Clare said she was going to stay with friends until arbitration was over.

"Is that your dickhead lawyer's idea?"

"I'm just doing what I think I need to do."

"What friends?"

"I don't want to say."

"Fine with me." Len gulped his drink. "I'm not leaving this place. Until feet first."

Arbitration day was set for the third week in May. Hannah instructed Clare that as part of her case, should she be granted possession of Loghaven, Clare must provide an alternative place for Len to live. Clare was able to rent a first-floor furnished apartment for the month of June on the outskirts of Ottawa. She met with the administrator at Chartwell retirement suites and confirmed there would likely be a vacancy there in later June.

In the remaining weeks, Len had done some things which Clare interpreted as foolish violations of the terms of their separation agreement. He followed her in his car when she moved to the cottage. She stopped by the side of the road to take a phone call when she knew that further along the road, cell service was unreliable. While on the phone, she saw Len's car go by her. And then a short time later, he came back, pretending he didn't see her.

He phoned her quite frequently and was nice to her on the phone. She warned him that phone calls were against the rules. "Not my rules," said Len.

Clare told Hannah about Len following her. Hannah took it as not foolish, but alarming. "He shouldn't know where you are."

Clare did not really believe Len would pursue and break in on her. She interpreted that he just wanted to know for sure where she was. Nevertheless, she kept her door locked.

The arbitrator declared, out of fairness, Clare should be allowed to live at Loghaven until arbitration was concluded, since Len had had it to himself for the previous weeks. Len moved to the motel he used in previous years.

One day, he used his key to go into Loghaven while Clare was absent in town. He took her backup laptop which was synchronized with her new laptop and contained all her legal and personal correspondence. Clare agreed that was an alarming violation. Len was ordered to return it immediately. He complied, leaving it at the law offices.

On arbitration day, Clare and Len were put in separate offices with large computer screens. Assistants were at hand to help them technically. Their lawyers could be viewed on their screens, also Tanya, the one witness. The arbitrator was not in view to Clare or Len. It was the first warm day of that cold May. Seeing Len appear in a shirt and old windbreaker, Clare wished she could have made him dress more smartly for what was essentially a court appearance. He did not look stiff or tense but was quite casual in attitude. She felt the seriousness of the occasion very much. Hannah had her well prepared and taught her to look into the camera.

She had read all the affidavits but was still not over the revulsion of Tanya's portrayal of her as a pathetic hysterical shrew. Never would be. Len's portrayal of her was more moderate, though in the same vein. But Clare could forgive him for it. He was a husband fighting for what he believed was his. He never saw marriage as an equal partnership and never would.

When Sadie cross-questioned Clare, Clare just gave her straight, honest, calm answers. But when she saw that Sadie was trying to form a picture of her as enjoying 'sparring' with Len, as though they fed off each other's antagonisms, that she, Clare never suffered from stress, even insinuated that Clare had never been seriously ill, Clare felt incredulous and rattled, then said flatly, "There are medical records of my cancer surgery and heart condition."

Sadie moved on to emphasize that they watched the sunset together. "Yes," said Clare, "But that was many years ago." She just felt sad when Sadie tried to round it off with an image of Clare frequently crawling into bed with Len since their separation. "Not so," she said quietly and shook her head slowly.

At the break, Hannah and her assistant commended Clare enthusiastically.

"Rockstar performance," said Hannah.

"Just the truth," said Clare feeling drained.

She found it hard to watch Len being questioned by Hannah. Hannah was firm and pointful with him, not tough and attacking. Clare pushed it out of her mind, not wanting to recall it. But the impression of Len coming off as cavalier, not taking the process seriously enough, remained. When asked about a bad consequence he had created, he replied with a shrug, "As it says on a baby's bib, 'Spit happens.'"

Jazuz! Len, thought Clare. But it did make her smile, weakly.

When Tanya verbalized her affidavit, Clare watched with reluctant amazement. What an expert liar, Clare thought. If you didn't know the truth you'd likely believe her.

Hannah got tough and made short work of Tanya's evidence. She asked Tanya how often and for how long she had actually witnessed Clare together with Len. The day of Len's eightieth birthday party was all she could muster. Then Hannah asked a question of Tanya that surprised both Clare and Len.

"Should Mr. Rekai be awarded possession of Loghaven, would you be willing to move in and be his caregiver and housekeeper?"

"Yes I would."

"Have you ever discussed this possibility with him?"

"Not yet."

In the closing arguments Sadie Pitblado emphasized that Clare and Len had a mutually tolerable relationship which did not cause harm to either and hence the terms of the separation agreement had not been violated. In fact they lived as they had lived throughout their forty-year marriage, with Clare voluntarily doing the laundry and making dinner for Len. She did not fear or feel harmed by his behaviour. She was not threatened by him.

Hannah rose from her chair. "This is 2020. We are all aware, or should be, that women who are abused and threatened, do continue to serve their intimate partners in habitual ways. The woman who was found in pieces in a suitcase had made dinner for her husband the night he murdered her."

Clare and Len were led out separately to their vehicles. The arbitrator, Mr. Whalen, informed their lawyers that he would have his report ready in one week. Clare went home to Loghaven for what could be her last week living there. She would not let herself dwell on that, or where else she might live. If Len were awarded possession of Loghaven, she could live in the rented apartment for the month of June and make her plans from there.

She got some spaghetti bolognaise sauce from the freezer and made herself her favourite comfort food dinner with as much wine as she felt like. She made extra spaghetti for Piji.

Len phoned the next day. "Your lawyer is not a dickhead." He sounded sober. "She sees right through people. I knew Tanya wanted something from me, some degree of inheritance. But she's right out of her tree thinking I would live with her. Not in a million goddamn years."

"It's so farfetched," said Clare. "I didn't see that either. But it would be a good deal for her. Never have to be a cashier again. But she sure has it in for me."

"Oh," Len was dismissive. "Most of that was made up by my lawyer. Sadie's a good scrapper, isn't she."

If you don't mind unethical, thought Clare. "Yeah, I guess good scrapper says it all. We'll see what Mr. Whalen makes of it."

"Yeah. I like him. So does Sadie."

"Me too. And Hannah."

Hannah phoned late Friday afternoon of the next week. Mr. Whalen was punctual with his summary and verdict.

"Clare, it's a big document, nearly five hundred pages, with a good outcome. Covers all bases and tightly argued. Should stand up to any appeals. You are awarded exclusive possession of Loghaven. You and Len maintain half interest in the value of the property. You have to pay maintenance costs but you share in the cost of property taxes and insurance. Repairs to the property costing over $1500 will be agreed upon and shared."

"I'm so lucky." Clare felt like bursting into tears.

"You make your own luck, Clare. You stuck to the truth. Len violated the terms of your separation agreement."

"How do you feel about it?"

"Couldn't be better. Mr. Whalen is exceptional. And this case has set a legal precedent."

"How so?"

"It was all done and recorded by video conferencing. The costs are less than half they would be for normal in person proceedings. This makes it more affordable to women on lower incomes. And men."

I was hoping to set a precedent for women not having to flee the marital home, thought Clare. Oh well. Can't win 'em all. "It's all thanks to you, Hannah. You were magnificent."

"Thanks. I can't wait to discuss this one with my colleagues. You're good to work with."

Clare had not heard such happiness in Hannah's voice and tone. She wished she could hug her. They talked a long time. Clare dared to ask questions about Hannah's upbringing. She had very smart and persevering parents, not at all wealthy but hard-working people who ran their own business. Her father had come from England as a six-year-old orphan child sent to work on a farm. He was born in 1900 and went through both World Wars, the Depression, and post-war prosperity. He didn't live to see Hannah graduate and become a renowned lawyer. Her mother did. Her mother had taken over the business and worked into her eighties. She was now nearing one hundred.

Clare phoned her daughters, who sighed with relief and congratulated her. She thought it best to steer clear of Len until he absorbed the blow. But she had Warren phone Len to make sure he was alright. She phoned Julie, Nesta, and Tory.

"I hope I didn't wake you up."

"No," Tory said. "I'm reading *The Economist*. It usually puts me to sleep. Any news at your end?"

"I've been awarded exclusive possession of Loghaven."

"Absolutely bloody marvellous! Len could never look after it on his own."

"I know. He'd let it fall into disrepair and disuse. He doesn't come outside the house, let alone use the tennis court, trails or lake. He needs to get into Chartwell."

"Maybe he will now. How are you going to manage on your own?"

"I haven't dared to let myself think much about that. I know I can't afford the maintenance on my own. I'll have to get a tenant."

"Who would you get?"

"I don't know. All my friends around here have their own places. I suppose I could run an ad in the paper."

"I don't want you doing that. Unsuitable, possibly dangerous people might apply. Why don't you ask me?"

"Really? Would you? You're always telling people you like it there in the Bradgate."

"Not since lockdown. I'm dying to get out of here. Well … I don't want to go that far!"

"Come to Loghaven."

"You need to think that through, Clare. I'm an old man. You need someone much younger. Think it over. Let's talk seriously about this tomorrow."

Chapter Thirty

The Last Chapter

It is July 1, 2022, Canada Day. Clare and Tory are hosting a party at Loghaven. They have been living there together for two years. Tory, now 96, had made pancakes for breakfast, with Megan and family gathered at the table for the long holiday weekend. Tory continues to amaze Clare daily with how helpful he is around the house and garden. He helps prepare meals and clear up. He likes to go shopping with her and does errands. He enjoys pruning shrubs and fixing things. They hire mowers and gardeners for the rest of the maintenance work.

Most amazing is how nice he is to her. Day and night. They hike and swim together. Tory works on another light mystery novel in his office. With the encouragement of Tory, Clare has set up a photography studio to take portraits of people and pets. Tory and Clare have many friends in Ottawa who enjoy visiting them at Loghaven. Word is spreading about Clare's talent for capturing the character of people and animals. Friends and clients enjoy the excursion to Loghaven. They are welcome to swim, play tennis, and picnic by the lake. The studio is closed November to May.

At the end of the day, Clare and Tory have drinks on the verandah, or by the fireside, discussing anything and everything, They both love music and singing though Clare is careful to sing a slight note behind Tory who sings on perfect tune. She can't. He sings in the shower, knows all the words to an entire Gilbert and Sullivan operetta. Sometimes they burst into song or dance in the kitchen while preparing dinner. They have nights of tender intimacy.

Peace and harmony, thinks Clare, I've never known such peace and happy harmony. Maybe it's because we're old and free from careers and from the family responsibilities of our younger years, that we can be like this. Whatever … I think I'm living with the nicest man in the world.

"This place has never looked so good," said Megan when she came for her first visit after Len had moved into Chartwell. "You've certainly expanded the calibre of art around here," Megan remarked to Tory. "It's not all wildlife on the walls." Tory's mother's paintings of scenes with children, grand old houses, and illustrations from *The Secret Garden* hung in the dining area. Tory's paintings and sketches and Clare's wildlife photographs hung on other walls. Tory's armchairs and lamps and small tables from countries where he had had mining projects replaced furnishings Len had moved to his suite at Chartwell.

This Canada Day of 2022, the sun is shining on the lake, cottagers are paddling around in canoes, waving to each other, wearing funny hats with Canadian flags attached in various ways. The rule is, no motor boats on this lake on Canada Day. Just a few people don't follow the rule. Everyone at Loghaven has had a swim. Tory and Clare swam to the raft and back as they do most days in summer. Tory swims early and late in the season, when Clare and others declare it too cold.

Neighbours have joined their party, including Catherine and Lynn. Friends have come from Ottawa. Nesta has brought Len with his walker and Joyce, a long time friend of Tory's who is a year older than him. Today is her ninety-eighth birthday. No walker for her. Joyce is a retired scientist who decided to learn to fly small airplanes when she turned eighty, just after her husband died. Her husband had been Tory's closest friend. Joyce still flies small airplanes, but no longer solo.

Len would not take his walker out of the car. "Don't need it," he said. "I brought my cane. Just need a chair."

Nesta signalled a look to Clare indicating 'best go along with what he says'.

Clare knew this all too well. She had visited him regularly when he moved into the rented apartment. He insisted he could look after himself, shopping and cooking his own meals. But his fridge held wieners, sliced ham, and bread gone moldy. He lived mostly on breakfast cereals and scotch. Clare brought meals he liked but he complained about large portions and wasted some of what she brought. After a couple of weeks, Len phoned her at night to ask if she had received his email. "I don't do emails at night," she said. "But I'll check them now if you want me to."

"I copied you on one I sent to Tanya. She's been driving me nuts with her phone calls. I think I've put a stop to her badmouthing you and telling me what to do. She was complaining that you have a tenant and I should sue for half his rent. I also wrote to Mr. Whalen."

"Why?"

"Just told him I appreciated him making me see what my drinking had done to me and to my family."

Clare was astounded. She read Len's email to Tanya. It said:

You've got it wrong. Tory Sanderson is a good guy. You think he pays twice as much rent as he actually does and I have no problem with Clare using that for maintenance. She needs it. She and I have been married forty years. There were good times and some bad, mostly because of my drinking too much. I now drink one-third of what I used to and I'm keeping it at that. I don't want to hear any more derogatory remarks about Clare. She doesn't deserve them. Don't phone me if you're going to go on against her. And don't think I will ever need you as my caregiver. I'm going to move into Chartwell. You're right. This living alone is no good for me.

Clare wept after reading it. That's the man I married, she thought.

The next day, Len drove to Loghaven to pick up his postal mail. Clare went out to meet him on the driveway. "Thank you," she said, with watery eyes and hugged him.

She helped him move everything he wanted into his suite at Chartwell. He grew weaker as he refused to go out for walks. His exercise was getting into his car to get his supply of scotch. He eventually had to use a walker to get around the halls of Chartwell. He made friends and ate well enough but never became close with the women there. He was always honourable about finances and remained amicable with Clare and Tory.

It was barbecued burger time on Canada Day. Beef burgers, lamb, or vegan. Nate took over the barbecue, with Catherine making sure he did them right. Tory and Clare kept the bar table replenished. Wilf, now a high school student, wore a red cowboy hat with a white maple leaf on it. He was showing neighbours' grandkids his skills with the kayak. Aurora, who would attend McGill University in the autumn and be able to ski in the Laurentians and visit her grandmother more often, took a refill scotch to Len.

Tory squeezed Clare's hand. He didn't need to say anything. It was a great day, a great party. A good summer ahead. Everyone had been vaccinated and boosted. The mask mandates were dropped. Tory's kids and grandkids would visit. Clare hoped that sometime Ali and family would come when Megan and family were here. But they were busy professionals. Maybe sometime, before we expire, Clare mused, I'll have both my daughters and families here together. But she was grateful for everyone who was there that day.

Joyce was holding court as she does, entertaining people with her stories punctuated with saucy swearing. Clare sensed something odd in the air, when Nate and Megan conferred at the barbecue, looked at their watches and left it for Catherine to tend. "There's one hell of a lot of burgers here!" Catherine exclaimed loudly. Tory went over to her and said something with his back to Clare.

Aurora and Wilf brought out the Indigenous drums which Clare had obtained years ago and used for announcements at parties. They beat the drums. Nate stood on the verandah steps to address everyone. He said greetings in Inuit language, then raised his glass. "Happy Birthday Canada!" he yelled.

Horns were honked in the driveway as everyone raised their

glasses yelling "Happy Birthday Canada!"

Aurora and Wilf beat the drums louder as they walked to the side of the house where suddenly, Ali and Ari appeared with their three boys. More yelling and bedlam ensued. Clare shrieked and choked as her eyes welled up. She held out her arms as Ali and family ran to her and she stepped forward to embrace them. "You little rats!" she said, smiling at her grandsons who had grown taller than her. "You know old people don't like surprises." She hugged each one of them.

"And teenage boys," retorted her oldest grandson with a smile, hugging her, "can't handle hugs."

When Nate could gain control of the party he gave a short speech about this being Canada's 155th birthday but for the Indigenous peoples of Canada it was the thousandth and something. But this was indeed an epochal birthday, because later this month, the Pope would arrive to make a formal apology to the Indigenous people of Canada for the destruction of culture and the deaths and harm done to children in the residential schools.

"About time!" someone shouted. "Genocide!" yelled another, "Call it genocide!"

"This is a birthday party!" Megan took over from Nate. The drummers settled people down. "I would like to welcome my sister, Ali, and her husband Ari and all my nephews."

Cheers were raised.

Tory took over the podium. "It is also Joyce Goode's ninety-eighth birthday. Happy birthday, happy birthday, my old friend. Will you say a few words?"

"Hell no!" she laughed. "I've been boring people all afternoon with my words. Besides I can't yell as loud as you youngsters."

Burgers were served and salads and more drinks. Then fireworks were set off from the dock.

"I always have fireworks on my birthday," Joyce said and cackled, holding her rye and water towards the sparkling streaks and stars soaring skywards from the dock, flying and falling into the calm, clear water of the lake.

Acknowledgements

My thanks to David Stover of Rock's Mills Press for expert and very respectful editorial treatment, also for quickly recognizing *Bear with Me* as a 'book that matters' and publishing it.

I learned early on in my writing career as a novelist that a lot of people wish to be portrayed in a novel, but what they're expecting is to be glorified. I write realistic fiction. It takes a good sport to approve one's portrayal in my novels, since I can only portray people from my limited perspective. The good sports bearing their real names in this novel are:

Wildlife photographer Michelle Valberg; Fort McMurray residents Lisa Schaldemose and her mother Annette; Randy the animal shelterer; photographer Tracey Holland; entrepreneur David Bouchier; heavy equipment driver Catherine Gaudet and her wife Lynn Thordarson; cancer surgeon Dr. Lisi; friends from Queen's University days, Liz Love and Nesta Scott; veterinarian Dr. Ardis Ardiel; Alison Postma of Wolfrunner Kennels, Malamute breeder of Yukon Sally, Yukon Jake, and, with Michelle Lavigne of Shelaskan Malamutes, breeder of Ike; real estate friend Christine Woodman; and ninety-eight-year-old practicing pilot Joyce Goode.

Dr. Judith Samson French is the veterinarian who read *City Wolves* and invited me to visit her and participate in her Dogs with No Names project near Calgary, Alberta. She did not invite me to portray her as my sister in this novel, but she laughed and went along with that too.

I have declared *Bear with Me* to be my final novel, as I now turn eighty. My first novel was published by Macmillan (London) when I was twenty-six and began teaching part time for Oxford University. I'm grateful to the many people who encouraged me as a writer over the decades. Especially:

My Oxford friends: Peggotty and Andrew Graham, the Fowlers, McLennans, and Lairds, Safie Ashtiany, my editor Marni Hodgkins, my agent Sheila Watson, my husband W. H. Newton-Smith, and barrister Barbara Simpson.

My many friends when I returned to Canada in 1980: those in the Writers' Union of Canada; my husband D. L. Gauer and Sun Life friends; my publisher of *A Shark in the House*, Anna Porter, and editor Barbara Berson; my publisher of *City Wolves,* Dundurn, and editor Dominic Farrell. My Queen's roommate, Shirley Tilghman, soared as the first female president of Princeton and has been my unpaid publicist. My buddy Anne Powlesland and pal 'Caitlin' Spenser always answered my calls. Artist, publisher, and editor Deena Dolan, my work and life advisor. My sisters Joan and Patricia see my faults, but we always support each other in our work.

Most serious thanks to my lawyer Julie Hannaford for getting me out of the long difficult years. Garth Martin and Carol Blasedale for guidance in getting me through them. Dear journalist friend Roberta Avery saw and gave me refuge at the most dangerous time. She died bravely of pancreatic cancer, just recently. Catherine Sinclair continues to give helpful literary criticism along with friendship as she battles a relentless illness. Talented young journalist and editor Erika Engel masters my website and keeps my laptop from driving me crazy.

Norman Paterson made writing again possible for me.

And always, my amazing daughters, Superior Court Justice Apple Newton-Smith and Rain Newton-Smith, chief executive of the Confederation of British Industry, have nourished and replenished my life. I bask in the limelight of them, with their dedicated husbands, Malcolm Jolley and Andy Goodwin, along with my grandchildren Alec, Will, and Hamish Jolley, and Willow, Autumn, Sky, and Indigo Goodwin.

—Dorris Heffron
September 18, 2024

Manufactured by Amazon.ca
Acheson, AB